# ZERO ZERO

(AN AGENT ZERO SPY THRILLER—BOOK 11)

JACK MARS

**Jack Mars**

Jack Mars is the USA Today bestselling author of the LUKE STONE thriller series, which includes seven books. He is also the author of the new FORGING OF LUKE STONE prequel series, comprising six books; and of the AGENT ZERO spy thriller series, comprising twelve books.

Jack loves to hear from you, so please feel free to visit www.Jackmarsauthor.com to join the email list, receive a free book, receive free giveaways, connect on Facebook and Twitter, and stay in touch!



ISBN: 9781094350288

**BOOKS BY JACK MARS**

**LUKE STONE THRILLER SERIES**
ANY MEANS NECESSARY (Book #1)
OATH OF OFFICE (Book #2)
SITUATION ROOM (Book #3)
OPPOSE ANY FOE (Book #4)
PRESIDENT ELECT (Book #5)
OUR SACRED HONOR (Book #6)
HOUSE DIVIDED (Book #7)

**FORGING OF LUKE STONE PREQUEL SERIES**
PRIMARY TARGET (Book #1)
PRIMARY COMMAND (Book #2)
PRIMARY THREAT (Book #3)
PRIMARY GLORY (Book #4)
PRIMARY VALOR (Book #5)
PRIMARY DUTY (Book #6)

**AN AGENT ZERO SPY THRILLER SERIES**
AGENT ZERO (Book #1)
TARGET ZERO (Book #2)
HUNTING ZERO (Book #3)
TRAPPING ZERO (Book #4)
FILE ZERO (Book #5)
RECALL ZERO (Book #6)
ASSASSIN ZERO (Book #7)
DECOY ZERO (Book #8)
CHASING ZERO (Book #9)
VENGEANCE ZERO (Book #10)
ZERO ZERO (Book #11)
ABSOLUTE ZERO (Book #12)

## Agent Zero - Book 10 Summary

*A minor terrorist group with few resources, looking to make their mark in the most impactful way possible, kidnaps a former president and holds him for ransom while placing the blame on Iran. Relations deteriorate rapidly as the US prepares for the possibility of an act of war. But Agent Zero faces his own personal battle: when he is targeted for assassination and Maria ends up the victim instead, it sends him into a downward spiral, his only course of action vengeance against those responsible.*

Agent Zero: With a new treatment plan for his neurological condition and a recent wedding to Maria Johansson, life seemed to be as good as it could get—until the second day of their honeymoon, when an assassin vying for Zero killed Maria instead. His mind muddled and hell-bent on vengeance, Zero tore a path halfway across the world before his daughter Maya confronted him and talked him down. Upon return to the US, Zero figured out where the former president William McMahon was being held and rescued him from Iranian captors, but in doing so allowed the assassin Stefan Krauss to slip away.

Maya Lawson: After completing the CIA's "junior agent" program, Maya was sent on her first op with new partner Trent Coleman, only to find that they had been recruited into SRM, also known as the "dark agent" program, to carry out strategic assassinations. Maya refused, and found herself face-to-face with John Watson, the man who murdered her mother. In exchange for his life, Watson offered vital information on the whereabouts of her father, who Maya found in Greece and brought home to the US. After Zero was taken into custody Maya located Mischa and saved her from near-death at the hands of Stefan Krauss, who narrowly escaped.

Sara Lawson: Despite her vigilantism against male abusers, Maria's murder leaves Sara feeling helpless and ineffective. With her dad, Maya, and Mischa all absent, Sara drove alone to Florida, where she murdered one of her own former abusers, a drug dealer, before returning home. She told no one of her whereabouts, or the growing darkness within her.

Mischa Johansson: The thirteen-year-old former spy was conflicted after Maria's death and reconciled the only way she knew how: by seeking out Maria's murderer and confronting him herself. A standoff with Krauss that was meant for Agent Zero almost saw her killed, had it not been for Maya's intervention. But Zero vowed that he was not yet done with Stefan Krauss, and Mischa—now legally his daughter—offered her help to find and kill him.

Stefan Krauss: The assassin who was supposed to eliminate Agent Zero was dismayed at Maria's act of sacrifice, and by his own bizarre honor code let Zero live to get his revenge. But Krauss instead found himself faced by Mischa Johansson, who shared information about a wealthy puppeteer and war profiteer who was pulling Krauss's strings behind the scenes. After a bloody fight, Krauss escaped with his life, vowing not only to see through his promise to kill Zero, but to follow up on Mischa's claims.

Todd Strickland: An attempt to bring Zero home in Morocco led to a fight in which Zero bested the former Army Ranger, leaving them on bitter terms. After the deaths of Chip Foxworth and Maria Johansson, and the resignation of Alan Reidigger and Agent Zero, Strickland is the only remaining member of the Executive Operations Team.

Mr. Bright: All that is known about the wealthy New York financier is that he was once the business partner of Mr. Shade, the incarcerated war profiteer who funded several of the terrorist operations that Zero personally shut down. Despite his lack of presence, Mr. Bright seems to have his hands in almost everything nefarious, including not only the plot to kidnap the former president, but also Stefan Krauss's contract to kill Agent Zero.

**Zero Zero:**

*Atmospheric conditions that reduce ceiling and visibility to zero; the ejection of the occupant of an aircraft from a grounded stationary position.*

# PROLOGUE

Too easy, Krauss thought. It had been too easy so far.

*Who is Mr. Bright to you?* That's what the girl had asked him, right before they had fought. Mischa Johansson, age thirteen, a slight girl short for her age, with blonde hair and a pink T-shirt, had nearly been the death of him.

Stefan Krauss was a world-class assassin with thirty-seven professional hits notched in his belt, not including the many more who had gotten in the way or saw too much. Yet an unassuming preteen had almost gotten the best of him. Well—physically she had almost gotten the best of him. Mentally, she certainly had.

*Who is Mr. Bright to you?*

The Buchanan Building in Midtown Manhattan was surprisingly less secure than he'd assumed it would be. Still, Krauss took precautions. He dressed in his best, a Giorgio Armani slim-fit suit, a two-button Italian wool jacket with notched lapels, and a navy blue Ermenegildo Zegna necktie. His shoes, leather Giuseppe Zanotti loafers.

Krauss was not all that particular about material possessions, but even he had to admit that if this was the day he died, at least his corpse would be an attractive one.

The Buchanan Building had doormen and a lobby clerk with a required sign-in and ID check and three armed guards, but Krauss was able to gain access under the pretense of an appointment with a hedge fund manager on the fifth floor—which was not a lie, at least not entirely. The hedge fund manager had an appointment with a Belgian by the name of Simon Woulters.

Krauss could not risk using his American alias, Patrick McIlhenney, again. After all, it was how the girl Mischa had found him in a hotel in Washington, D.C. It pained him slightly to bid adieu to a persona he enjoyed, in a manner he imagined was akin to American elitists getting a kick from mimicking southern yokels. The more he leaned into the stereotype, the more it seemed people bought the act.

Oh well. At least the Belgian allowed him to use his native German accent, with only a slight adjustment to account for a Dutch influence.

*Who is Mr. Bright to you?* Mr. Bright was no one to him. He hadn't even heard the name until four days ago and his fight with Mischa Johansson.

*Mr. Bright, out of New York. The business partner of Mr. Shade. He funds the operations that paid you to kill Zero.*

The girl had more information than he did, which was concerning. Stefan Krauss had spent months tracking down the defunct terrorist cells that Mr. Shade had been bankrolling, relieving them of their funds in exchange for killing Agent Zero.

Not only had he failed to kill Agent Zero, but now he'd learned that someone else had been pulling the strings the whole time. This Mr. Bright knew what Krauss was doing and fed the meter, as it were, kept Krauss believing that he'd done it all on his own.

No, not on his own; Krauss had help from the Kiwi. A former smuggler from New Zealand who went by the name Dutchman. They'd met three years earlier in a bar in Jakarta. Dutchman had agreed to use his underworld network and extensive contacts in exchange for fifteen percent of Krauss's take.

It had never occurred to him before how strange it was that Dutchman was always able to come through, without fail.

Stefan Krauss was a world-class assassin with a record of thirty-seven professional hits. Twenty-nine of those had been in the time he'd been working with Dutchman. Had they all been at the covert behest of this Mr. Bright? Had he really been behind Dutchman the entire time?

"No one controls me," Krauss murmured to himself in the elevator. "I control them."

The girl's words rang in his ears: *What I hear is a man who does not realize when someone is pulling his strings.*

The elevator, Krauss noted, only went up to floor twenty-six, despite there being forty-eight floors in this building. That likely meant that what he was after was above that.

The Buchanan Building, he'd learned, was owned by a company called Sunshine Realty, a trite name. Mr. Bright might as well have been advertising.

The Kiwi was dead now. Krauss had seen to that first. It was not a pleasant death, either. Krauss was not an enthusiast of torture; he preferred quick deaths, because it meant quick jobs. But he made an exception for Dutchman. To the New Zealander's credit, he held out for as long as he could. He refused to talk, to admit Bright's influence, for far longer than Krauss would have thought. It wasn't until his eyelids had been removed that he sputtered out the name of the building that Bright operated from. By that point speaking was difficult for him, on account of so many missing teeth, but "Buchanan" eventually became clear.

The elevator doors opened on the fifth floor and Krauss stepped out, following a sign to the office of the hedge fund manager.

"You must be Herr Woulters." As Krauss stepped into the office, a man with hair plugs and a bleached smile hurried over to shake his hand. "Zane Thompson, pleasure to meet you. You can call me Zane. I prefer to keep it informal around here." The man chuckled, as if he'd told a joke.

"Simon, then," said Krauss.

"Please, Simon, have a seat."

The office was white and glass with black furniture. Krauss lowered himself into a leather chair.

"Can I get you something to drink? Water, coffee, tea?"

"No, thank you," said Krauss. He crossed a leg, right over left.

Zane's bleached smile widened. "Those are sharp shoes, Simon. Say—you strike me as a scotch guy. I know it's only eleven, but I won't tell if you don't."

Zane winked. Krauss feigned a smile of his own.

"That would be agreeable."

"Terrific." Zane zipped over to a minibar in the corner of the spacious office. Krauss noted through the window that he had a partial view of Central Park from here, just a sliver of green but probably enough to triple the cost of a similar office on the opposite side of the building.

It felt strange, doing this in the daytime. But it was necessary, not only for his cover but because he assumed it would be unexpected.

"So, Simon," said Zane as he dropped a large cube of ice into a pair of rocks glasses. "Before we can begin, it seems that my office did not receive your financial records. Now, I'm fully prepared to admit that it could have been a clerical error on our end, for which I apologize. Would you be able to—"

"Do you know a man who calls himself Mr. Bright?" Krauss interrupted as he rose slowly from the chair.

Zane's back was to him as he poured two fingers of scotch into the first glass. "Can't say that I do. Should I?"

"No," Krauss told him, "I suppose not." It just meant that if Zane was being honest, he was innocent in this. "I am sorry."

"For what?" Zane poured the second glass.

It took only two long strides to reach him. The moment Zane set the bottle back down, Krauss cupped the man's chin in one hand with the other flat on the back of his head and cleanly broke his neck.

He lowered Zane to the floor. He took no pleasure in the act, yet it was a necessary expenditure if the people downstairs were to believe Simon Woulters was still in a meeting.

Atop Zane's black desk was a slender, sterling silver letter opener. Krauss put it in his sleeve and then hurried back to the elevator. He pressed the button for floor twenty-six.

Anyone else might have thought that going into the Buchanan Building unarmed was foolhardy, but Krauss needed to ensure that he was not captured or worse before he reached his target. He could not risk being frisked, or metal detectors, or dogs—though none of those had happened, and he was again surprised by how much less secure the building was than he'd assumed it would be.

Bright seemed to be the sort of man who did not think anyone would dare to come for him. A man who thought himself untouchable. A man who conflated wealth and power into authority. Krauss had met many such men before, and he had no issue teaching them their final lesson: when hands are tightening around your throat, wealth and power mean nothing.

"No one controls me," Krauss growled under his breath, his shoulders tense as he drew nearer to his target. "I control them."

The doors opened on the twenty-sixth floor. Krauss stepped out into a corridor painted a light gray and softly lit by dim sconces in the walls, giving a silent, ambient glow. There were doors lining the hall, bearing numbers as if they were apartments, but there was no sound. No voices, no muffled televisions, nothing.

The carpet beneath his Zanotti loafers was pristine, not a scuff or fiber out of place. The twenty-sixth floor, it seemed, was meant to look like apartments, but was likely nothing more than a buffer between the accessible floors below and whatever was above.

He followed the hall as it wound left and right, leading near to the other side of the building before he spotted another pair of elevator doors, the ones he was certain would bring him up where he needed to be.

Between the pair of doors was a plain metal chair, and seated upon that chair was a man with a suit and a thick neck.

He stood when he saw Krauss, and he scowled.

"Sir. You're not permitted on this floor."

Krauss frowned. "Apologies," he said, donning a British accent. He liked the British accent; it made everything sound polite and disarming. "I am trying to find a friend's apartment. What floor am I on?"'

"Twenty-six," the man told him. The scowl remained. "You need to go back downstairs, sir."

"Certainly." Krauss gestured to the pair of steel doors. "Can I take that elevator?"

"No, sir. Authorized personnel only."

He frowned. "I'm afraid I'm going to have to insist."

The guard's hand moved to the interior of his jacket.

Krauss sprang then, the fingertips of his right hand reaching for the man's thick neck. The silver letter opener slid into his palm. The tip of it was in and then out of the guard's throat in an instant.

Krauss sidestepped quickly to avoid the thin jet of blood that erupted from the guard's carotid. Stefan Krauss was not all that particular about material possessions, but this was an eleven-hundred-dollar jacket, and had been tailored to his frame. It would be a shame if it was ruined.

The guard was unconscious in eleven seconds and would be dead in under a minute. Krauss located the weapon holstered at the man's armpit—a Sig Sauer P226. The same firearm that was standard issue for Secret Service agents. The magazine held twenty 9x19mm Parabellum rounds.

He hoped it would be enough.

The pair of elevators had no up button to press, but rather a thin slot on the panel between them. He located a keycard in the guard's breast pocket and inserted it. For a few seconds he wondered if there was a missing step to the task, but then he heard a soft ding and the door on the left slid open.

Krauss entered. The numbers on the panel ranged from twenty-six up to forty-eight. He pressed the topmost one. He had Bright pegged; men like him needed to be at the top, in more than just the metaphorical sense. Besides, even if he was wrong he would rather work his way down than up.

He had no idea what to expect when he reached the top. A dozen armed guards ready to lay down their lives to protect their employer? Or perhaps only a nebbish man behind a desk, assuming his identity was safe?

Whatever his mind could conjure, it was nothing like what was waiting for him on the forty-eighth floor.

The elevator doors slid open, and Krauss stepped out to the scent of sawdust. There were no electric lights on; only daylight lit the topmost floor of the Buchanan Building. The floor was bare concrete, and plastic sheets hung from the ceiling. Sawhorses, makeshift workbenches, and an array of tools littered the area.

The top floor, it seemed, was under construction. Yet there was not a sound. There was no one here, despite it being eleven o'clock in the morning on a weekday.

Krauss raised the Sig Sauer and stalked forward. He carefully pushed aside a plastic sheet. In the silence, the crinkling sheet was as intrusive as an air horn. He stepped between the unfinished skeleton of two-by-fours framing a wall.

There was nothing here. He needed to find stairs; taking the elevator again could prove risky. He needed to…

Krauss heard soft footfalls and quickly crouched behind the nearest workbench. The footsteps were approaching his position, carefully and slowly. He slid the Sig Sauer into the back of his slacks and reached up, lifting a claw hammer from the top of the bench.

A gun came first, the black barrel tracking center mass from around a plastic sheet. Then a hand, and then the sleeve of a suit jacket. Krauss sprang, smacking the man in the kneecap with the hammer. He yelped, but it was short-lived as the assassin swung the hammer up into the bottom of his jaw. The guard's teeth clacked together. His head snapped backward, and his body followed.

Rapid steps, behind him. Krauss turned and flung the hammer. It sailed end over end and struck the second assailant in the forehead.

He didn't wait around to see if the man was unconscious. They knew he was here; staying on the top floor was a death trap. He dashed across the floor in search of stairs and found them—and heard the thumping of boots coming his way. More than one pair.

"*Scheisse.*" He spun and rushed back to the elevators, only to curse again, louder, when he realized he had not taken the downstairs guard's keycard with him.

It seemed, however, that wouldn't be a concern. One of the cars dinged, and the door on his left slid open.

Krauss yanked the Sig Sauer free and open-fired into the doorway, caring little for who was on the other side. He fired in tight pairs, *pop-pop! Pop-pop!*

The first two men fell instantly without so much as a shout. Behind them three others tried to take cover near the panel as Krauss fired six shots, then eight.

Hands wrapped around him from behind and squeezed into a bear hug. Krauss whipped his head back, his skull connecting with the bridge of his captor's nose and collapsing. The arms loosened but held their grip.

A man whirled out of the elevator with a pistol in his hands and bleeding from the shoulder. He aimed at Krauss, but did not shoot.

From the stairs on the southern-facing side of the building came three more, these men in dark uniforms and tac vests. They drew nightsticks as their boots pounded the bare concrete.

Krauss threw out both elbows, forcing the arms around him up, and spun out of the grip. He jammed the Sig Sauer in his assailant's ribs—it was the man he'd thrown the hammer at—and fired twice into his abdomen.

Arms grabbed at his gun hand and forced it upward.

There were two men on him, struggling against him. Then three.

A nightstick slammed into his midsection.

The breath rushed out of his lungs as Krauss doubled over.

The gun was wrestled from his hand.

The nightstick came down on his back, and Stefan Krauss collapsed to the floor, breathing hard.

"No. I do not die here," he tried to say, but it came out hoarse and unintelligible.

He waited for the nightstick to come again. To break his spine or crush his skull.

He waited for the man with the pistol and the shot shoulder to put a bullet in him.

He thought of the life he'd lived. No one would know the things he'd done. No one would know how he died.

He looked up, or tried to, and saw that the black boots and wingtips surrounding him were standing still.

He heard a single pair of footsteps and saw a pair of soft brown loafers approaching. Leather Giuseppe Zanotti loafers, ironically.

"Nice shoes." He spat on them.

The man sighed. "Come on. Get to your feet."

With some difficulty, Krauss pushed himself up to one knee, and then grunted as he stood. The pain in his midsection was intense, but not nearly as intense as it could have been. They had not shot at him. They had pulled their strikes. Why?

*For this moment,* he realized. They knew he was coming. He had been surprised at how lax security in the building was. Now he knew why—they had let him come.

It was strange. The man before him was not at all how he would have imagined Mr. Bright, yet he had no doubt that the man before him was Mr. Bright. He was younger than Krauss would have assumed, mid-forties at best. He wore large aviator-style eyeglasses and there was a slight hook to his nose. He wore his hair long, pushed back off of his forehead and past his ears, and had a day's worth of sandy-colored stubble on his chin.

"Stefan Krauss." Bright leaned against the workbench and folded his arms. He wore no jacket, just a starched white shirt with the sleeves rolled to the elbow and a red tie loose around his neck. "It is a pleasure to finally meet you face to face."

"How?" Krauss demanded.

Mr. Bright shrugged one shoulder. "I know all your aliases, Krauss. Even Simon Woulters. Even the ones you don't think anyone knows about. I have to admit—I have a lot of assets out there, but you're my favorite. I bet I know things about you that you've never told anyone in your whole life."

Krauss shook his head. "I am not impressed or intimidated by your hubris."

"Oh, it's not hubris, Krauss. It's the truth. My problem is, I don't know how to separate business and pleasure. I like what I do. I've become quite good at it. Just like you. One might even say we're kindred spirits, in a way—"

"You are a warmonger who hides in an office building," Krauss spat. "We are nothing alike."

"War." Bright sighed. "War is two or more sides fighting each other. War is… well, it's pedestrian. Yes, I deal in war. But more importantly, I deal in terror, Krauss. It's not enough to create a conflict that has a clear beginning and an eventual end. People need to believe that something is always behind them. That the boogeyman is under their bed. That something awful is lurking just around the corner. Always. *That's* my business."

Krauss rubbed at his sore abdomen with his left hand. He had met Mr. Bright, and he was already tired of this man's conceit. He shook his right hand, just slightly, just enough for the silver letter opener to slide into his palm.

"Business has been booming," Bright continued. "No thanks to our current administration. Partially thanks to you. No thanks to Agent Zero, who is still alive, no thanks to you." Bright arched an eyebrow. "I assume Dutchman is dead?"

"He is," Krauss confirmed. *As you will be, in a moment.*

"Shame." Bright took off his eyeglasses and wiped them on his tie. "I liked him. He told good jokes. And that accent was just a bonus." He pushed the glasses back onto his nose.

Krauss lunged. His right hand shot out, the letter opener aimed at Bright's larynx.

Bright shifted slightly, twisting at the shoulders. He was fast, faster than Krauss would have imagined. The letter opener grazed the skin of his neck, not even enough to draw blood.

Arms were on him in an instant. Two men dragged Krauss backward. A third pried the letter opener from his hand. Krauss struggled but could not free himself.

One of the uniformed guards drove the tip of his nightstick into Krauss's stomach again. He coughed and groaned with the impact.

"Hey!" Bright scolded sharply. "Enough of that." He touched the spot on his neck and looked at his hand to make sure he wasn't bleeding. Then he smiled. "You almost got me, Krauss. Almost."

The German-born assassin breathed hard. He'd tried, and he'd failed. He'd always known, or at least suspected, that his life would not end at a ripe old age. He would not retire, or die peacefully in a bed surrounded by loved ones. He'd always suspected that one day he would fail, and he would die for it, he had long since accepted that.

There were worse things than death.

"I am not afraid to die," he told Bright.

"I know." Bright chuckled. "Did you really think I let you get all the way up here if I was just going to kill you? No, no. I would have had my door man shoot you in the lobby."

"I will not work for you."

Bright held up both hands. "You already have been for the last few years. You just didn't know it." He chuckled again. "I'm not going to kill you, Krauss. I enjoy you too much. I'm just going to kill a little part of you." He patted Krauss on the cheek twice. "And you *will* work for me." To the men holding him he said, "Take him to forty-four."

Krauss struggled and thrashed against their grip as they dragged him toward the elevator. The door on the left was still open, the bodies he had shot blocking it from closing. One of Bright's thugs swiped a keycard in the slot, and the elevator on the right opened. It took three of them to get Krauss inside. When the door slid shut again, he felt a sharp pinch in his neck—a needle.

He tried once more to fight his way out of their grip, but he grew weaker by the second. His vision turned fuzzy, dark at the edges. His chin lolled to his chest.

*Who is Mr. Bright to you?* Krauss had been wrong about Bright in almost every way except one. Bright was a puppeteer, and he'd made Krauss a puppet.

*No one controls me,* he reminded himself. That was the last thought that Stefan Krauss ever had.

# CHAPTER ONE

Zero leaned against the closet door in the bedroom of his home, a one-story bungalow in the unincorporated suburb of Langley, Virginia.

*His* bedroom. *His* home. It had been Maria's house, as far as law and taxes were concerned. But it had been *their* bedroom, *their* home. Their home, and their three daughters—*his* daughters now, even Mischa, the adopted thirteen-year-old former assassin and sparrow that Maria had taken in with boundless patience and empathy.

He had lost her. But he hadn't been the only one who lost her. They'd all lost her…

*No. Not lost,* he reminded himself. She'd been taken from them, and he couldn't lose sight of that. Maria had been murdered, and her murderer was still out there. Maya and Mischa had found him, confronted him, and had come so close, *so* close to killing Stefan Krauss.

They hadn't—but they would. Together. That was the promise.

Zero stuffed a few pairs of jeans into the open suitcase on the bed. He'd never been one to care much for fashion, at least not since his days as a professor of European history, and even then he'd thought tweed with leather elbow patches was a good look for him. After the jeans came some shirts, socks, the necessities. A toothbrush, unceremoniously tossed in. It wouldn't be a long trip, but it was one that Zero couldn't put off any longer.

Funny, that he still thought of himself as Zero even if he wasn't Zero. And he wasn't Zero, not really, not anymore. He was no longer employed in the Special Activities Division or the Executive Operations Team or in any capacity of the CIA. The file was closed on Agent Zero, and he planned to keep it that way.

He couldn't go back. Not after what had happened. Not after *everything* that had happened.

*Then who am I now?*

He packed his phone charger. He packed deodorant. He tossed in a Robert Ludlum novel that he'd been about halfway through, and then thought the better of it and took the book out of the suitcase. There was a trash can in the bathroom. He dropped it in.

It was a fine book. The problem was that he'd been reading it the day it happened. On the beach that day, not more than two weeks ago, with her, under an umbrella with the steady sound of crashing surf a tranquil soundtrack.

*Who am I now?*

Zero was a widower now. He was a father. That's who he needed to be. Money wasn't an issue; despite the scores of laws he'd broken in the service of his country and the world, the CIA could not simply disavow or sever ties with Agent Zero. They couldn't pretend he'd never existed. They couldn't pretend he wasn't living less than a twenty-minute drive from the George Bush Center for Intelligence.

Instead they'd offered a not-insignificant pension. And when Maria's life insurance paid out, a tidy sum to say the least, it would ensure that he and his daughters could live comfortably. He could buy a new house, perhaps a bigger place, so that Sara didn't have to room in the basement, as much as she seemed to prefer it.

He planned to do that as soon as possible. Sell this house, get out of Langley. There were too many memories here. Too many reminders of her. Yet there were lots of things he planned to do as soon as possible but hadn't yet done. He hadn't yet taken her clothes out of the closet. Her jewelry and makeup still littered the top of the bureau with the mirror. The sheets… he hadn't even changed the sheets yet, because the pillow still smelled like her.

"Penny for your thoughts?"

Zero spun, startled, as his eldest leaned against the frame of the open bedroom door. It shouldn't have been that easy to sneak up on him, but he hadn't realized how long he'd been standing there, staring at the pillow that still had a small indent in the center from the last time she'd laid her head there.

He forced a smile. "Just… thinking about how annoyingly long this flight is going to be."

Maya nodded slowly in a way that suggested she didn't believe him for a second but wasn't going to push it. She was nineteen now, legally an adult even if she'd been mature far beyond her years for longer than either of them would care to admit. Every day she looked more like him; she had his brown hair, his keen eyes, his half-cocked smile and snarky sense of humor that fell just short of caustic. It was Sara whose words had teeth. It was Sara he worried about.

"Are you sure you'll be okay with those two?" he asked, even though he knew she would be. "I could put it off a bit longer—"

"Absolutely not," Maya insisted. "You've put it off long enough. You are getting on a plane tonight and going to Zurich." Maya may not have inherited many of her mother's physical characteristics, but Kate Lawson lived on in other ways—in Maya's authoritarian tone, her increasingly commanding yet reassuring presence.

"Yes ma'am." She was right; he'd delayed the trip another week and a half out of what he claimed was necessity and none had argued, with Maria's death being so recent. But now he was just spinning his wheels. He had made a promise to Dr. Guyer, the Swiss neurosurgeon who had been working to reverse the deterioration of his brain—and, ironically, the man who had installed the memory suppressor that caused it. Guyer believed he had promising news, a possible treatment that he had developed in cooperation with Dr. Eugene Dillard, head of the Department of Neurology at the George Washington University School of Medicine in Washington, D.C.

"You have your passport?" Maya asked.

"I do."

"Toothbrush?"

"Yes."

"Phone charger?"

"Check."

"You'll call me when you land?"

This time his smile was genuine. "While I appreciate your concern, I'm not sure how much I care for the role-reversal. I'm supposed to worry about you, remember?"

"Last I checked, we worried about each other." Maya took a couple steps into the room. Hesitant steps, as if crossing sacred ground. "Listen. Before you go. I was thinking of, uh, doing a little housekeeping while you're gone. Might be the best time to do it, you know?"

"You shouldn't have to do that. I should be the one…"

"Can you, though?"

It was a valid question. So far? No. Not at all. He couldn't even bring himself to pour out the almond milk in the fridge, even though she had been the only one who drank it.

"Eventually." He zipped up his suitcase, just a single small carry-on. He'd only be gone two days. "Did you feed the animals?"

Maya chuckled softly. "Yeah. Well… one of them."

Zero frowned at that. He carried the suitcase out of the bedroom, Maya on his heels, and set it down in the kitchen, where Mischa sat on a stool at the counter with a bowl of pasta in front of her. She was so engrossed in whatever was displayed on the tablet screen she was reading that she nearly missed her mouth with a forkful of ziti. As it was, there were already two sauce stains on her Hello Kitty tee.

"It seems that Krauss has fully abandoned his Patrick McIlhenney alias," she reported.

"How do you know?" he asked, and then immediately followed it with a wave of his hand. "Never mind, I don't want to know." He had to keep in mind that he no longer enjoyed the amnesty that being a covert CIA operative afforded him; if Mischa was using some illegal means to track Krauss, then it was probably best if he could claim deniability.

Besides, she was nothing if not thorough. He didn't need to check her work.

"So where do we go from here?" he asked.

"I think we should try to locate the elusive Mr. Bright," said Mischa, still not lifting her gaze from the tablet. "Unfortunately that may prove difficult. My only connection to him was the sleeper agent who called himself Pin, and he was found in a dumpster three days ago." She said it candidly, as if reporting on her day at school. But Mischa was no stranger to death. "All I know is that he operates out of New York City. Midtown Manhattan, to be precise."

"But that doesn't exactly narrow it down," Zero remarked, rubbing his chin. "I'll talk to Alan, see if he can check his network." He and Reidigger still weren't on the greatest of terms, but he knew that his best friend would still help him when he needed it—especially if it was to expedite the delivery of a bullet into the head of Maria's killer.

"Hey." Maya snapped her fingers twice. "Look, I want to find him as much as you two. But right now, you"—she pointed at Mischa—"need to focus on eating. You're making a mess. And you are getting on a plane to Zurich in less than two hours."

Mischa glanced down at her shirt, only now seeming to notice the stains there. Zero nodded tightly.

He didn't want to get on a plane to Zurich. He wanted to find Stefan Krauss.

But he had responsibilities. Chief among them, being the single father to three girls. He had put revenge over family in the past, had seen the grave mistake of it. And the only way he could continue being a single father to three girls was to not die young from the slow deterioration of his own brain, and the only way he could do *that* was to see Guyer, let him run his tests, and pray to anyone listening that this experimental treatment might work.

"Fine. Then I'm off." He squeezed Maya's arm gently. "Keep this place from falling down while I'm gone, okay?" To Mischa he said, "And you—go to school tomorrow. No more skipping."

She looked down at her bowl as if its contents were suddenly very interesting.

"I mean it." His throat flexed, but he managed to add, "It's what Maria would want." It was still difficult to say her name aloud.

"Yes," Mischa agreed quietly. "It is."

"I should say goodbye to Sara quick. Where is she?"

"Where do you think?" Maya said flatly.

Of course. In her underground lair.

Zero pushed open the door to the basement and gently knocked twice on the wall. "Can I come down?"

"Sure," came the dull reply.

He made his way downstairs. It was nearly dusk outside, but with the single window covered in dark curtains it might as well have been midnight. Sara sat by the light of a single lamp, scratching a pencil against the page of a sketchbook.

"You're drawing?"

"No," she said without looking up, "I'm perfecting a triple lutz into a backflip. Really think I might have a shot at gold in ladies' singles."

Zero let the sarcasm slide. Sara had been distant for some time, but ever since Maria's death it felt as if she'd slipped away from them. She came and went like she was a hotel guest rather than a member of their family. She rarely came up for meals with them, if she was even home, and trying to force her only resulted in scathing blow-ups. He couldn't actually recall the last time he'd seen her eat something.

"I'm leaving," he told her.

"Okay?" The pencil continued scratching.

"I mean, I'm going to Zurich for a couple of days. I'll be back late Tuesday night."

"See you then."

He sighed evenly. Dealing with Sara lately required more patience than he would have thought himself capable of. "I love you," he said, and before she could say anything sarcastic he quickly added, "And if there was anything you ever wanted to talk about, I'm here for you."

"Actually, you'll be in Zurich."

Frustration bubbled inside him like rising bile, but he pushed it down. He wasn't about to leave the country on a sour note. "Fine. Then if not me, maybe someone else."

The pencil stopped scratching. Sara looked up at him without moving her head. Her gaze met his, and it made his heart break a little. She looked more like her mother every day as she grew into adulthood.

"Like who?" she asked.

"Like a professional."

"Ah. Someone paid to listen."

"Yes, Sara. Someone whose job it is to listen to you, heed your problems, and help you work through them."

"And what exactly would I say to them, Dad?" Sara slowly set the pencil on the page, closed the sketchbook around it, and set it upon her bedside table. "Maybe I could start with how I was kidnapped by an assassin and sold to human traffickers because my father had been a secret agent for the CIA my entire childhood?" She rose from the bed as she spoke, staring daggers at him now. "Oh, I know—maybe I'd ask how to reconcile the fact that the man who murdered my mother, who I thought died of natural causes, also saved my life twice."

Zero opened his mouth to speak—to apologize, not to argue—but she wasn't finished. Her voice rose an octave as she said, "Or maybe I should talk to a professional about how my stepmother was only my stepmother for all of two days before being killed by yet *another* assassin that was trying to kill you."

Zero squeezed his eyes shut, fighting against the urge to shout back, to make some excuse, to do anything other than try his best to be compassionate. "Please, don't talk about—"

"Don't worry," Sara interrupted, "I'm through talking. It doesn't fix anything. It doesn't solve anything. It doesn't bring anyone back from the dead or change anything that's happened. It doesn't make up for lies or crimes or murders." She strode to the base of the steps. "Talk to someone? Get real."

Sara stomped up the stairs. His first instinct was to go after her, to… well, to try to talk it out, but she'd made herself clear. So instead Zero stood there, and he sighed. He found his gaze drawn to the sketchbook she'd been working in, her page kept by the pencil.

He opened it.

It was a rough drawing, just graphite on paper, but Sara had talent when she opted to use it. In this case, she'd sketched a first-person perspective: an arm, extended, ending in a pistol. Sharp, angry lines represented the muzzle blast. Beyond the gun was a man, wearing a tank top, his eyes wide in surprise and his mouth open. There was a hole in his forehead, and behind him was the product of the exit wound, penciled brains and dark lines of presumably blood spatter.

"Jesus," Zero murmured.

*It's just a drawing,* he reminded himself.

Still, it was concerning.

Still, the man she'd sketched seemed somehow familiar.

He dropped the sketchbook back on the table. Maya was right; he had to go. He'd deal with this later. He was only one person, could only do one thing at a time, and right now going to Zurich and seeing Guyer was what he needed to do.

Zero trudged back up the steps to the kitchen, where neither Maya nor Mischa were even attempting to pretend they hadn't heard the argument.

"Where'd she go?" he asked.

"Stormed out," Maya told him. "Must have been one hell of a goodbye."

He shook his head. "I don't know what to do."

"You pick up your suitcase," she said simply. "Get to the airport. Don't miss your flight."

"Yeah." He did so, grabbed up the small carry-on and his car keys. "I'm off. See you in a couple days."

Maya walked with him to the door. "Before you go… here. Some light reading on the plane." She pulled something out of her back pocket and handed it to him.

It was a brochure; that much was obvious, but still it took him a moment to recognize what Maya had handed him. It was a brochure for a psychiatric treatment center in Fairfax County.

“Maya…” He kept his voice low so Mischa wouldn’t hear. “Are you thinking what I think you’re thinking? Are you suggesting we have your sister…” He lowered his voice another register. “Committed?”

Maya scoffed. “That’s an ugly way to put it. Think of it as involuntary psychiatric help.”

Zero shook his head. “I couldn’t. She’d hate me forever.”

His eldest shrugged a shoulder. “Not if it works.” She sighed, though it came out more as an impatient huff. “Look, you know I love Sara deeply. I would never suggest this if I thought there was an alternative. I just want her back. Don’t you?”

“Of course I do,” he agreed quietly. But this didn’t seem to him like the way to get that done.

“Just think about it. Have a safe flight. Call me when you get there.” She squeezed him in a brief hug.

In the driveway, Zero tossed his suitcase in the backseat of his SUV and then climbed behind the wheel. Before he started the car, he looked at the brochure once more.

Then he tucked it into the glove compartment.

He couldn’t do that to Sara. He wouldn’t.

Maya’s heart was in the right place, but she was thinking, as she almost always did, in the manner of most logical and efficient. While he admired her ability to do so, not every situation called for it, and this didn’t seem like one of them. There was a way to handle this; he just hadn’t figured it out yet.

Zero made a to-do list for himself in his head.

One: go to Zurich, see Guyer, start treatment.

Two: come home, deal with Sara.

Three: find and kill Stefan Krauss.

# CHAPTER TWO

Sara pedaled harder, pretending she didn't know where she was going even as she headed there, the breeze whipping at her hair. She wished she'd had the foresight to grab a hair tie from her bedside table before she'd stormed out, but anger had gotten the better of her and some sort of potentially misguided pride kept her from going back for one.

It was a minor inconvenience. She hadn't grabbed a sweater or light jacket either, but it was still early in September, not even officially fall yet, and even though the streetlights were flickering on, the air was still warm, pleasant even.

It was irritating how pleasant it felt. She didn't want to feel pleasant.

The evening was clear, cloudless; she could see a few stars already overhead. That bothered her. She didn't want a nice night for a bike ride. She wanted a shadowy, dusky night, with rolling clouds and thunderheads, possibly even some rain to fuel her anger and frustrations.

This was no ordinary life, and she was tired of being expected to pretend that it was. This was no ordinary teenage angst, and she was outright exhausted of people pretending that she could talk her way through it, or lose herself in a hobby, or whatever other ridiculous ideas they had that might work for normal people with normal problems. Normal people's parents hadn't been murdered. Normal people hadn't been lied to about it. Normal people hadn't been tortured and forced halfway around the world with the intention of being sold as a sex slave for some stranger.

More than that, she was just so tired of her family pretending that they could be normal. At least Mischa was understandable; she'd never even had a shot at normal to mess anything up. But Maya, the way she tried to channel her pain and anger constructively into academics and athletics and then a career, it was infuriating. Her dad, the way he tried to run a normal household, to get the kids off to school and work, the way he could pretend a wedding on the beach was something that people like them were allowed to have. Like it was something they deserved.

She pedaled harder, pretending she didn't know where she was going even as she headed there.

Sara was seventeen years old. She should have been starting her senior year of high school. She should have been begging her dad to buy her a car, worrying about her social life, deciding what art schools to apply to. She should have been flirting with boys and sneaking out to go to parties where she'd have her first beer.

Instead, she was an unemployed dropout with a GED. A recovered drug addict who thought at least twenty-five times a day about going back to the pills. When she looked in the mirror, it wasn't to adjust her lip liner or eye shadow; it was to make sure that the broken, soulless girl looking back could still fake a smile if she needed to.

To make sure she could look convincing if she ever had to lie about shooting her former drug dealer several times in the chest.

Hell, she'd never even had a boyfriend.

She'd left her phone behind at the house. Most teenagers would probably freak out without their lifeline to the world, but Sara had done it intentionally, for fear that her dad or Maya or even Mischa would be able to track her with it.

This was *not* normal. This was *not* okay. *She* was not okay.

She pedaled harder, pretending she didn't know where she was going even as she got there. Third Street Garage was an unassuming place, three wide garage bays with an adjoined office that smelled of motor oil and a small apartment behind it so that the flat-roofed building looked like an L from a bird's-eye view. It was both home and workplace to Mitch, a burly bearded mechanic who wore the same sweat-stained trucker's cap so frequently Sara simply assumed he slept with it on. But she knew that Mitch, the grunting, un-emoting proprietor, was just an alias for former CIA Agent Alan Reidigger, her dad's best friend and a man who had been friend, guardian, and, on more than one occasion, a life preserver to her.

The lights were off in the office but on in the garage.

Sara walked her bike into the small office, with its green Astroturf carpet and two folding metal guest chairs, and then let herself into the garage. The fluorescent lights overhead made her wince almost as much as the old stereo in the corner blaring a song, "Run Through the Jungle," the name of which she knew thanks to her dad's preprogrammed radio stations, but the name of the band it was by relegated in her mind to "Some Old Guys."

Alan's legs, wrapped in stained jeans and ending in big brown boots, stuck out from beneath the jacked-up front end of a car that was easily older than Sara. He sang along to the song, poorly and off-key and not caring at all even though she was certain he knew she was there.

He was harder to sneak up on than her dad was.

"Go ahead and turn it down if you want," he told her from under the car.

"Off is better." She cranked the volume knob to the left until it was entirely muted.

"To what do I owe the pleasure, Sara?" he asked her.

She skirted the question. "How'd you know it was me?"

"Lavender vanilla," he replied from his half-hidden place, referencing the body spray she preferred.

"Ah. Do you actually fix cars here?"

Alan chuckled. "Sometimes. Have to keep up appearances, don't I?"

"Guess so."

He lifted one of his bulky boots. "Pull me out."

She obliged, grabbing onto the boot with one hand. He rolled out from beneath the car, lying on his back atop a mechanic's… dolly, or gurney, or whatever it was. "What's that called? The cart thing."

"A creeper." He grunted as he sat up.

Sara grimaced. "Seriously?"

"Seriously." Alan grunted again, more significantly this time as he rose to his feet. He pulled a rag from his back pocket, already gray from use, and wiped his face. She grimaced again. "Does your dad know you're here?"

"If I say no, are you going to call him?"

He shook his head. "No. Just curious. You don't usually come down here by yourself."

She shrugged a shoulder. "Just had to get out for a bit. Dad left for Zurich and I didn't feel like suffering through a Maya lecture."

"Yeah, she's getting real good at that. How is he, anyway? Your dad. Haven't seen him in at least a week."

How was he? She wasn't sure how to answer that. Mourning? Overbearing?

"Pretending," she muttered.

"What's that?"

"He's fine," she said louder. "All things considered."

"Good. And how are you? All things considered."

Sara said nothing. She wasn't as good with words with her sister or her father. She knew she'd struggle to articulate what was going on in her head without getting frustrated, or angry, or a combination thereof.

Alan seemed to sense that. He gestured to a metal stool. She sat as he leaned against a workbench. "It's tough, for people like us."

"Like us?"

"Yeah. People that have…" He thought for a moment. "That have gone through things that are harder to relate to. Things that don't seem so… ordinary."

She arched an eyebrow. "You think that's what I want to be? Ordinary?" Maybe it came out a bit too defensively. Sometimes she hated how good he was at reading people.

Alan shrugged in response. "Don't know. But I know I do, sometimes. You know, I've spent more than four years now as Mitch. There are less than a dozen people that know who I really am. There's at least triple that number of people who'd want to kill me—or worse, people close to me—if they knew who I really was. This is the face I show the world because I have to. You see what I'm saying?"

Sara saw, but she said nothing.

"I go to the grocery store," Alan continued, "or the pharmacy, or I fill my car up at the pumps, and people probably think, 'look at that guy, he's just your everyday blue-collar mechanic.' They have no idea what's going on up here." He tapped a finger to his temple. "Or in here." Alan put a hand over his heart. "And that's tough. Gets lonely. So even though that number of people who know who I really am, what I really am, is small, I'm all that happier to have them. You need that. Everyone needs that."

Sara nodded slowly, staring at the concrete floor of the garage. She licked her lips, and at last opened her mouth. "I just… I think sometimes…" Then she sighed.

"Tell you what. Think for a minute about what you might want to say. I'm going to grab a beer, be right back. You want something to drink?"

"Make it two?"

Alan chuckled. "Sure. Root beer, or birch beer?"

It was worth a shot. "Root beer sounds good."

"Back in a flash." Alan headed toward the door that connected the garage and the office.

As soon as he was through it, Sara stood from the stool. She strode quickly to the workbench at the furthest end of the garage. The top of it was littered with tools; underneath was a gas-powered generator and an air compressor. And behind the compressor, she knew, was a rectangular steel toolbox. She reached for it, pulled it out, opened the clasp.

Inside the old toolbox was a loose socket set, a messy assortment of both metric and standard sizes, but the tray they sat in was a false bottom. She'd seen Alan pull this toolbox out once before, saw that the socket tray lifted easily, and she already knew what she would find beneath it.

She didn't care about the money, a bundle of emergency cash held together with a red rubber band. She didn't care about the fake ID or passport; they had Alan's picture on them anyway, a clean-shaven one from his younger years, showing what he used to look like before he grew the beard and became Mitch. He was thinner then, had fewer lines around his eyes, more color to his cheeks and no gray streaks in his hair.

There were only two things in the toolbox that interested her. First she took the compact black handgun. It was small, the barrel stubby, but it fit nicely in her hand and thin fingers. She didn't know what this gun was called but she knew enough to be able to find the release for the magazine and how to tell if it was fully loaded.

It was.

The second thing she took from the toolbox was a black cylinder. A screw-on suppressor.

Sara shoved the suppressor in her pocket and the gun in the back of her pants and closed the toolbox and pushed it back into its spot behind the air compressor, and then she hurried toward the office. She retrieved her bike and pulled open the office door and almost ran right into Alan Reidigger, who took a quick step back with two glass bottles in his hands.

"Oh! Sorry," she said quickly. "You're right. What you said. And, uh, I think I should get home. Thanks."

"Sure thing." He stepped out of her way as she walked her bike out into the night. "Get home safe. Come see me anytime."

"Thanks," she said again, and then she pedaled away from Third Street Garage as quickly as she could.

She did feel a small pang of guilt, taking advantage of Alan like that. He kept his guard up naturally, all the time, around everyone—almost everyone. He had a soft spot for her and Maya, always had. Ever since he'd revealed his identity to them, ever since he'd saved their lives in a Nebraska safe house, he'd been like a trustworthy uncle, the one they could run to when they needed to talk, when life at home got frustrating.

He'd never suspect what she had been there for, what she'd done.

*

Sara wasn't lying. She was going home. There was just one brief stop to make on the way.

Her dad had suggested she talk to someone. A professional, he'd said. That was a good idea, now that she thought about it. She had just the person in mind.

His name was Wesley. Wesley Strode. But he went by Wes. Wes was a professional, in his own right. He was a security guard at one of the fifty-something high schools in the surrounding D.C. area. Sara didn't know which one. But she knew where Wes lived.

Her dad had a slightly different idea of the type of professional she should talk to. But that wasn't the type of professional she needed. Someone like Wes, that's who she needed to speak to.

It took her more than an hour to pedal to Wes's one-story ranch-style house just outside the Mount Pleasant neighborhood. She didn't care; it was a nice evening and she was feeling better after her talk with Alan. She was in no rush.

She would talk to Wes. But talking, she knew, solved nothing. There was a whole saying about it and everything. Actions spoke louder than words.

Sara let her bike fall to the patchy grass of Wes's small front yard. She strode up to the front door and knocked on it. It just before ten o'clock at night and there were lights on inside.

"Yeah?" Wes yanked open the door, wearing boxer shorts and straining a white T-shirt with a beer belly that hung over his waistline. When he saw who it was he bristled instantly. "I'll call the cops," he told her quickly.

"No you won't." She had warned him, not two weeks earlier, not just with words but with two black eyes as a reminder. Wes was a big guy who used his size and strength to intimidate. But Sara had been training with Mischa for months. And if there was one thing she could learn from a thirteen-year-old former assassin, it was how to use someone's advantages against them.

Wes took a cautious step back. "This is my house, you're trespassing."

"I warned you," Sara told him. "Didn't I warn you?" She was reminded of a joke, an old sexist joke she'd heard somewhere, that she mentally tailored for her own use.

*What do you tell a serial abuser with two black eyes?*

*Nothing. He's already been told twice.*

She reached for the pistol at the small of her back. She'd already screwed the suppressor tip onto it.

Wes's eyes bulged at the sight of the gun. He tried to turn, to run, but Sara had it up, aimed, and fired a single shot at his abdomen. It hit as he was turning, entering right around where a kidney would be.

A tingle went up her spine as the gun chirped. She got a small thrill from the way it jumped in her hand.

"God!" Wes shrieked and fell to a knee. "Dammit!"

Words solved nothing. Actions spoke louder than words. Or they would, unless the action was silenced by a nine-millimeter suppressor and the words were screamed in agony.

Sara took a step over the threshold, through the open door. The TV was on in a quaint, wood-paneled living room, tuned in to some sitcom rerun from the late nineties.

"Wait," Wes panted, both hands pressed over the bleeding wound. "Wait, wait, don't—"

Wes had an ex-girlfriend, a lovely young woman named Becca who used to be a regular at the trauma group Common Bonds. Sara had long since stopped going to group but she still kept tabs on the women there as best she could. Becca's absence was notable; everyone there had heard the stories of Wes's abuse after Becca tried to break it off. His late-night drunken visits to her house. Having his friends threaten her on social media. Leaving her voicemails from payphones and intimidating her family.

Becca had stopped coming to group, not by choice, but because she was in the hospital.

Sara had warned him. She'd even gotten violent. It hadn't stopped him. It would never stop him.

"But this will," she said quietly. She shot him three more times. Wes stopped moving. Then she tucked the gun back into her pants and retrieved her bike.

She hadn't lied to Alan. She was going home. She'd just had to make one brief stop on the way.

# CHAPTER THREE

Zero's first instinct upon landing in Zurich was to head straight to the hotel and check in. But after he gave it some thought he realized that he knew very little about what it was that Dr. Guyer actually wanted to do with him, how long it might take to examine him, or how much of it could be done with the assistance of Dr. Dillard back home. Guyer was a hands-on sort of guy; Zero was all too aware that the only reason he was here in Switzerland was so that the neurosurgeon could get a direct look at Zero's head and not have to rely on being sent scans and reports.

In short, if Guyer didn't need him there for more than a day, Zero would catch an earlier flight back. As silly as it sounded for him to fly to and out of Zurich again in the same day, and as much as he had to realize that this trip was about potentially saving his life, he couldn't help but feel like it was a bit superfluous considering everything else going on at the time.

Almost funny, he thought, how often taking care of himself seemed to take a backseat.

He took a cab from Zurich Airport to within just a few blocks of the Swiss National Museum. He knew Guyer's address—he'd been to the office before—but it felt criminal to visit such a beautiful city and not get at least some cursory sightseeing in. Guyer's practice wasn't far from the museum, so Zero took his time, meandering down Löwenstrasse, parallel to the Limmat River. He admired the green-capped cathedrals, the centuries-old architecture. The air was a bit brisk; even in early September, at this altitude and latitude it wasn't even sixty degrees, but the views more than made up for it.

He did not venture inside the Swiss National Museum, as much as he would have liked to, but rather admired it from the outside. The building itself was stunning, unlike any museum he'd ever seen; the original museum was designed in 1898 by architect Gustav Gull, very much resembling a medieval monastery, while a modern expansion had been built in 2016, comprised of windowless angles and a palette on the beige end of the spectrum. The result looked something like a Hogwarts outbuilding had been added to by Elon Musk.

Last time he was here had been with his girls, a few years earlier. Before they really knew who, or what, he was. He'd left them in a movie theater watching a documentary about the history of Zurich from the Middle Ages to the present while he snuck off to see Dr. Guyer for the first time. Well—for the first time that he could remember.

*Dad of the Year,* he thought glumly.

And then…

Then Maria had shown up. She'd tracked him there, to Zurich. She knew what it meant, him being there, and she'd cared enough to fly there, all the way to Switzerland, to ensure that his appointment with Guyer had gone well.

And then she and he and Maya and Sara had spent the day together. The girls were, of course, a bit suspicious about the nature of Maria's sudden appearance in a foreign country, but they had taken a surprising shine to her. It was then, that day, when he first thought that they could have a real shot at normalcy. That they could have a life, even though at the time he hadn't fully known it would mean together.

*And what an idiot you were.* Normalcy? He didn't deserve normalcy. If he could go back in time to that day, he'd slap himself to his own senses. Where had attempts at normalcy gotten him? A murdered spouse. An addict for one daughter. A CIA agent for another, and he couldn't decide which of the two latter fates was worse.

He'd done enough sightseeing, enough recalling for now. Those memories, painful as they felt now, were all he really had left of Maria, and he couldn't lose them too. Zero crammed his hands in his pockets and doubled his pace toward the neurosurgeon's office and the treatment that he hoped would fix his brain.

Guyer's practice was located on the third floor of a wide, four-story professional building two blocks off Löwenstrasse and across a courtyard from a cathedral. This might have presented a strange sort of dichotomy had the structure, which couldn't have been more than twenty-five years old, not been built in a similar Romanesque style. It was as far a cry as could be from the bland, even uninspired sort of medical buildings that Zero was accustomed to in the US.

The modern interior of the building made the effect of its appearance all the more dizzying. There was even an elevator. Zero took the stairs.

On the third floor he found the dark oak door with a bronze knocker and the doctor's name inscribed on a metal plate above it. He chuckled then, at the sight of the honest-to-goodness knocker, recalling that on his last visit, Alina Guyer had electronically locked this door from the inside with just the push of a button.

He didn't bother with the knocker. The door wasn't locked anyway.

Zero pushed into the small reception area of the neurosurgery practice. It was instantly familiar; it looked like nothing much had changed since the last time he was here. Dr. Guyer's keen eye for art—or perhaps his wife Alina's keen eye—was on full display in colorful Impressionist paintings on the walls. The swirling textures of a Van Gogh, undoubtedly a print of course, was eclipsed only by the sinewy sculpture in the corner that Zero had since confirmed for himself with Guyer during a video chat was indeed a genuine Giacometti.

Even so, the hairs on the back of his neck stood on end. His instinct kicked in before his senses did, but it was there. A scent, at least an undertone of one, a layer just beneath the floral air freshener plugged into the wall. A coppery, metallic scent that would only be perceived for what it was by those who had smelled it before, yet every mammal brain was programmed to know it, to be repelled by it, to fear it.

Guyer's office smelled of blood.

Zero dropped his suitcase on the seat of a cushioned waiting-room chair and crossed the small room in three vaulting strides. Opposite the door was Alina Guyer's cocobolo desk, carved from a single reddish-brown irregularly shaped piece with dark, swirling patterns in the grain. On his first visit, the desk had been the second-most stunning thing in the room, the first being the natural beauty of Dr. Guyer's Swiss-born wife, Alina.

She had been the kind of woman who would leave any man breathless, perfectly arched eyebrows and pouting lips. Blonde hair that perfectly framed a heart-shaped face. Eyes that appeared too crystalline blue to be real.

She had been.

Those eyes stared up at him, wide and blue, deep as the ocean but vacant now. The trail of blood that ran from her desk to the hall to the place where she'd fallen, just outside the closed door of her husband's office, told Zero the story of what had happened.

But now was not the time for stories. Zero had no weapon but his own two hands but still he took a breath and threw open the door to Dr. Guyer's office.

It was still and silent in there and smelled even more of death than the reception room had. Guyer was there, seated behind the desk, his cheek lying atop it and arms at his sides. When Zero had last been here he had been impressed by the number of framed records of achievement that adorned Guyer's walls, among them certifications, diplomas, photographs of travels. They told of a life well lived, a life of curiosity and exploration and accomplishment.

Here, now, the arc of arterial spray across the walls and frames told Zero that Guyer had not been killed in his chair, behind his desk, but rather posed there.

There would be time for shock later. There would be time to mourn the loss of a friend, of two innocent lives—if he was even capable of more mourning. But the blood was fresh, still bright and wet, not yet dark and dry. This had happened recently. Less than an hour ago by his best guess.

Whoever did this might still be here.

Zero bolted out of the office, past Alina's body a second time, further down the hall and into a wide white room with dim blue lighting. This was Guyer's examination room, the largest of spaces in his practice to accommodate the array of medical equipment he used—*had* used—for his consultations. He did not perform actual surgeries here (those would be done in a hospital setting with specially trained assistance) but still the room contained an X-ray machine, a magnetic resonance imaging scanner, and an ultrasound generator. Along the furthest wall were monitors and computers and a mounted light box for reading scans.

Broken. All of it was broken. Anything glass had been cracked or shattered. Metal had been dented. Wires, exposed and torn out.

Why?

*To make it look like a robbery?*

No…

*To make it look personal.*

Zero frowned.

*Was this personal?*

He quickly checked the washroom, the utility closet, and a small kitchenette before determining definitively that whoever did this was long gone.

He hurried back to Alina's desk, which required passing her body a third time. He recalled that the button to electronically lock the door was affixed to the underside of the beautiful Brazilian rosewood desk. He pressed it, and heard the lock slide into place.

He sat behind at the computer and clicked the mouse. Their appointment bookings were digital, open on the desktop. A quick glance told him that Guyer had cleared the entire day for him, for Zero's appointment. The killer was gone, and no one else would be showing up here unexpectedly.

At last the tension ran from his shoulders. He took a deep breath, let it out slowly in a long sigh, and rubbed his face with both hands.

"I'm sorry," he said hoarsely to the empty office, the blood on the floor, the two bodies.

He immediately wondered why he did that. Why had he apologized? Because, simply, he assumed that he had something to do with this. Yet he knew he shouldn't jump to conclusions. Guyer could have had enemies. Other clients with dangerous associations.

*Like who? The Swiss mafia?*

At last he rose, wiped the mouse clean of his prints, and returned to Alina's body. He knelt beside her and let her tell her story.

She had no defensive wounds. In fact, she had only one wound at all. It took some careful inspection to confirm it, as her hands as well as the front of her were covered in blood, but the narrative became clear.

Someone had entered the practice. Someone unassuming enough that they had not raised any alarms. Alina had probably smiled at them, asked how she could help. They might have smiled back, for the sake of their cover, as they approached the desk. That's when they struck, just once, an incredibly well-placed and clean shot straight into the jugular vein of her neck.

Zero retrieved an ice cube from the kitchenette and rubbed it gently against the woman's throat until he cleared the puncture site of excess blood. It was thin, tiny, like a keyhole. Whatever sort of blade had done this was narrow and smooth, not serrated…

A scalpel, he realized. Someone had murdered her with a surgical scalpel.

Alina had stood then. One hand, maybe both, would have flown to her throat as she realized with horror what had just happened. Maybe, in that same instant, she even realized that she was going to die. And in her very last moments, with literally seconds before she passed out from blood loss, she had tried to run down the hall to warn her husband. She had gotten to the door of his office.

Had it been open at the time? Had she been able to cry out with a hole in her throat and blood running down the front of her?

Zero stepped back into the office. He studied the spray of Dr. Guyer's blood on the wall, streaking down the glass-framed diplomas and photos of fishing trips, hikes, climbs, getaways. The door had been open, most likely. Guyer had heard his wife, or seen her, or both, and came running. She fell in view of the open door. He ran to her. And the assailant merely stepped over her, and one clean slash to the doctor's throat was all it took. Guyer must have turned then, partially, spraying the wall. The killer waited until he was dead, until they were both dead, and then he dragged Guyer's body to the desk and sat him in the chair.

Zero shuddered. Behind his desk, Guyer looked like he could have been napping after a long day. His prematurely white hair was still impeccably parted, barely disturbed. He might have dozed off during paperwork. If it wasn't for all the blood, he might have just been resting his eyes for a few minutes, waiting for Zero's arrival.

Whoever had done this was not afraid of a mess, but they'd made it quick. Clean kills, at least in the sense of effort. They'd used a blade instead of a gun. No excess. No need for pain or explanation or prolonging the inevitable. They had come here with an express goal, carried it out, and got out. The broken machinery was to throw off investigators. Make it seem like a jilted patient, perhaps.

This had Stefan Krauss written all over it. He might as well have signed his name in Guyer's blood.

Zero shook with anger, but he felt the chill of something else—fear. If Krauss knew about Guyer, he might know about Eugene Dillard. He certainly knew about the girls, and might know about Alan Reidigger.

He had to make calls, and now. But even as he reached into his pocket he noticed something—a single drawer of the wooden filing cabinet in the corner of Guyer's office was open, just a couple of inches. All of the other drawers were closed firmly, except for that one. He crossed the room quickly and yanked it open, using all of his fingers to rifle through the manila tabs. The one he was looking for, the one he already knew with a sinking feeling would be there, was the last in the row, all the way at the back of the drawer. Its tab had only one character written on it, in black felt-tip pen: a circle with a slash through it. A zero.

He pulled it out, opened it, already knowing just as he knew it would be there that it would be empty.

Of course Guyer was the sort who would keep hard copies of Zero's records. And he would have been equally keen to keep Zero's name, real or otherwise, out of the records. But if whoever now had them already knew who he was—as Stefan Krauss did—then they'd be as valuable as they'd be damaging.

Killing Guyer and his wife wasn't the goal here. Killing them was a necessity to get to the files on Agent Zero. Not personal, but an obligation. And now they would know about the memory suppressor, about its removal, about the deterioration in his brain, about the slow death that Guyer was trying to stymie or stop and now never would.

And that truth hit him just as hard. He'd come here hoping for a solution, or at least the hope of one, and would be leaving with less than he came with.

Zero shoved the folder back into the filing cabinet and slammed the drawer shut. As he reached again for his phone he heard three thunderous booms from somewhere close by. He froze, confused for a half a second about what he'd heard.

Then he ran back to the small lobby. The booms came again—a fist, pounding on the locked door. Angry voices from the other side, loud but muffled, foreign words. Zero's throat ran dry. And then they kicked in the door.

"*Einfrieren!*"

# CHAPTER FOUR

There were three of them, in the dark uniforms of the *Kantonspolizei Zürich*, the city's municipal police force. The jamb of the locked door splintered and two came in almost at the same time, pistols out, up, aimed. The third behind them, a bald officer, was the one who shouted. And even though Zero's German was more conversational than fluent, Swiss German as a dialect was close enough that he understood the command.

"*Einfrieren!*"

*Freeze!*

He threw both hands up over his head. "*Bitte,*" he stammered, "uh, *warte—*"

*Please. Wait a moment.* That's what he wanted to say, was trying to say, but there was a pistol in his face and behind it, a scowl, and he fell silent.

The killer had called the police. He had probably reported the murders. Had he watched Zero go into the office? Was he still nearby, even now?

The two armed officers kept their guns on him as the third hurried down the hall.

"*Lieber Gott,*" he heard.

*Dear God.*

"*Englisch,*" Zero pleaded. "English?"

In response, one of the two officers put a heavy hand on Zero's shoulder and forced him to his knees.

The third officer returned, shaking his head. "Two dead," he said in accented English, more to Zero than the others, his tongue clicking with the forcible pronunciation.

He was all too aware of how bad this looked. Two freshly murdered corpses, and Zero behind a locked door. If the building had cameras, and he suspected it might, they would show him entering several minutes earlier but hadn't called the authorities.

The two guns remained on him as the third officer pulled a pair of handcuffs from a pouch on his belt.

He couldn't fight his way out of this. If he was still with the CIA, and on an operation—if his actions were in service of country or the world, if there were lives at stake—then perhaps he could get away with fighting police officers. But he wasn't an agent anymore. He wasn't on an operation. He was here for a doctor's appointment that no one outside of his immediate influence knew about. Even his pal, US President Jonathan Rutledge, wouldn't be able to get him out of an international incident involving a dead neurosurgeon and an altercation with Swiss police.

Switzerland didn't have a Miranda warning, but they did have an equivalent, the reading of rights upon arrest that dictated the right to remain silent and the right to legal counsel. Zero got no such warning as the metal cuff ratcheted closed around his left wrist.

That was his first sign.

These cops hadn't radioed anything in. They hadn't called for backup, or to report a double homicide, or to call for emergency services of any sort.

That was his second sign.

And the third— *Einfrieren.* That's what the cop had shouted at him when they kicked the door in. At the moment Zero had been blindsided, hadn't thought twice about it. But *einfrieren* meant "freeze." And in German it was literal. No German-speaking cop would say "freeze."

"*Halt,*" Zero said.

The cop behind him paused. "What did you say?" he hissed.

A German-speaking officer would have told him to *halt.* Same in German and Swiss German as in English.

"You're not the police," Zero said quickly. He jerked his wrists to keep the second cuff from closing around it. "You're not even Swiss, let alone German. Mercenaries, I'm guessing? Maybe friends of Krauss. What, he couldn't face me himself?"

"Keep still or I'll have them shoot you!" the fake cop behind him barked.

"No you won't." Zero's heart pounded as he called their bluff. He had no other choice; he was on his knees with his wrists behind him, already in execution position. "If you wanted to shoot me you would have done it by now. You were supposed to burst in here, pretending to be cops, arrest me, and take me somewhere. Is that right?"

The shadow of a glance, an uneasy one, passed between the two in front of him.

“Shots fired would be loud,” Zero rattled on. “They’d attract attention. Maybe even the real cops. Besides. I don’t think you’re supposed to kill me.”

“Shut up!” The one behind him grabbed a fistful of Zero’s hair and yanked his head back. He winced as the cop hissed in his ear. “Smart, huh? You have it figured out, yes? But you are wrong about something. We are not *supposed* to kill you… but if you give us trouble, we will just say you gave us no other choice.”

The two mercs in front of him reached for their belts. Each pulled a silver tube, about six inches long, and set about screwing them to the ends of the barrels. Silencers.

The one behind him let go of Zero’s hair with a short, braying laugh.

The barrels were off of him, but they would be for only a precious few seconds.

He had to act now.

Zero threw himself forward from his kneeling position and shoulder-rolled between the two men. They shouted at each in alarm as he leapt to his feet and reached for the only available weapon at his disposal.

It was almost painful to do so. His late (first) wife had been a restorations expert and a lover of all things art. He wouldn’t have even recognized the lanky sculpture as an Alberto Giacometti if it hadn’t been for Kate, and wherever she was now she would be sorely disappointed as he grabbed the figure by its shoulders and hefted it upward.

The sculpture was bronze, waist high on Zero, and substantial in weight. Still he swung it, two-handed, like a golf club. The wide base caught the closest of the trio where his jaw met his neck before he could reposition his aim.

The impact sent shockwaves up both his arms. The smack of it was as satisfying as the crack of a whip; the man’s head twisted at an odd angle and his body followed limply.

The statue completed its arc back to the ground and Zero went with it, letting its weight pull him down as the other Glock chirped twice.

*Thwip! Thwip!* Two suppressed shots cracked the wall where Zero’s head was a half-breath ago.

He grunted as he lifted the statue again, as if to swing it, but this time released it and sent it sailing into the arms of the second armed man. He caught it awkwardly but didn't expect the weight to be what it was, sending him collapsing backward.

Zero sprang up, noting the ache in his legs—he hadn't even stretched that morning, much less expected a fight—and kicked out with the heel of a sneaker. The bald cop who'd tried to cuff him was ready for it and caught his foot.

Suddenly Zero doubted these guys were affiliated with Krauss. They were amateurs.

While both the cop's hands were busy with the captured foot, Zero leaned forward and grabbed his lapels with both hands. Then he leaned back, letting himself fall, and the cop fell with him. With his foot still planted against the bald cop's abdomen, Zero rolled back, pushed off with the planted leg, and threw the man upside-down into the wall in a stupendous crash.

*Someone will have heard that,* he noted.

The man he'd hit with the statue lay motionless, his eyes open and vacant, neck at an odd angle and his gun within reach. Zero grabbed it, rose to one knee, and fired two shots at a downward angle. Then another two shots. Chest, head, chest, head.

And then there were none.

He sat on the floor and breathed for a moment before he realized he needed to move. The crash against the wall might send someone investigating. Even silenced shots were not completely silent.

He scrambled over to the bald cop and located the key to the handcuffs. He wiped the cuffs and key on his shirt and left them both on the reception room carpet. The gun he tucked in the back of his pants; he could ditch it in an airport bathroom if need be.

Then he grabbed up his suitcase and scooted out the broken door.

He kept alert as he reached Löwenstrasse, checking and rechecking his periphery to see if anyone might be following him. When he was fairly sure he was in the clear, he stopped a passerby, a Swiss man in his fifties with silver eyeglasses, and asked, "English?"

"Yes?"

"Please call the police," Zero told him. "There was a shooting in that building." He pointed. "Five dead."

The man frowned deeply. "Pardon me?"

But Zero didn't wait around. He strode on quickly, suitcase in one hand as he pulled out his phone with the other. He wasn't sure what the real *Kantonspolizei Zürich* would think of the crime scene. He hoped they wouldn't assume that the dead fake cops had anything to do with Guyer's and Alina's deaths. He knew those three weren't the culprits; they were sloppy, favored guns. They were probably former military, or militia types, not professional assassins.

Not like Krauss.

And if the wrong conclusions were made, then the only one looking for Guyer's killer would be Zero.

He made the first call. Alan answered on the second ring.

"Alan? I'm in Zurich. Guyer's dead. I'll be on the first plane back, but…"

"I'm on it," Alan said quickly and ended the call.

Zero said a silent prayer for good friends. They hadn't spoken more than a few sentences to each other since Maria died, but in the event of an emergency nothing would stop Alan from coming to his family's aid. He would make sure the girls were safe.

Maybe it was unnecessary. If Krauss was behind this, he'd be a thousand miles from their home. But the assassin's network was vast, and if German mercenaries could come for Zero then they could come for them.

His second call was to the doctor.

"Dr. Dillard's office," said a pleasant-sounding receptionist whom Zero knew as Tricia.

"Put Dillard on please," he said urgently.

"I'm so sorry, Dr. Dillard is with a patient at the moment. If you'd like to leave your name and number—"

"Tell him it's Zero. He'll want to take this call."

"I'm… so sorry," the woman said again, "but as I said, he's with a—"

"This is a matter of life and death, Tricia. Put Dillard on. Now. Please."

She was silent for three irritating seconds. "One moment," she said tightly.

Zero continued his brisk pace, heading back toward the Swiss National Museum. As soon as he was off the phone he'd call an Uber to take him back to the airport and hop the first flight back to Dulles.

"This is Dr. Dillard."

"It's Zero. I'm sorry, there's no time to soften this blow. Dr. Guyer and his wife are dead. My files were stolen from his office—"

"Good lord," said Dillard. And then, "Are you certain?"

It was a ridiculous question, but one borne of bewilderment.

"Very," Zero confirmed. "Pretend everything is all right but you're not feeling well. Close your office. Get your family and go somewhere safe. Tell no one where you're going. Lay low for a bit. Stay off the phones. Got all that?"

"I…"

"Dillard," he said sternly. "Guyer is dead. My files are gone. You and your family may be in danger. Do you understand?"

"I… yes. Yes, I understand."

"Good. I'll be in touch." Zero ended the call, and hoped against hope that this was all paranoia, and that everyone else he knew, everyone he loved, would be perfectly safe.

# CHAPTER FIVE

Maya paused for a moment on the marble floor of the expansive lobby at Langley. Under her sensible flats was the seal of the CIA, the eagle and shield, the arcing words across the top and bottom that read *Central Intelligence Agency. United States of America.*

She'd made it. Her goal had been to become the youngest field agent in the history of the agency, and here she was, just shy of twenty years old—an impossibility, most would say, but they didn't have her background and experience. Her age alone was enough to raise questions about how she'd gotten so far, about her deservedness of a seat at the table. But she'd done the work. Tested out of high school early. Got into West Point on a recommendation from none other than the current President of the United States. Gained favor with the dean, Brigadier General Joanne Hunt, and was granted early graduation from the academy (a first, to her knowledge) by virtue of being accepted into an experimental CIA training program. She'd done her dues as a dark agent—and by "dues" she meant that she'd refused to kill someone without evidence of their crimes—and had been recommended as a field agent.

And finally, accepted as a field agent.

If there was a bitter taste on the back of her tongue it was because she knew, no matter how hard she tried not to acknowledge it, that her current status was partly due to one Agent John Watson, the man who had murdered her mother. A man whom Maya had assumed had fled the country in favor of anonymity only to reappear as a dark agent with the CIA, the division that handled "specialized removals."

Calculated assassination was what they were. Murder, if she was calling a spade a spade.

She'd prided herself on getting as far as she had on her own merit, without her father's help. In fact, just the opposite—her dad had been very vocal quite often regarding his feelings about her joining the CIA. She doubted he would have helped even if she'd asked.

So the knowledge that it was Watson who ultimately had a hand in making her dream a reality, a man she was inclined to loathe out of necessity, a man she wanted very much to die by her own hand and ideally soon, was an indelible stain on her otherwise impeccable record.

But—she was here. She had done it. And if she had any hope of finding Watson again, to make her new dream a reality, she was in the right place to do so.

"Don't tell me; I know what you're thinking."

The male voice behind her was chipper, jocular, and Maya bit her lip at the sound of it in an attempt to keep herself from smiling. She didn't want to give him the satisfaction.

She turned. "Good morning, *Agent* Coleman."

"Right back at ya, *Agent* Lawson." Trent Coleman had been her partner on their sole dark agent op, another inductee of the CIA's program and the only one besides her to pass it. He was twenty-two, tall, handsome, with movie-star genes and equally award-worthy cheekbones. He was as smart as he was affable. It seemed that everyone loved Trent Coleman; there was hardly anything at all to dislike about him, which was why Maya had entirely detested him when they'd been forced to partner.

Since then, she could admit that her feelings had softened a bit. But only a bit.

"So?" she asked as she folded her arms. "What am I thinking?"

"You are thinking about how incredibly, *devastatingly* unfair it is that I look this good." He grinned his boyish grin and spun once to show off the dark blazer, red tie, white shirt, all bespoke to his frame by the looks of it.

"That so?" Maya raised an eyebrow. "Then what are you thinking right now?"

"I'm thinking," he said slowly, taking a step toward her, "about how incredibly, *devastatingly* unfair it is… that I look this good."

She couldn't help it. A thin smile cracked. "Ass."

"Harpy."

"Let's go."

"After you, partner."

Maya led the way to the security checkpoint, where they swiped keycards and walked through metal detectors, all very procedural and professional. Just the way she imagined it would be. Just the way she wanted it to be.

For her first official day on the job, she'd chosen a charcoal blazer with light pinstripes and matching slacks. She was grateful that her dad was in Zurich, or else he might have noticed that she was old enough to fit in her mother's old clothes. She'd had little time to shop lately and needed a wardrobe expansion, so last week she'd raided a box in the attic that her dad had kept and secreted it away to the dry cleaners and back again.

She thought of Maria's clothes, still hanging in the bedroom closet at home, and her offer to handle them for her dad while he was away. But he'd declined, said he would take care of it. She doubted it would be anytime soon.

"So where are we supposed to go?" Trent asked her as they walked side by side down a wide corridor.

"I get the feeling you were the kind of guy who had no idea where his classes were on the first day of school," she mused.

"What's your point?"

Maya rolled her eyes. "Conference room C. It's right up here."

Her phone buzzed in her pocket as they approached the door. She checked it; it was a call from Mitch. Which meant Alan Reidigger.

"One sec," she told Trent. "Hello?"

"Where are you?" There was an urgency to Alan's voice she instantly disliked.

"Langley."

"Good. Stay there. Possible trouble brewing, I don't have the details. I'm going to get the girls, keep them with me until I hear otherwise. You have somewhere to go that's not home if need be?"

She glanced over at Trent Coleman, who was checking his hair in the reflection of a framed portrait of former President George W. Bush.

"Uh… yeah. I guess I do. You need me?"

"I've got it," Alan told her. "Might be nothing anyway, and Langley's pretty much the safest place you can be. Just steer clear of the house until you hear from me or your dad."

"Will do." She ended the call and resisted the urge to turn on a heel and march out of there. While it seemed like there was a crisis in their household every other week, she still couldn't help but worry for her sisters and her dad. But Alan had a handle on things. And he was right; no one would try to get to her here.

"Everything okay?" Trent asked.

"Family drama."

"Say no more." He didn't push the issue. Trent knew that her dad used to be Agent Zero. He knew that a dark agent had killed her mother, and he knew that she'd been trafficked when she was younger. Apparently those meager facts were enough to keep him from prying into her personal business.

She entered the conference room first, Coleman on her heels. She paused abruptly and he nearly ran into her. She hadn't expected to see so many faces. There were nine others in the room, every one of them clearly and significantly older than her, some possibly even as old as her dad, in pressed suits and combed hair with thin lines for mouths.

Maya suddenly felt like a child. For all her academics and accolades and experience, she felt every bit the amateur among pros.

It certainly didn't help that she was the only female in the room.

"Well!" said Trent behind her, louder than it felt the somber audience warranted. "If this isn't a party."

"You must be my rookies," said the man at the head of the long rectangular table. He stood, and Maya blinked; he was short, five-seven at best. Even she had a couple inches on him. "Sit."

There weren't any two available seats next to one another, so Maya took the closest vacant swivel chair and Trent sat across from her.

"Hi," he murmured to the agent to his left. "Hi," to the one on his right.

Neither responded. Maya shook her head at him.

"For our tenderfoots," said the man at the head of the table, "allow me to introduce myself. I am Deputy Director Walsh. I run the CIA's Special Operations Group of Special Activities Division."

To her, Walsh looked more like an accountant than a deputy director. He was short and slight of build, wore black-framed glasses, and his nose and chin were angular, almost pointed, in a way that was reminiscent of a rodent.

"And you are?" Walsh asked expectantly.

Trent sat up straight in his chair. "Trent Coleman, sir."

"Sorry?" Walsh leaned forward and tilted his head as if he'd heard wrong.

"Agent." Trent cleared his throat. "Agent Trent Coleman. Sir."

"Agent Maya Lawson," she said loudly and clearly.

"Lawson?" A devilish smirk crossed Walsh's lips, though it looked foreign there, as if it hadn't been used often. "I believe I may have known a relation of yours."

"I believe you may have, sir."

"Big shoes to fill," he remarked.

He was toying with her. He knew damn well who she was before she walked into this room. He'd no doubt read her file.

Maya stared back at him, unblinking. "I'm not here to fill anyone's shoes. Brought my own. Sir."

Walsh nodded slowly. "We'll see, Agent." He clapped his hands together once and kept them tented. "All right. You've met the newbies. You have your assignments. SOG2 team, you'll take Lawson. SOG3 will take Coleman. Use them as you see fit, break them in—"

"Sir." The syllable slipped out of her mouth like a sneeze, unwillingly and forcefully. "With all due respect, Coleman and I work well together. We were partners… we *are* partners."

Walsh took a deep breath in and out through his nose, flaring his nostrils dramatically. "Lawson, I honestly expected to last more than three minutes in this meeting before I likened you unfavorably to your father. Yet here we are."

Maya's throat flexed. Obviously some bad blood had passed between this man and her dad, and now on to her. Despite its vulgarity she was reminded of an old saying: *shit always rolls downhill.*

"What I'm saying, sir, is that either team would benefit more from having both of us than each would from only one of us," she said quickly.

"You're suggesting that I put not one, but two green agents on one of my Special Activities teams? Hmm? Teams responsible for operations that ensure the safety and freedom of not only the people of this United States, but the world over?" Walsh leaned on the table with both hands. "Is that what I'm hearing, Agent Lawson? That you and Coleman are such a great team that no security threat could possibly surmount your… what, power of friendship?" He scoffed.

"Yes," Coleman joined in, though he didn't meet Walsh's stare. "That is what she's suggesting. Sir." He nodded to her once.

To Maya's surprise, the man to her left straightened in his chair. "SOG2 will take them both if it's agreeable. I've read their files; seems they can handle themselves—"

"Ah." Walsh held up a hand and the agent fell silent, though Maya noticed a slight curl of his lip. "I appreciate the sacrifice, Agent Fisk, but I'll run this show, thank you." Walsh straightened his tie. "SOG2, SOG3, dismissed. The two of you—stay put."

"Thanks," Maya said quietly to the agent at her left, apparently called Fisk.

"Good luck," he muttered back.

The eight other agents filed out of the conference room, the last of them closing the door behind him and leaving only Trent, Maya, and the deputy director at the table.

Walsh unbuttoned the top button of his suit jacket and sat on the edge of the table. Maya gritted her teeth; in her experience, it was a gesture typical of adults who wanted to show affinity or camaraderie right before they talked down to someone.

"I don't like you much," Walsh said candidly.

*Well, so much for camaraderie.*

"Was just thinking the same, sir."

"I didn't like your father, either. If I'm to expect the same tactics from you, I'm sure it's just a matter of time before you blow up a city block or something."

Trent coughed. Maya smiled.

"Depends on the city, sir."

Walsh smirked mirthlessly. "But in the meantime, we're at an impasse. I can't transfer you right out of the gate and I can't fire you without good reason. I'm sure you'll give me one, sooner than later, but until then the only thing I can do is suffer you. Certainly doesn't help you're female; human resources is all about the diversity hires these days."

Maya wondered if an arrest for assault would be worth the satisfaction of breaking his jaw.

"But you two want to stick together? Fine by me. A few hours ago the NSA handed over some chatter that suggests a possible Islamic sleeper cell in Paris. Ninety-nine times out of a hundred, it's nothing. Some guy tries to order falafel in Arabic and it gets mistranslated. But someone needs to look into it. Ordinarily that'd be Interpol, but if our president's treaties are on the line here and someone is planning something, we make it our business."

"You want us to go to Paris," Maya said flatly.

"I do. Yes. Ideally as soon as possible. You look too much like your father for this conversation to go much longer without triggering my PTSD."

She knew precisely what this was; Walsh was assigning them a low-level throwaway op and trying to get a rise out of her. Trying to get her to react negatively, maybe even physically. If she did, he'd have immediate grounds to fire her. If she didn't, they'd be relegated to an operation that should have been assigned to a tech who was used to cold coffee and surveilling for hours on end.

And even though her first instinct was to argue, there were far worse things than a few days in Paris eavesdropping on a Muslim man who was probably flagged just for using the word “bomb” out of context.

Besides. No way would she give Walsh the satisfaction of getting under her skin.

“We’re on it, sir.”

“We are?” Coleman asked.

“We are,” she told him.

“Terrific,” Walsh said with no inflection. “Get your briefing from Agent Fisk. Then head down to R&D and gear up. Fisk can show you where—”

“I know where it is.” Maya stood and buttoned the top button of her blazer.

“You do?”

She allowed herself some gratification from Walsh’s surprise; she knew Dr. Penelope León well, and had even on one occasion used Maria’s keycard to access the subterranean level of Langley where Penny’s lab was located.

“Of course I do.” She smiled as sweetly as she could muster at the deputy director.

“Come on, Agent Coleman.”

“Um, yup.” Trent stood quickly and followed her out.

But Walsh, it seemed, was not yet content to leave it be.

“Right,” he said loudly behind her. “Dr. León is chummy with your family, isn’t she? Speaking of—”

Maya stopped in her tracks, one hand reaching for the doorknob.

“I heard about what happened. So sorry for your loss. Maria Johansson was… well, she was really… *something.*”

*Son of a bitch.*

She could hear the smirk in his voice. The wry satisfaction of knowing just where to jab. Try as she might, she couldn’t let it go. Walsh had just stepped in it.

“Go ahead, Trent.” She nodded to him. “I’ll be there in a minute.”

“Maya…” he said in a low voice.

“It’s fine,” she promised.

Trent looked from her to Walsh and back again, and then he left the conference room, closing the door behind him.

Maya turned back to the deputy director. She didn't dare step closer to him out of fear that her urge to relieve him of a few teeth would be too great.

"Let's get one thing straight," she said. "You may be my boss. You can order me around, chastise me in front of other agents, send me on shitty assignments. But you don't get to say her name to me, ever again. Understand?"

Walsh dug a pinky in his ear. "Are you threatening me, Agent Lawson?"

"I am. And you can tell whoever you want that I did so, and you can tell them *why* I did so." She looked him up and down, and she scoffed. "On your best day you're not half the person she was." Maya turned on a heel and pulled the door open.

"For now," Walsh said.

"Sorry?"

"I'm your boss… for now." He smiled wide. "Good luck in Paris."

Maya joined Trent in the hall, and they headed to the elevators wordlessly. It wasn't until she had pressed the down button that Trent finally said, "That guy… is a world-class dick." He let out a ragged sigh. "Are we really going to Paris all for some chatter? You know that's almost always nothing."

"Oh, I know it's almost always nothing." The elevator doors opened and she stepped in. She would go to Paris. She would do the job. If nothing else, it would give her some time to figure out what to do about her deputy director problem. "But sometimes, it's something."

# CHAPTER SIX

Mischa had a game she liked to play. She sat up straight in her chair, eyes open, attentive, nodding every now and then when the teacher said something particularly meaningful.

It was a game like any child might play; make-believe or playing pretend or whatever they might call it. In her game, Mischa was pretending to be an undercover agent. She'd recently discovered several spy novels on Zero's shelves (and another, curiously, in the trash of his bathroom when she'd gone in there in search of Q-tips), burned through them in a few days, and decided she would become a spy.

In order to be a spy, she had to be undercover. In order to be undercover, she needed an alias. And her alias, she decided, was that of an ordinary eighth-grade student, eager to learn, one who didn't know the material being taught. She sat up straight and stayed attentive. She jotted down notes in the spiral-bound notebooks that Maria had bought for her. She wore ordinary clothes like any other girl in her class, and she pretended to be a spy, because otherwise school would have been terribly insufferable.

"Now, who can solve for x?" Mrs. Court asked, gesturing to the equation she'd written in black marker on the dry erase board. "And remember, you must be able to show your work."

Mischa might have scoffed, but she could not blow her cover. Of course she already knew that x was 9. She'd been solving algebra tougher than this since she was seven years old. And show her work? Why? Wouldn't it be far more impressive to know the correct answer *without* showing her work?

"Anyone?" asked Mrs. Court.

Mischa did not raise her hand, because her alias did not know the answer. Knowing the answer might give her away. In her game, she suspected that Mrs. Court was feeding intel to the Serbians, names and possible locations of her fellow undercover agents in Europe.

While her history teacher, Mr. Blankenship, droned on and on about the American Civil War, Mischa suspected that he was part of a cabal that owned a construction company and had laced the cement foundation of several new buildings with explosives.

When the wood shop teacher, Mr. Heder, commended her on a near-perfect cut with a miter saw, Mischa knew he was speaking in code that would translate into coordinates leading to the last-known whereabouts of Stefan Krauss.

Of course it was just a game. Equally of course was that Krauss invaded even her imagination. There were few times when she didn't think of him; school barely held her attention, and every glance in the mirror showed her the fading vestiges of the bruises that Krauss had left her when they'd fought in the courtyard of a downtown DC hotel.

She'd had him. She'd *had* him.

And now he was gone.

She would have much preferred to skip school and spend her time in search of him anew, but Zero insisted on her formal education, which up until now had been decidedly informal.

*It's what Maria would have wanted.* That line was growing tiresome, even if no less true.

A tone sounded from overhead. Not the bell; class wasn't over for another twenty-three minutes. The tone was a PA announcement, and it was followed by a flat female voice who said, "Mischa Johansson, please report to the main office. Mischa Johansson to the office."

Mischa frowned. The last time she'd been called to the office, the guidance counselor, a thin woman with frizzy hair named Ms. Biggs, had spent thirty minutes asking her gentle questions about the bruises on her face.

Mrs. Court nodded to her. "Go ahead, Mischa. Take your things with you."

She closed her textbook and notebook and shoved them into her backpack, and then slung it over her shoulder as she strode to the door. Children whispered to each other behind her, as they would when a classmate was called to the office, speculating on her possible offenses.

She had been honest with Ms. Biggs. Mostly honest. She'd told the guidance counselor she had gotten in a fight with a boy, and that her sister had come to her aid, and that the boy ran off.

Mischa walked down the empty hall, glancing into rooms with open doors as teachers lectured and students took quizzes.

Ms. Biggs had asked her about things at home. Of course the school knew that Maria had died. An American tourist being murdered on foreign soil was a big deal; even the CIA had some trouble with the cover story. Ultimately what came out to the press was that the murderer was a crazed homeless man that the police had apprehended two days later.

Ms. Biggs had asked her about that too. If she wanted to talk about it. The guidance counselor asked if she fought with the boy because she was lashing out.

She asked Mischa about her feelings no fewer than eight times in their meeting.

*How does that make you feel?*

To which Mischa had finally asked, *Why is that important to you?*

She wasn't a danger to herself or others unless others were a danger to her first.

Mischa reached the administrative office and immediately saw why she had been called.

"Hey, kiddo," said Alan Reidigger. He wore his sweat-stained trucker's cap and overalls and brown boots, looking remarkably out of place in the white office with fluorescent lights. "I'm here to pick you up for your dentist appointment."

Mischa had no dentist appointment, but she nodded anyway. "I almost forgot."

"Your uncle has already signed you out," said the woman behind the administrative desk. "We'll see you tomorrow, Mischa."

Perhaps they wouldn't. When Maria had registered her for school, she had put down "Uncle Mitch" as a family member in the event that Alan had to pull her out for any reason. His presence there could mean only one thing.

Something was wrong.

But neither of them showed it. Alan held out a hand, and she took it, and they walked out of the office and down the hall.

"What is it?" she asked, keeping her voice low.

"Not sure yet."

"It must be something if—"

"Just wait 'til we get to the truck," he told her.

They walked in silence out of the school, down the concrete steps, across the parking lot to Alan's rusting pickup. It was at least twice Mischa's age and looked as if it might fall apart at the seams at any moment, though she knew that it topped out at a hundred and forty miles an hour and could outmaneuver most sports cars.

She climbed into the passenger seat and waited for him to explain, but Alan said nothing as he turned over the engine, backed out of the parking space, and left school grounds.

"Well?" she said impatiently.

"Well." Alan scratched at his beard. "I don't have details. Zero called, said we should hunker down. So I'm getting you and Sara, and we're going to hunker down."

Mischa thought for a moment. "He found something in Zurich."

"How do you figure that?"

"It is obvious," she reasoned. "He no longer has CIA affiliation so it is unlikely intelligence was given to him. Yet going into hiding means there must be some perception of imminent threat. He could not have landed in Zurich more than… ninety minutes ago. Therefore—he must have arrived and found something. Or something found him."

"Nothing gets by you, does it," he muttered. "All right, look. The doc he was supposed to see? Zero found him dead."

"Murdered?"

"I assume."

"Krauss," she said immediately.

"Now, we don't know that—"

"It is obvious," she said again.

"Not exactly his style," Alan pointed out. "Last time he had the chance to kill Zero he didn't, because…" He trailed off, but Mischa knew exactly what he meant.

Krauss had accidentally killed Maria instead, and had let Zero live with the intention of hunting him another day. If Krauss knew that Zero would be visiting the doctor, he would strike at Zero, not those close to him…

"Unless it is retaliation," Mischa pointed out. "I attacked him. Maya and I fought him off. Perhaps killing the doctor is sending a message."

"If that's the case," Alan countered, "then the message is 'hunker down, stay safe.' That's what we're going to do."

"But," Mischa argued, "Krauss is smart enough to know that Zero would assume the same, that those close to him might be in jeopardy and that he would return home immediately. Which stands to reason that Krauss would then come here. Which means that we should not, as you say, 'hunker down,' but set a trap. Be where he expects us to be, and spring on him."

Alan scoffed as he rolled to a red light. "And how well did that end up for you last time? Springing on him? You're gonna sit there before those shiners he gave you are even healed and tell me you're keen for round two?"

"Yes," she said forcefully. And then she added in Russian for good measure, "Stupid fat man."

"I speak Russian, kid."

"I know."

Alan sighed. "Just… humor me here, okay? Zero's probably at Zurich Airport right now hopping a flight home. Once he's back, we'll convene, and we'll plan. Together. Isn't that how you were supposed to do this?"

He wasn't wrong. But she wouldn't admit that. It had been more than two weeks since Maria's murder, and they had done nothing. Gotten no further on Krauss's trail. And now, having him reappear like this, having the possibility of a legitimate lead and… hunkering down? It was unconscionable.

The light turned green and Alan eased off the brake.

Mischa made her decision.

As the truck picked up speed, she shoved open the passenger-side door and threw herself out. She rolled into it, landing on the pavement with her right shoulder, onto her back, and coming up on both feet.

Then she ran.

"Ah, dammit!" she heard Alan Reidigger shout behind her. Brakes screeched. When she looked back, the truck was parked right in the intersection and Alan was giving chase.

She had to give him credit; he was faster than she'd imagined he would be, light on his feet for a larger man.

"Mischa, stop!" he shouted after her. Car horns honked at the vacant truck. Passersby gawked at the large man in overalls chasing a teen girl down the street.

Up ahead was an apartment complex. She could vault the fence, lose him in there.

"Mischa!" he yelled behind her.

He wasn't yet winded. She put on a burst of speed. Her legs were shorter than his, her strides double-time.

"Mischa," she heard him shout behind her. "Is this what Maria would want?"

She reached the chain-link fence at full speed, but instead of leaping it, she crashed against it, grasping with both hands, stopping herself suddenly as anger washed over her.

Alan slowed to a trot behind her, panting hard.

Her cheeks burned. She spun on him. "No more!"

"What?"

"That is not an excuse anymore!" She pointed at him. "I am exhausted of people telling me what Maria would have wanted. We don't know what she would have wanted! She's dead!"

"I know, kid. I know. I'm sorry." He put his hands on his knees and stared at the ground. "Just wanted you to stop."

Mischa wiped her eyes. "I want to kill him."

"We all do. But… I need your help." Alan straightened with a grunt. "Maya's at work. I don't know when Zero will get back. And we both know Sara can be a handful. She listens to you. Help me out? Please?"

Mischa shook her head. He was right, again, annoyingly. Sara was, it seemed, at odds with the whole family in one way or another. Except for her.

"Fine," she relented. "Just until Zero is back."

"Just until he's back."

Mischa walked past him wordlessly, back toward the truck still parked in the intersection. She would be true to her word and go with him to retrieve Sara. She would, as he put it, "hunker down" until Zero returned from Zurich.

Maria was dead. But still, it's what she would have wanted her to do.

But if she caught even the slightest scent of Stefan Krauss, no force on this earth would stop her from pursuing him.

## CHAPTER SEVEN

Most days, President of the United States Jonathan Rutledge enjoyed his position. He hadn't, at first, having been the Speaker of the House when the previous administration had been impeached and suddenly finding the Oval Office foisted upon him. He'd had no long-term delusions of presiding over the country, especially because he was fairly certain that anyone who pursued the office must be delusional.

And yet here he was. And most days, Jon Rutledge enjoyed his position. But sometimes, he found the pageantry of it a bit ridiculous.

Case in point: the executive order currently before him. Executive orders from the president were (generally) absolute, could only be turned over by Congress after the fact, and yet he could not simply wave a hand say, "I decree…" like some medieval monarch. There were procedures, the first of which involved meeting after meeting with key personnel involved in said order. Then the White House legal team drafted a formal document for the order—in this case, two small paragraphs on a single sheet of white paper. That sheet of paper was then mounted on the right-hand side of an honest-to-goodness black leather portfolio emblazoned on the cover with the seal of the President of the United States. Finally, the executive order (which had been Rutledge's idea in the first place) was then delivered to him as he sat behind the Resolute Desk in the Oval Office so that he could put pen to paper, deliver unto it his John Hancock before an audience, and make it official.

Sometimes he wished he could just wave a hand and say, "I decree…" like some medieval monarch.

His audience today was only two people. Vice President Joanna Barkley sat in an armchair on one side of a round area rug, while the Director of National Intelligence David Barren sat on a loveseat opposite her with his left leg crossed over his right.

Rutledge had never seen that loveseat before. They'd gone and replaced the furniture, rearranged the office once *again*, a process that seemed to happen at least once a month and that he had little doubt his wife, Deirdre, had a hand in. She'd always wanted to be an interior decorator.

He wished he knew what either of them was thinking. Barkley, he was certain, was always thinking something; her mind seemed to work like a clock, one cog turning another turning another and turning another, an efficient machine. Despite her relative youth—thirty-seven and in the office of vice president—there didn't seem to be a problem she couldn't solve.

And then there was Barren. The reason for their meeting today was a poignant one given his presence. His only child, a daughter who had worked in the service of Rutledge himself, had been murdered not two weeks prior, and yet here he was, to bear witness to the signing of the executive order.

There was a knock at the door, and Chief of Staff Tabitha Halpern stuck her brunette head between the doors. "Sir? He's here."

"Send him in, Tabby, thank you."

Depending on the nature of the order, there might be cameras. There might be more bodies in the room. The text of the order might be published to a government website. None of those would happen today.

A moment later the door opened again, and a young man in a suit entered. He looked immediately uncomfortable, likely due to the clothes as much as the pageantry. His eyes darted left to right—to Barkley, to Rutledge, to Barren, and back to Rutledge. Had there been another exit in the room the young man's gaze might have swept over that too.

Then he saluted the president.

"Agent Strickland." Rutledge chuckled as he rose from his chair. "Put that hand down and come in. No need for formalities, we're all friends here."

Todd Strickland nodded. "Thank you, Mr. President." He stepped forward, nodding to Barkley. "Ms. Vice President." And in turn to the DNI. "Director Barren."

Strickland was thirty-one, a former Army Ranger turned CIA agent, as clean-cut as they came. He kept his hair short, his face smooth, his nails trimmed. The collar of his white dress shirt was starched and impeccable; the top button was hidden beneath a blue tie but undoubtedly straining over his thick neck. Strickland was loyal; he'd been a member of Rutledge's Executive Operations Team since its inception, serving alongside Maria Johansson, Alan Reidigger, and Agent Zero.

Now Maria was dead. Zero had retired. Reidigger had quit as well. EOT needed rebuilding, and Todd Strickland was lead agent.

"You know why we're here," said Rutledge warmly, still standing.

"I do, sir."

"Actually," the president corrected himself, "you know *half* of why you're here. So let's get that part out of the way, sound good?"

"Yes sir."

Rutledge put his pen to paper, and he signed the order. There were no cameras, no photo ops, no quotes for the press. No pomp and/or circumstance. Just the scratch of a pen. "There. Done. He's all yours."

The first paragraph of the order, the two-paragraph single sheet of white paper in a black leather portfolio, effectively released one Preston McMahon from the remainder of his duty with the United States Army, specifically the elite 75th Ranger Regiment headquartered at Fort Benning, Georgia.

The second paragraph, equally immediate, made McMahon a member of the Executive Operations Team, a small and unilateral division of the CIA that answered only to the three people in the room: the president, the vice president, or in the event of their absence, the Director of National Intelligence.

DNI David Barren was there in a professional capacity. But he was also there to witness his deceased daughter's replacement.

"So that makes four," said Rutledge.

"It does, sir."

"Are you comfortable with four, Strickland?"

"I am, sir."

Strickland had personally vouched for and vetted the other two new members of EOT. First had been O'Neill, a former Blackhawk pilot with three tours under her belt who had garnered national attention two years prior when she rescued an eight-man special ops team from an Afghan hot zone. Second had been Hauser, a Secret Service agent who Strickland hadn't served with but knew personally. His actions at the bombing of the Queensboro Bridge had saved dozens of lives.

They were young guns, all of them. In fact, Strickland was now the eldest member of EOT. But they were loyal, they were patriots, they were fighters.

Still—Rutledge wondered what Zero was doing right now.

"Sir?" said Strickland.

"Speak your mind, Todd."

"Shouldn't McMahon be here for this?"

Rutledge chuckled. "It's his last night with his pals. He doesn't need to see me sign my name. He'll be on a red-eye to DC tonight, and by morning you'll have a full team again."

He winced internally when he said "again." Strickland had lost friends. Barren had lost a daughter.

Rutledge lowered himself to his chair again. "Now then, on to the second item of business, and I'll turn it over to Vice President Barkley for that. But first, have a seat, Todd."

Strickland nodded, and then sat beside Barren on the loveseat, his back straight.

Joanna Barkley cleared her throat and leaned forward. "As you're well aware, Agent Strickland, our administration has been working fervently toward strategic alliances with no ulterior motive other than peace with nations that have been historically… tumultuous."

Strickland nodded. "Peace with the Middle East."

"Moreover," Barkley corrected, "peace *in* the Middle East. While many of the pieces, as they say, have been falling into place, it's that one little word—'in'—that has managed to elude us so far. It's not enough for the United States to ally with them. One might even argue it is more important that they ally with each other as well as us. And the fact is, only Israel and Palestine have made that successful union as of yet. A significant accomplishment, to be sure, but not enough."

"We're making a push," Rutledge chimed in. "A big one. There's going to be a summit."

"A peace summit?" Strickland asked, but he nodded even as he did, answering his own question.

"Egypt will host," Barkley told him. "In just two days' time. And if all goes according to plan, leaders from all of the Middle Eastern nations allied with us will sign the Cairo Accord, guaranteeing peace, free trade, and shared resources between them."

"The accord," said Barren, speaking for the first time since greeting Rutledge, "will also expand the joint task force that was established between the US, Israel, and Palestine to create a new international organization to facilitate cooperation and maintain the peace."

"Like Interpol," Rutledge added, "with a bit more specificity." He stood, came around the desk, and sat upon the edge of it in a manner he hoped was more genial. "This is the big show. Everything we've been doing, everything we've been working towards, has led to this."

"Which is why," said Barkley, "the summit is and *must* remain top-secret. It's why we couldn't tell you, or anyone else, sooner. Based on recent events, there are too many out there who might want to attempt a… disruption, of some sort."

Strickland nodded. No one had to expand on the type of possible disruption Barkley was referring to; the young agent had been there when Rutledge had been kidnapped by a Palestinian terror group during the signing of a treaty in Jerusalem.

"You want EOT there as security," Strickland said in a way that was almost a question.

"More than that," said Rutledge, "I want you and EOT in *charge* of security. I want you to vet every single person who will be in attendance. I want you to ensure that everyone there belongs there and no one's there that doesn't."

Strickland nodded, though he glanced away, toward a lamp, and frowned slightly as if he was working out an equation in his mind.

"There's not a lot of time. We'd need help," he said at last. "Dr. León. If the CIA is willing to loan her."

Rutledge suppressed a smile, recalling the time Dr. Penelope León had cut the power to the entire White House and appeared in his bedroom to deliver a personal message from Zero. "Director Barren can see to that."

The DNI nodded. "Consider it done."

"And once again," Barkley reminded him, "we cannot stress enough that this is as top-secret as secret can be. The public will know about the accord the day it happens and not a moment sooner. That includes the media."

"Of course, ma'am."

"Good." Rutledge stood, and Strickland did as well. "Director Barren will get you everything you need, including Dr. León. Thank you, Agent Strickland."

"Thank you, Mr. President." They shook hands, and Strickland marched out of the Oval Office.

"You think he's up for the task?" asked Barren once the door was closed again. "He's young."

"So am I," said Barkley casually, though the intent behind it was enough for Rutledge to chuckle slightly. The Cairo Accord had been almost entirely Barkley's brainchild; she had even drafted the first version of the document herself.

"I have every faith in him," said the president. "And in EOT."

The Cairo Accord would be a historic first. It would go down without a hitch. Even if his own confidence waned now and then, he was confident in the people he'd surrounded himself with.

Still—he wondered what Zero was doing right now.

# CHAPTER EIGHT

"Zero's on the plane," Alan reported.

"Don't text and drive," Mischa scolded.

Alan scoffed and put the phone down. He'd once changed clothes, head to toe including shoes, while out-driving intelligence officers in Hamburg. He could handle reading a text.

"Sara is still not answering," Mischa told him as she tried a third time to call her. They were only a few minutes away from the house. "Will we tell her the truth?"

"If she asks." Alan knew they were far past the point of keeping information from the girls. Time was that the less they knew, the better, but Maya was an adult now and Sara was right behind her. The only reason he'd refrained from telling Maya what he knew was that she had a job to do, needed to stay focused. Despite the disdain that Reidigger had for the CIA, not to mention its current management, he knew that Maya had worked hard to get where she was. She didn't need to jeopardize that over what might turn out to be nothing.

His phone buzzed again. He read the message and frowned.

"Don't text and drive," Mischa told him again.

"I'm not texting, I'm *reading* a text." He didn't elaborate, but Zero's latest message was concerning.

*Flying to NY. Will call from there.*

Why was Zero going to New York? Maybe there were no direct flights available from Zurich to Dulles and connecting in New York was his fastest way home. But even as he thought it, he doubted it. Zero was resourceful and Alan had connections. If he needed to get home fast, they could find other means.

*So what's in New York?*

He pulled into the driveway of the one-story suburban bungalow. Mischa already had her house key out. She unlocked the door and punched in the six-digit code to disarm the alarm. The fact that the alarm was still armed was promising.

Alan stood in the foyer and listened for a moment. He heard nothing. No signs of a break-in or even an attempt of one. He went to the basement door and pushed it open. It was dark down there, almost pitch-black, and from somewhere in the space below he heard gentle snoring.

She was asleep. Of course she was asleep.

"Sara?" he called down. "Sara."

"Sara!" Mischa shouted sharply from his side. Alan jumped a little.

"Mm? Who?" came the groggy reply.

"It's Alan and Mischa," he said loudly.

A moment later a light clicked on. Sara appeared at the foot of the stairs, barefoot in pajamas and a ponytail. But her eyes were alert. She knew what this might mean.

"What is it?" she asked.

"I need you to throw some things in a bag and come with us."

Sara instantly looked annoyed, and opened her mouth as if to say something, but then she looked to Mischa standing beside Alan. The younger girl nodded just once, and Sara shut her mouth.

It was a good thing she hadn't outrun him.

"Fine." Sara turned and vanished from sight.

"You too," Alan told Mischa. "Grab some essentials, change of clothes for at least two days…"

The girl scoffed lightly. "As if I don't have a go bag." She scurried to her bedroom and reappeared not thirty seconds later with a small duffel. Sara took only another minute before she trudged up the stairs, still in pajamas but her feet in sneakers and a black backpack over one shoulder.

She didn't ask any questions as Mischa re-armed the alarm and locked the door behind them. Mischa sat in the center of the truck's bench seat as Alan pulled out of the driveway.

"So?" Sara asked at last. "What is it this time?"

Alan was about to give her the standard "not sure yet" reply, but Mischa spoke first.

"Zero's doctor in Zurich was murdered—"

"We don't know that for sure," Alan pointed out.

"Fine. He was found dead. But probably murdered, and probably by Krauss—"

"We don't know that either."

"And he wants us to… what was it, Alan?"

"Hunker down."

"Yes. We will hunker down until Zero is back."

“Ain’t that swell,” Sara said flatly. “So might be something, might be nothing.”

Alan eased to a halt at the stop sign at the end of their street. He glanced in his rearview, and kept his foot on the brake, frowning.

Three blocks behind them, a black cargo van rolled to a stop outside Zero’s house, coming from the other direction.

“Alan?” Sara said.

“Hang on,” he murmured. At least four men climbed out of the van—four that he could see. They marched briskly up the walkway toward the house. He didn’t see guns in their hands but had little doubt they were armed.

“So it’s something,” Sara said quietly. She saw the van too, in the angle of the side mirror.

Mischa twisted in her seat. “We should go back. Get answers from them.”

In response, Alan made a right-hand turn and headed up the street going about five miles over the speed limit. He didn’t want to draw attention but wanted to put some space between them and the men in the van before they realized no one was home.

“Did you not hear me?” Mischa said indignantly. “They might know—”

“They won’t know anything,” Alan argued. Whoever was behind this, Krauss or otherwise, knew that Zero couldn’t possibly be back in the US by now. The men in the van were lackeys, foot soldiers, goons, whatever the term might be. And Alan knew from experience that giving men like that more information than they needed was often dangerous to the perpetrators of whatever plot was in play. “Even if they did,” he added, “they don’t exactly look like they’re going to share.”

“We could make them!” Mischa countered.

Alan said nothing. Between the two of them, him and her, they probably could. But he’d made a promise, and that promise was to keep the girls safe, not run headlong into a fight.

As it was, they’d gotten Sara out of there without a minute to spare. He didn’t want to think what might have happened if they’d arrived and found her alone and asleep.

“So what’s next?” Sara asked. “Where do we hunker?”

“First we’re going to the garage for some supplies,” Alan told her. “But we’re not staying there.” Few people knew about his identity, but those few were still a few too many when their adversaries were unknown. “There’s a safe house about an hour away, in the sticks. I set it up a little while back for an occasion like this. We’ll go there, wait to hear from your dad.”

Sara just nodded. Mischa had her arms folded over her thin chest defiantly. He had no doubt that if he’d let her, she would have rushed right back into the house—and probably would have won. But “probably” was too far from a safe bet.

And despite how close a call it was, they were safe. For now.

*

Alan parked the truck in the alley behind Third Street Garage so it was off the street and out of sight. Only the middle of his garage bays was being used, but he didn’t want anyone to see him pulling in or out. He and the girls entered the office through a back door. He grabbed a canvas bag from under the desk and pushed into the garage. The old beater he’d been working on was still there, a renovation job he’d been doing for an acquaintance in return for a favor. He hadn’t disclosed what the favor would be; just that he’d be owed a favor.

He didn’t need money. But favors, those could always come in handy.

“This won’t take long,” he told the girls. “Go into my apartment and grab whatever food and necessities you find. There’s a first-aid kit in the bathroom and two gallons of water in the pantry. I’ll meet you there.”

Sara and Mischa dutifully hurried off. Once they were gone, he tore a poster of Dale Earnhardt off the wall. Behind it was a pressboard panel that pulled away easily, and behind that was a small hollow in the wall that contained a Heckler & Koch MP5. The German submachine gun was small for its capability, elegant, and admittedly looked a bit out of place in his large, calloused hands.

Alan had nine guns hidden throughout the garage. Some might call him paranoid—and he’d concede it, all things considered—but he had spread them throughout so that he was never more than an arm’s length away from one if need be. Some were easier to get to than others, like the Glock 17 that was hidden in a holster bolted to the underside of his workbench, right under a pneumatic vise so he knew just where to reach. Others were a bit more secured, like the small black Walther

PPK he had hidden in a steel toolbox behind the air compressor on the far side of the garage.

He opened the toolbox and lifted away the false bottom.

The PPK wasn't there. Strange, he was certain that's where he'd left it. It couldn't have been discovered and stolen; there was a few thousand dollars in cash in the toolbox that had been left behind.

Eight. Alan had eight guns hidden throughout the garage. He couldn't concern himself with where he'd misplaced the PPK right now. There were enough others.

He had five guns in the canvas bag when he heard the sound. Just outside the garage bays. The slightest squeal of brakes. Boots on the ground.

Alan threw himself to the floor and landed hard on the concrete. Automatic gunfire erupted an instant later, shredding all three of his garage doors. He covered his head and stayed flat as debris fell, as glass shattered. The old beater was buffeted by bullets.

*So much for that favor.*

After what felt like a full minute but was only seconds, the gunfire finally ceased. Alan crawled forward on his elbows and knees until he reached the bag and pulled out the MP5. He dared to rise to a kneeling position and aimed at the open doorway between the office and the garage.

Glass shattered again as the assailants forced open the office door. But he didn't fire, not yet.

He heard their footfalls. They were coming. He could only hope that the girls had made a run for it. But he knew they hadn't. Mischa wouldn't run from a fight and Sara wouldn't leave him behind.

*Just stay where you are,* he hoped.

He saw a barrel track in the doorway, about to spin on him.

Then he fired.

The MP5 rattled like the beater's engine. The first two men trying to come through the door fell dead before half a yelp.

Alan ceased fire. He didn't move an inch from his position. From the office he heard a harsh whisper of warning, which meant there were at least two more. If these were the same men he'd seen at the house, there were at least four. Hopefully only four.

And he was pretty certain he knew where one of them was.

Alan took careful aim at the thin span of drywall separating the office and garage, and he squeezed the trigger again, tracking left to right. Parabellum rounds pounded the wall, sending chunks of chalky sheetrock airborne.

A scream. A body thudded to the floor.

There was movement in the office through the holes he'd made, someone getting out of the way quickly.

Alan knelt there. He waited.

So did whoever was on the other side. He couldn't see him, couldn't hear him, but now he was fairly certain he'd been right. There'd been four. Now one.

"If you put it down," said the man in the office, "I won't hurt those kids."

Alan said nothing in return. These men had already made it perfectly clear they weren't there to take anyone alive.

"You want something to happen to them? Huh? So how about we—"

*Thwip!*

Alan heard the telltale chirp of a silenced gunshot. The dull thud of a body hitting the floor. Then silence.

He was bewildered. Was there another one of them out there? Had Mischa gotten her hand on a gun?

"It's… it's just me." Sara's voice. "I'm coming in."

She rounded the corner. In her hand was a stubby black pistol with a suppressor on its end. A Walther PPK.

It struck him suddenly and painfully. The real reason she'd visited the night before wasn't to talk to him. The reason she'd run off in such a hurry wasn't because he'd given such good advice.

And now Sara had killed someone, shot them dead, and stood there just as lucid and plain as could be.

*This is not the first time Sara has killed someone,* he realized dully. But now was not the time to deal with that.

"We have to move," he said urgently as he stood and hefted the canvas bag. He traded the MP5 for the Glock 17 and sidled to the office door. The entire neighborhood would have heard those shots; the police had undoubtedly been called, but still he had to make sure there had only been four.

"Are any still alive?" Mischa asked from the open back door.

"Just meet me at the truck," Alan told them. "Go." Sara wouldn't meet his gaze.

He peered out through the broken glass of the office door. The black van he'd seen earlier was parked sideways right outside the garage, the engine off but the doors open. He didn't see any movement, so he cautiously stepped outside and had a quick look around, keeping the gun pointed downward.

He brought it up level as he cleared the van. It smelled of stale cigar smoke but was empty, other than a black rectangular utility trunk on the floor of the backseat.

He flipped the clasps and opened it.

Then he ran.

Alan Reidigger knew a bomb when he saw one, even if it didn't have an active countdown at six seconds. He didn't have time to shout a warning; he simply bolted back to the office, across its small span in three strides, to the back door.

Mischa stood there, just beyond the door. Why was she there? She was supposed to go back to the truck. No time. His mind registered her like a photograph, frozen there, brow furrowed in confusion about why he was barreling toward her as fast as he was capable of moving.

The explosion was so loud it jarred every sense at once. The shockwave pushed him off his feet, through the open rear door, into Mischa. He landed hard with a grunt of pain and rolled on the concrete just outside the entrance to his apartment.

His ears rang as flaming debris rained down around him. He coughed as he pushed himself to his elbows and knees.

The garage was burning. What was left of it, anyway. A failsafe, he realized; a bomb on a timer in case their assailants failed to kill them. Had they been successful one of them probably could have disarmed it with a flip of a switch.

Whoever was behind this wanted them dead, and they were willing to sacrifice their own people to get the job done.

"Mischa," he said breathlessly. The girl had landed a few yards from him. She lay on her side with her eyes closed and her mouth open. He scrambled over to her and felt for a pulse.

It was there. She was alive. Just unconscious.

No time. Police would arrive soon. Others. They'd want to ask questions. They'd want Mischa to go to a hospital and Alan to go to the precinct. And if that happened, whoever was after them would know exactly where to find them.

He slung the canvas bag over his shoulder and scooped Mischa up in his arms. She felt like a frail bird in his hands, limp and barely weighing a thing. He hurried toward the alley, the waiting truck, and Sara…

And found only two of those things.

"Sara!" he called out, his voice hoarse. "Sara!" He didn't see her. He didn't hear her. She wasn't inside at the time the bomb went off. Where was she?

He quickly put Mischa in the cab of the truck and reached for his cell phone. Then he groaned; the screen was cracked and it refused to power up. He'd crushed it when he was thrown by the bomb's impact.

Sirens wailed. They weren't far off. Alan had a decision to make, a difficult one. Sara was alive somewhere. She hadn't been inside. He just knew it. Had Mischa been conscious, maybe he'd choose a different route. But as it was, he had no choice. He couldn't lose them both.

Alan climbed behind the wheel with a grunt and started the truck. He'd have to take Mischa to the safe house. Get her secure, and then find Sara.

He would just have to hope she'd still be alive when he did.

# CHAPTER NINE

Her ears still rang from the explosion. It had happened so suddenly she still felt disoriented. Still felt the dense, congealed fear in the pit of her stomach. One moment she'd been crossing the small concrete courtyard between Alan's apartment and the alley.

"Wait," Mischa had said. "The bag." She'd left a bag in the office. She turned to go back for it. Sara took one step closer to the alley. And then…

And then she'd been forced to the ground as if she'd been hit by an invisible truck. The sound of it was so loud it could hardly even be described as a sound at all, more like a force, one that shook her bones and rattled her teeth and made her instantly nauseous. Her head swam; stars swirled in her vision.

When she climbed to her feet she was dizzy, taking staggering steps. The office and the garage behind her were on fire.

She was three blocks away before she even realized that her legs had carried her away from the scene. That tight fear in her gut had taken control, urged her to get away from that place before it happened again. Her brain finally took over. She'd abandoned them. She'd left Alan and Mischa behind. She had to go back.

Were they even alive?

They had to be alive.

Of course they were alive.

She had to go back…

Sirens screamed toward the scene. It was easy to spot, black smoke billowing high into the sky above what used to be Third Street Garage. If she went back now, she'd be facing the police and all their questions.

She still had the gun in her hand. She was standing on a street with people around and she still had the gun in her hand. Fortunately anyone around was far too concerned with the nearby explosion to look her way. She quickly tucked it in her pants.

She still had the gun. And she still had her phone. She pulled it out and tried to call Alan. It went directly to voicemail. She tried to call Mischa. No answer there either.

Sara joined the gathering crowd of rubberneckers at the corner as a fire truck blared past them. Then another one. A police cruiser. An ambulance. She couldn't go back. They'd find bodies.

How many would they find?

Alan had told her about a safe house. But he didn't tell her where it was. She could never find it on her own. Who else would know? Her dad, maybe.

She tried his cell. It went straight to voicemail. She didn't leave a message.

"Okay," she told herself. "Okay. Okay."

She was walking again before she knew it. Who else could she call?

Maya. Call Maya.

She tried her cell. It went straight to voicemail. She didn't leave a message.

Sara still had the gun. She still had her phone. The phone—whoever was after her could probably track her that way.

But her family might try to contact her.

She turned it off.

*Where am I going?* she asked her feet.

*Home. We're going home.*

There was nowhere else to go.

*

Sara didn't know how long it took her to walk home. She didn't know what time it was, only that it was still day. And she was tired.

At last she reached her street. The black van was gone. She approached the front door carefully. At a glance it looked perfectly normal. Upon closer inspection she could see the cracked jamb where it had been kicked in. She gave it a push and it swung open easily, the locks broken.

In the foyer, the panel of the alarm system had been torn off. Colorful wires hung out, cut. Whoever did this knew about the alarm and had quickly disarmed it. She doubted the emergency signal had gotten out. The police would be here if it had. Or there'd be some evidence that someone was here, other than the broken door and the vandalized panel.

She kicked off her sneakers and padded softly to the kitchen. Nothing was tossed; the men who had come here had been looking for people, not things.

It was quiet.

She wondered if the same men who had come to the garage were the ones who came here first. It seemed likely.

Who were they?

They were dead now. She might never know.

Sara pushed open the door to the basement and went downstairs. She liked it down there in her cave-like room. The natural light all but snuffed. It could be nighttime down there. It could be anytime down there.

She heard a sound over her head. Water running through pipes. She knew that sound; she heard it every time someone flushed the toilet upstairs.

Someone was here.

Sara slid the gun from the back of her pajama pants. She went to the base of the stairs. She knew she should stay put, stay silent. Whoever was here probably already checked the basement.

But her shoes were in the foyer. If they saw them…

She took one stair up. Then another. At the top of the stairs she heard another familiar sound; the bathroom faucet running. She turned the corner from the kitchen to the short hallway that led to the bathroom and, at its end, Mischa's bedroom.

A man came out of the bathroom. He was dressed all in black but she couldn't see his face because he was rubbing a towel against it.

She raised the gun.

He lowered the towel.

The man's eyes went wide. He had bushy eyebrows and a black beard.

"Now, hang on—"

She shot him twice. His body jerked and he fell to the floor on his back just outside the bathroom.

"This is our *home*," she told him.

She was just so tired. She took the gun with her and trudged back down the stairs, closing the basement door behind her. She set the gun on the nightstand, along with her inert phone.

*You're in shock,* her brain told her. But it was such a small voice, like someone whispering from behind a wall. Easy to ignore.

And her bed, it looked so inviting. She climbed into it, pulling the comforter over her head.

Comforter. What an apt name.

Someone would come find her. Eventually.

Or maybe they wouldn't. Maybe anyone that would try would be dead. Maybe she could sleep for a hundred years, like the man in that fairy tale, and she would wake to a world where no one knew who she was or what she had done.

She could be anyone, in a world like that.

# CHAPTER TEN

Zero was grateful he didn't have any luggage other than his small carry-on. He was off the plane and in the backseat of an Uber in less than fifteen minutes. He had the address he needed, a brownstone in the Flatiron District of New York, near Gramercy Park on the Upper East Side.

It wasn't until they were on the way that he powered his phone back on. He had no new voicemails, but he did have a single text, and from a surprising source, no less.

*Call me ASAP* was all that Penny had said.

First he tried to call Alan, and then Sara, and then Mischa. All three went to voicemail and he didn't bother leaving a message. He had to assume that no answer was good, that it meant they were in hiding, together, and that they'd shut off their phones to avoid being traced.

He called Penny.

"Zero!" she answered. It was almost a shout. "Where are you? Where are your girls?"

"I'm in New York," he told her. "The girls are… with Alan. Why?"

"Are you sure?"

His blood ran cold.

"Penny, *why*?"

"There was an explosion," she told him somberly. "At Third Street Garage."

*No…*

"Penny, what are you telling me?" he asked hoarsely.

"It's not what you think," she said quickly. "Bodies were recovered, all male, four of them. They were shot before the bomb went off. The device was in a van parked just outside."

Zero frowned as he put it together. Four men had assaulted the garage in a van. They'd all been killed—at Alan's hand, most likely. Mischa might have helped. But then a bomb had gone off?

*In case they failed,* he realized. That was how badly someone wanted them dead.

*Why?*

"You're *sure* no one else was found?"

"I'm sure," Penny confirmed. "But I haven't been able to reach Alan."

"Me neither. Which hopefully means the girls are with him and safe." Their phones weren't active. But… Zero had told Reidigger he'd call from New York. Maybe Alan was just playing it safe. He was, at times, known to be a bit paranoid.

"The tracking device!" he said suddenly. He recalled that Maya had found Mischa and saved her from Stefan Krauss because Maria and Penny had installed a tracker in Mischa's arm, under the guise of a flu shot. "Can you use it?"

Penny sighed. "To be honest, I tried. I made a promise I wouldn't, but then I saw the explosion, and…"

"And what, Penny?"

"Inactive. She must have dug it out recently."

"Okay." Zero rubbed his face. He hadn't slept on the flight to Zurich, or from Zurich, and the exhaustion was wearing on him. "Until we hear something to the contrary we have to assume they're okay."

"Should I send someone to your house?" Penny asked. "Call in an anonymous tip to the police at least?"

Zero was tempted to say yes, but if the garage was compromised, home definitely was as well. That would be the last place Alan and the girls would be.

"Thanks, but no," Zero said. "If anyone had tried to get into the house, the alarm company would have notified the authorities and me." He didn't say it aloud, but he also didn't want the police poking around his place with no one there. He had several guns stashed around the house, only two of which were registered, not to mention some other "keepsakes" from his time as an agent, and he would much prefer to not have to explain them. "Just keep an ear to the ground as best you can. Alan will check in when he's able. I've got something I have to do here and then I'll be heading straight back."

"Will do."

"And what about Maya?"

"One sec and I'll tell you." He heard fingers clacking against a keyboard, and a moment later Penny told him, "She's en route to Paris. Some low-level op investigating NSA chatter, possible insurgent cell."

"Paris? Who knows about that?"

"By the looks of it? Her, her partner, Walsh. Me. And now you."

"Good. Let's keep it that way." At least one daughter was out of the line of fire. "Keep me posted and I'll let you know when I'm back in town."

"You got it."

"Thanks, Penny." He ended the call and rubbed his eyes again. When he opened them he noticed that his Uber driver was arching an eyebrow in the rearview mirror.

"Everything okay, pal?" he asked.

"Just another day in the life," he murmured. He opened his wallet, pulled out a fifty-dollar bill, and passed it over the seat. "Say, how much faster do you think we can get there?"

*

Zero had never met Dr. Howard Bliss. It had been Maya who had discovered him, tracked him to New York, and confronted him. It was Maya who found out that Bliss had been hired by the CIA to install an experimental device, a memory suppressor, into the now-deceased Seth Connors, the first CIA agent who had volunteered to test it after the tragic death of his daughter.

Maya had told him everything, including where to find Bliss. Zero stood on the front stoop of the handsome three-story brownstone on the Upper East Side. He examined the place before knocking; it was daylight but he saw no lights on inside, no movement or evidence of anyone home. He glanced upward—the small black dome of a security camera stared down on him. A small white panel to his left indicated a doorbell and intercom.

He pressed it and waited.

After ten seconds he pressed it again.

Then he tried the door. It was unlocked. Not a good sign, even in a nice neighborhood like this one.

*Wish I had a gun.*

He glanced around quickly but didn't see anyone watching him. He almost laughed at himself; this was New York. There was undoubtedly someone watching him. But he stepped through the doorway anyway and gently closed the door behind him.

The house was quiet. He heard the hum of a refrigerator and nothing else. He stood in a high-ceilinged foyer, a chandelier high over his head and a hardwood staircase leading up to the second level. To his right was a home office with a dual-monitor setup. On his left was a pair of French doors, through the glass of which he could see some sort of parlor or sitting room.

Both were empty.

Zero resisted the urge to call out, to warn of his presence. He'd had a hunch back in Zurich, a last-minute decision just before booking his plane ticket. Guyer and his wife had been killed and the files on Zero had been taken—which could align with his kneejerk assumption that it was personal.

Or it could mean something else.

He stepped into a wide, impressive kitchen that would have made any professional chef giddy. A dual-range induction stove, solid-piece granite counter space, an apron sink nearly the size of a bathtub. But no people. No scents of recently cooked meals. The coffee machine was dry as a bone.

He went upstairs then, treading softly, listening intently. Bliss lived well; Zero passed a bathroom almost as big as his entire bedroom with a claw-foot tub and an eight-foot vanity. The master bedroom had vaulted ceilings, a four-poster bed, and two bodies lying atop a sheet.

"Dammit," Zero said softly. He'd been right, but it was the last thing he wanted to be right about now.

Bliss was in silk pajamas, his hair thoroughly gray, and had been stabbed in the chest and neck several times. His wife had high, shapely cheekbones positioned between wide, unblinking eyes and a slit throat.

Just like Guyer, it was evident they hadn't been killed in bed. A window was partially open but there was no broken glass; Bliss must have had it open to enjoy the breeze, and the assailant climbed through it. A glance outside told him it would have been no easy feat. Bliss must have heard them coming and leapt out of bed. The signs of a struggle were apparent. Bliss's murder had been sloppier than the others; he'd tried to fight off his attacker, but lost. His wife had probably jumped for her phone, or tried to get out of the room before she was set upon.

Zero's hunch had been right. Dr. and Mrs. Guyer hadn't been killed just because of a personal connection to Zero. It wasn't simple retaliation. Howard Bliss had no connection to Zero. But he did have a connection to the Guyers, though none of them knew it.

They all knew about the memory suppressor. Whoever did this was eliminating anyone who knew about the CIA program to create a device capable of suppressing memories.

Suddenly Stefan Krauss seemed increasingly unlikely. He didn't have motive. He killed for money. He worked for no one but himself, and manipulated others into believing he was working for them. This didn't fit his MO or his worldview.

But at the moment, the whodunit of the equation seemed less important than the potential victims. If targets were anyone who knew about the suppressor, then the list included Alan Reidigger. Penelope León. Todd Strickland. All three of his daughters.

And of course, Zero himself.

He pulled out his phone to make the call when something caught his eye. A white envelope, on the nightstand beside Mrs. Bliss's body. But it wasn't the envelope itself that caught his eye, but rather the mark upon it. A circle with a slash through it.

A zero. Just like the one on Dr. Guyer's file folder in Zurich.

Zero reached for it as if it might be burning hot. The zero was written hastily in black marker, the slash fading to a jagged edge like a knife. Every logical thought in his head screamed a symphony for him to get the hell out of there. Instead, he dared to open it.

Inside was a single sheet of paper folded in thirds. Upon it were four handwritten lines, in a neat scrawl, perfectly parallel, almost mechanical. It said:

*You can't go back home to your family, back home to your childhood...*

*back home to a young man's dreams of glory and of fame...*

*back home to the old forms and systems of things which once seemed everlasting but which are changing all the time –*

*back home to the escapes of Time and Memory.*

Zero stared at it for far longer than he should have. He knew those words, had heard them before—no, not heard, but read. It was an excerpt from Thomas Wolfe's novel *You Can't Go Home Again*, published posthumously in 1940. Not just any excerpt, but the novel's denouement, and perhaps the most quoted and well-known excerpt from the book.

*You can't go home again.*

Home.

This was a threat.

He had to get home, now.

Zero stuffed the sheet and the envelope into his back pocket and raced out of the bedroom, down the hall, barreling down the stairs. At the front door he stopped himself briefly, took a breath, and exited the brownstone as casually as possible, as if nothing was wrong, as if he had not just found two dead bodies and an obvious warning to go home…

He was halfway down the block, phone in hand, when he stopped himself.

*You can't go home again.*

*You can't go back home to your family.*

*Back home to the old forms and systems of things which once seemed everlasting.*

*Back home to the escapes of time and memory.*

He kept walking, his feet moving automatically in some direction while his brain spin-cycled the words over and over.

He had just given Penny reason to believe that his home in Virginia was not a concern. Alan would have gotten the girls out and somewhere safe. Someone wanted him to come here, to find the doctor and his wife, to know what sort of game was afoot.

The note was right; he couldn't go back home. Because the home where he had tried to escape time and memory was not in Virginia. It was here, in New York.

# CHAPTER ELEVEN

Thirty-five minutes later Zero found himself standing outside a familiar yet simultaneously foreign house. Whoever owned it now, they'd painted the brick; what used to be brown was now white.

It was strange, like running into an ex who had dyed their hair.

*What am I doing here?*

He'd called Penny on the way, warned her about his theory, that anyone connected to the suppressor technology was being eliminated. He warned her to warn Strickland. He tried to call Alan again, and Sara, and Mischa, to no avail.

He would give anything to know where they were, that they were safe.

*What am I doing here?*

Zero was certain he'd deciphered the note correctly. Now he stood outside a white-bricked, two-story craftsman in Riverdale in the northern end of the Bronx. His former home. It was here that he'd lived with Kate when she was still alive. It was here he'd lived when she wasn't anymore. It was here he'd lived when the memory suppressor was installed in his head, and here he'd lived for two blissful, ignorant years thinking he was nothing more than an adjunct history professor at Columbia University and a widower, and a single father raising two daughters.

In this house, Sara had been so bright-eyed and inquisitive. She had wanted to follow her mother's footsteps and go to art school. Maya had been a high schooler with a mind as sharp as her wit. He'd hoped she would get into Columbia, or at least NYU, and stay local.

But he couldn't go home again, because it was here he'd lived when three Iranian terrorists, members of the fanatical faction called Amun, had kidnapped him and torn the suppressor out of his head.

*What am I doing here?*

He had to know. His feet were already propelling him forward toward the front door. Whoever had left that note was pointing him here, and if it was anything like he'd found in Zurich or Manhattan, he needed to know.

He knocked on the door and waited. A few moments later it was opened by a man who smiled awkwardly but politely back at him.

"Can I help you?" the man asked.

He was about Zero's height, slight-framed, nebbish, his hair combed, and dressed as if he was just about to go somewhere.

Funny; in another life, he almost could have been Professor Reid Lawson.

Zero realized that he hadn't thought for even a moment about what he might say. He'd been so concerned that no one would answer the door, that the current residents of the home would be dead, that he hadn't even considered what he'd say if he found himself facing someone.

"Hi. Um, this is going to sound strange, but, uh, my name is… Reid, Reid Lawson, and I used to live here. In this house." Zero was rambling, and at the same time imagining himself in the other man's shoes and declaring himself a lunatic. "I found myself in the area, and…" He cleared his throat. This was going very poorly. No one was dead here. This was a dead end, or possibly a distraction. Or maybe he'd interpreted the note wrong.

"You know what?" Zero said, forcing a smile. "Forget it. Sorry to bother you." He turned and started back down the walkway. It was foolish of him to come here.

"Hang on a sec," the man called after him.

Zero paused and turned, and the man's smile was still polite but not awkward. If anything, there was some compassion in it.

"I get it," he said. "You wanted to see the old homestead. You raised a family here?"

"I did. Two daughters. My…" Zero sniffed. "My wife passed away."

*Both of them.*

"Gosh, I'm so sorry." The man shook his head. Then something appeared to dawn on him, as his eyes opened wide. "Hang on, did you say Lawson?"

"That's right. Reid Lawson."

"Well!" He stuck out a hand. "Reid, you can call me Carl." They shook hands briefly. "Tell me, do you believe in fate, or are you more of a coincidence sort of fellow?"

Zero frowned at that. "Mix of both, I'd say."

Carl smiled wide. “Then try this on for size: last night I had a package delivered to this address, but with your name on it.”

“You don’t say,” Zero murmured.

“And the very next day you show up at my door. How about that?” Carl chuckled and shook his head. “I was going to bring it down to the post office to get forwarded, but how about you come on inside and I’ll give it to you myself?”

An alarm blared in Zero’s head like a klaxon red-alert. This was no coincidence. He’d been led here. What if this man wasn’t what he appeared to be? What if he was some sort of assassin or agent, and the real family that lived here was dead inside? Was there even a package, or was it a ruse to get his guard down?

“Come on in.” Carl retreated through the open door and waved him on.

Zero had made a lot of bad decisions in life, and he was still standing. What was one more?

*Wish I had a gun.*

He followed Carl inside and closed the door behind him. His muscles were tense, ready for anything—except what he found.

The first thing he noticed, he was surprised to find, was that the house still smelled the same. Or close to it. It was a scent he couldn’t quite pin down, something too nebulous to name, but familiar, warm, and welcome as a hug.

But other things were strange, like seeing photos of another family on the walls rather than his own. A young son, no more than ten, and a daughter, around Mischa’s age. A wife with a dazzling smile. Carl was in the photos; if he was some kind of agent then this was all well-staged.

He took a few cautious steps into the living room. The furniture was all wrong; anyone with two eyes would have known that the sofa was in the wrong corner of the living room, the television faced in the least optimal way. At that angle the afternoon sun would create a terrible glare through the windows.

“Let me just grab it for you quick,” Carl said as he disappeared into the room that used to be Reid Lawson’s study. Zero watched the hall carefully, in case Carl emerged with a knife or a gun, in case he tried to get the drop on him.

But instead the voice called out, “You caught me just in the nick of time, too.”

Sudden as a heart attack, a sensation gripped him. A recollection, like déjà vu, of him, Reid Lawson, standing exactly where he was standing at that moment, halfway between the kitchen and living room where the corridor ended, looking down the hall toward the door of the study.

"I was about to run some errands…" Carl said.

But in his mind, he heard another voice. A memory.

*"Zero-four-one-bravo, checking in. Status: routine."*

"Another fifteen minutes and I would have been out the door with your package, to forward it to you," Carl said.

But in his head, it was Kate's voice he heard down the hall.

*"No changes in speech pattern or behavior. Physical and mental health, normal. Memory, maintaining."*

This had happened before, sudden memories resurfacing—like the time he had, without warning, recalled his past as a dark agent, the time that he spent in his early years with the CIA carrying out targeted assassinations.

But this was different.

In his mind's eye, he stood there stock-still as Kate poked her head from the doorway of the study. He saw her there, in perfect detail, her blonde hair that she typically kept shoulder-length. Her blue eyes, full cheeks, a roundish, girlish face that kept her young despite being a mother of two.

*"Hey, you're home. Didn't hear you come in."*

*"Just a minute ago,"* he heard himself say. *"Who were you talking to?"*

*"Oh." A short laugh. "Just a work thing."*

Then there was a soft grunt, and Carl exited the study with a sturdy cardboard box in both hands, no bigger than a shoebox.

Zero leaned against the wall with one hand.

"You okay?" Carl asked. He set the box down on the kitchen counter with a thud.

"Yeah… fine. Mind if I use your bathroom quick?"

"Not at all." A short chuckle. "I suppose you know where it is."

Zero nodded, and then left the kitchen to the small half-bath between it and the back patio. He closed the door and turned on the cold tap and splashed water on his face.

What was that memory? What did it mean? Was it even real? He'd had false flashbacks before. Guyer had warned him early on about such things, hopes or fantasies or even ideas forming in his deteriorating brain and masquerading as memories.

But this wasn't any hope or fantasy he'd ever had. Kate had been talking like an operative. He heard the words himself, clear as day.

He couldn't even tell when the memory might have taken place. Years earlier, obviously, but how many?

"Not real," he told his reflection. He had bags under his eyes from lack of rest. His skin looked waxen. "It's not real."

It certainly had felt real.

Zero took a deep breath. Now was not the time to concern himself with that. He dried his hands and rejoined Carl in the kitchen as he busied himself with a few errant dishes in the sink.

"Heavier than it looks," he noted, gesturing with his chin toward the box.

Right. The box. Carl hadn't been lying; there was a box, and it had this address on it, and it was indeed addressed to Reid Lawson.

"Who dropped this off?" Zero asked.

"I didn't see," Carl shrugged, "but I assume it was a delivery driver, right?"

"Right," he murmured. "Last night, you said?"

"Mm-hmm."

The same night that Bliss and his wife had been murdered in their bedroom.

He carefully tested its weight. The box was indeed heavy, probably fifteen pounds or so. Whatever was inside was dense, possibly metal, or otherwise…

"Oh." The sound came out like a deflating hiss. He set the box back down slowly but didn't take his eyes from it as he addressed his host. "Carl. Is anyone else in the house?"

"Um…" Carl frowned at the question. "No, just us. Why do you ask?"

"We're going to leave," Zero told him, trying to keep his voice measured and not panicked. "We're going to walk outside and across the street, and from there you should call the police." Already Zero was backing up slowly, toward the hall and the foyer.

"I'm confused, Reid. What exactly is it you're talking about?"

Zero bumped into the front door behind him. He reached back for the knob. "Carl, please just step outside with me, leave the box, and I'll explain…"

He twisted the knob and pulled the door open.

The heat came first, an intense wave of it that brought with it an invisible force that took him off his feet, sent him through the open doorway, tumbling through the air.

Then he hit the ground. His body bounced once over the front yard. He was vaguely aware of the sensation of grass on his cheek as a fireball plumed above him.

He wanted to stand, to leap up and see if Carl was alive or dead, but he already knew the answer. He couldn't seem to lift his head, and then darkness consumed his vision.

# CHAPTER TWELVE

"Penny? It's Alan."

"Oh my god. Alan! Thank god you're all right," the tech gushed through the phone. "Are the girls all right? Are they with you?"

Reidigger sighed. He was on a landline in the safe house he'd set up, about an hour outside of D.C. The neighborhood was far from the best, but the old row house had come dirt cheap and the neighbors were not the sort that talked to authorities.

He'd stopped only once since leaving the shelled-out remains of Third Street Garage, to call in one of his owed favors. He swapped his truck for an old Buick with fake tags and a full tank and drove the rest of the way to the safe house, worrying every second about Sara and what had happened to her and resisting the urge to turn around and search for her.

Mischa had awoken, and tried to protest her sister's absence, but she'd suffered what seemed to be a minor concussion in the blast and couldn't protest much. She struggled to even keep her eyes open, as the daylight hurt her head.

When they'd arrived, Alan had pulled into a narrow, cracked driveway, and then he got Mischa inside and settled on a dusty sofa. He went back outside and pulled a tarp over the Buick. Then he'd tried to call Sara from the landline rotary phone in the kitchen. And then Zero. Both went to voicemail.

*What the hell is the point of cell phones, anyway?*

Finally he called Penelope León.

"Mischa's with me," he said at last. "Sara… she was with us too. But when the bomb went off, we… we got separated." He tried to keep the tremor out of his voice thinking about what might have become of her.

"Alan, listen to me," said Penny, "there were only four recovered in the blast. Four males, all with gunshot wounds. She wasn't there."

"I know," he said, more for his own sake than for hers. "She got out. I know that."

"She turned her phone off. She's a smart girl. Put yourself in her shoes; where might she have gone?"

Alan thought for a moment. No way would Sara have gone back to the house; it was compromised. They had seen the men and the black van pull up. "Uh… she's got a friend around here, Camilla something. Maybe there. Or to one of her friends from the trauma group."

"Exactly," said Penny. "Sara is smart, and she's independent. She'll keep her phone off, lie low for a couple of days, and poke her head out when she thinks it's safe again."

"Right," Alan agreed, more for his own sake than for hers. "But still—I should look for her."

"No," Penny said immediately. "I heard from Zero. He's in New York, and he has reason to believe that whoever's behind this is eliminating people that know about the memory suppressor."

Reidigger frowned. That made sense for Guyer. And for himself, and the girls. But what had Zero found in New York? He recalled the time that Maya had hijacked his cherry Skylark and left it in a Manhattan parking garage…

Right. There'd been a doctor there. A doctor who, Alan could assume, was now dead.

"But if that's true," he said, "then our lead suspect isn't our lead suspect anymore." That wasn't Krauss's style. He didn't even know about the suppressor, presumably, and even if he did, he had no motive.

"True," Penny conceded. "It also means you're a target—"

"And you," he reminded her.

"I'm bunkered down in R&D. No one's getting me here. But if you go out there looking for Sara, and they find you, the girls will lose their best ally."

Alan glanced over his shoulder at Mischa, who was dozing on the sofa. He shouldn't be letting her sleep. "Hey," he called out gently, "stay awake."

"Stupid fat man," she said groggily in Russian.

As much as he hated it, Penny was right. He couldn't run out there in search of Sara without a solid lead of her whereabouts. He couldn't go around asking about her to friends who might talk, or post something on social media. And he couldn't leave Mischa alone.

"Fine," Alan relented. "We said we'd hunker down, so we'll hunker. If you talk to Zero, give him this number, yeah?"

"Will do," Penny agreed. "Now I have to go. I have something else going on here that's… well, it's pretty much as classified as classified gets, and duty calls—"

"Hang on," Alan interrupted. "If Zero is right… there's only a handful of people on the planet that would know about the memory suppressor tech. You don't think the agency has anything to do with this, do you?"

"No," Penny said, as quickly as she did adamantly. "I don't. Just stay hidden and stay safe. I'll try to keep in touch."

"All right," Alan agreed. "Thanks, Penny." He hung up, his hand lingering on the receiver.

Penny had reason to distrust the CIA, he knew. Not as much reason as he did, but reason all the same. Both their reasons stemmed from things they knew that they shouldn't know, and now their lives were in danger over it. And they certainly both knew that killing innocent people just because of something they might have known was not exactly above the agency, as a whole.

He would stay hidden, and he would keep Mischa safe, but he wouldn't discount the notion that the CIA had a hand in this. But he understood why Penny would; because if it was true, then she, and Todd, and even Maya were not in the safest place they could be.

They were in the worst.

# CHAPTER THIRTEEN

Zero opened his eyes. A dull roar was in his ears; his own blood, rushing in his pounding head. At least that's what he thought at first. He pushed himself up with a groan, first to his elbows and knees, and then to his shaky feet.

Everything hurt. But that was nothing new.

He turned slightly, and he saw the source of the dull roar. The house behind him was burning. The house that used to be his. Someone had painted the brown brick white, and now the white brick was black with soot and smoke and char as flames rolled from burst windows.

*You really can't go home again.*

The interior of the house was completely ablaze. The roof hadn't yet collapsed. Two things were evident: first, that Zero hadn't been unconscious for long; no more than thirty seconds, tops. Still, emergency crews would be on site soon.

And two: Carl was certainly dead. He had been innocent in all this. Even more so than Alina Guyer, or Sharon Bliss. But still, he had died for it. Just for buying the wrong house.

"Sweet Jesus!" a female voice cried. Zero spun. His vision was still a little fuzzy but he noticed that a small crowd of people was gathering across the street, neighbors and a couple of kids on bicycles. Out of them, a white-haired woman in house slippers, was the only one to dare to get closer to the blaze, to check on the man who had risen from the debris scattering the front lawn.

Zero recognized her. Her name was Mrs. Gorman, and she lived four doors down.

"Are you all right, son?" She hurried to him, gripped his elbow.

"Been worse," he muttered. Then he waved a hand. "I'm okay. Thank you."

"Ambulance will be here anytime," she assured him. "Come along where it's safe, have a seat…" She gave his elbow a gentle tug, and then wrinkled her nose as she peered into his face. "Wait one second now. Reid…? Reid Lawson?"

*Dammit.*

“Sorry, I think you have me confused with someone else.” He shrugged her off. “Thanks.” He trotted across the yard, away from peering eyes, away from the confused older woman who could now easily identify him at the scene if she wanted to.

What was he supposed to do? Threaten her?

No. But she did give him an idea.

There was pain in his left leg and it took a lot of effort not to limp on it. Being blasted out of the house and into the yard would take a toll on any body, let alone a forty-year-old body that just didn’t know when enough was enough.

*So this is retirement,* he thought glumly.

Didn’t seem like it was all it was cracked up to be.

With Mrs. Gorman at the scene, her house would be empty. He recalled that she was a bit of a busybody, so he was certain she’d stick around until the police and firefighters and EMTs arrived, and then tell them everything she saw as if she’d been involved in the blast.

While she was there, Zero hurried down the block, up her walkway, and into her house. Her front door was unlocked, of course, on account of her rushing out to see what had happened. He imagined the tremendous boom of it scaring the daylights out of her, and then her stuffing her feet into slippers, rushing out to the street.

Her keys were in a basket just inside the front door and her car was in the driveway. He slid behind the driver’s seat as the sirens shrieked closer. Not fifteen seconds later a convoy of emergency vehicles arrived, parking at any odd angle available and blocking the road between his former home and Gorman’s. No one would see him leave.

So he backed her car out of the driveway and eased up the road as if nothing was wrong, as if there weren’t a hundred flashing lights in his rearview.

“Sorry, Mrs. Gorman,” he muttered. “But I need it more than you do right now.”

The old woman drove a practical sedan, good gas mileage, couldn’t have been more than three or four years old. She’d kept it clean and in good shape; it still had the new-car smell, at least a little bit, under the veneer of old-lady perfume.

He wouldn’t need it long. A half hour, tops, long enough to get to the airport and hop a plane. With any luck, Mrs. Gorman wouldn’t mention the name Reid Lawson. Maybe she’d be confused about who she thought she saw, and he could get back to Virginia before…

*Before what, exactly?*

Before the police tracked him down and arrested him? Before the CIA caught wind of several deaths that all pointed firmly in his direction? Before whoever was after him finally killed him, or his family, or his friends?

He rubbed his face. Everything hurt. Nothing made sense. And on top of it all, the memory lingered, the déjà vu sensation from the house, of Kate on the phone talking in code…

"It wasn't real," he reminded himself.

Still. Even if it wasn't real, he didn't know what it meant. His brain must have produced it for a reason. He didn't feel like himself. He didn't feel like Zero anymore. The irony was that both of those things depended on him being Zero. But he wasn't Zero, not anymore, not really.

"Pull yourself together," he scolded himself. He guided the car onto the highway, and then leaned over slightly to the glove box to see if Mrs. Gorman had any Tylenol stowed away there. The glove box was as neat as the rest of the car; it contained only the registration, insurance card, vehicle manual, and spare napkins.

"Think," he told himself.

Whoever was doing this knew about the memory suppressor. Guyer, Bliss, Zero's former home—that suggested someone from his past. Krauss checked that box, but none of the others. It had felt like him at first, but now it felt far more conspiratorial. Bigger than him. Bigger than one person.

Guyer. Bliss. His former home. Who would know those things?

Or: who could dig that deep if they wanted to? If they needed to?

Who might have reason to eliminate anyone associated with, or who had knowledge of, the memory suppressor?

There was only one answer to all of those questions, and he didn't like it at all.

*The CIA.*

But that only raised more questions. The agency didn't toy with people. They didn't leave cryptic notes or lead people on wild goose chases. They didn't take chances with bombs or make that big of a mess if they didn't have to. If they wanted someone dead, they'd employ someone like John Watson to kill them without hesitation or question. Ideally from a distance.

Whoever did this was into theatrics. The CIA didn't fit that bill. Neither did Krauss.

An idea hit him, or just the kernel of one, and he pulled his phone out of his pocket. It wouldn't power up. He didn't know if the explosion had killed it or if the battery was dead, and he couldn't remember the last time he'd charged it.

Mrs. Gorman may not have had Tylenol, but she came through this time. There was a USB charging cable in the center console. Zero steered with his knees as he plugged the phone in. It powered on this time. At least something was going in his favor.

But his optimism waned quickly as he tried to call Alan, then Sara, Maya, and Mischa in turn. Not one phone rang. Every one of them went to voicemail.

*What the hell is the point of cell phones, anyway?*

He called Penny at the lab.

"Zero!" she answered with some urgency. "You really shouldn't be using your own phone right now…"

"Someone just tried to kill me," he told her. "With a bomb. At my old house in the Bronx."

"Jeez. Hang on." He heard the keyboard in the background, clack-clack-clacking. "I see," she said softly. "One casualty."

"The current homeowner. Pretty sure he had nothing to do with this. The girls?"

Penny's moment of hesitation was not lost on him. "With Alan. He has a number you can reach him at."

"I'm driving."

"I'll text it."

"Great. Safe?"

"Safe. Yeah." Something in her voice suggested there had been some kind of trouble, but he didn't ask her to elaborate. "Where are you now?" she asked.

"You're not tracking me?" he mused.

"Kind of doing two things at once here. I have a… let's just say, an 'executive order' on my hands. Any idea who's behind this?"

"A notion," he admitted. "Where's Todd?"

"Abroad. Busy."

"Another 'executive order,' I take it?"

"The same, actually," she told him. "Don't ask me any more than that."

"I won't. Listen, I have a hunch about who might be—"

The car jolted roughly. Zero pitched forward, bracing himself against the steering wheel with a forearm. The phone tumbled from his hand. The sedan swerved, almost sideswiping a car in the next lane before Zero quickly righted it.

He looked in the rearview. A broad, black sports car was directly behind him, late model, so close he couldn't see anything but the tinted windshield.

And he didn't think for a moment that it was just an aggressive driver.

The phone had fallen on the floor somewhere near his feet.

"Penny!" he said loudly. "If you can hear me, I've got company!"

The sports car behind him revved its engine and bumped him again. Mrs. Gorman's little sedan lurched.

"Son of a…" Zero pulled the wheel to the left and the sedan jumped onto the shoulder, just as the muscle car behind him sped up for another ram. Zero took his foot off the gas, just for a moment, just long enough to pull parallel to the sports car, and then slammed the accelerator again to keep pace.

He glanced over.

The passenger side window was tinted, but rolled halfway down.

Through it, he could see the face of the driver. The man looked back at him, and their gaze locked for just a moment. He had short stubble on his chin, and his sandy hair was disheveled, but Zero recognized him all the same.

The man behind the wheel was Stefan Krauss.

# CHAPTER FOURTEEN

A cold fury rose in Zero's chest at the sight of the man who murdered Maria. The man who had almost killed Mischa.

Krauss did not smile, or glare, or snarl; he simply glanced, his face utterly impassive.

And then he pulled the sports car onto the shoulder.

The instant he saw the shift, Zero hit the brakes. The muscle car slid in front of him, mere inches from the guard rail, almost bouncing off of it. Zero hit the gas then in an effort to ram him, but the sports car leapt forward.

He desperately wished he had a manual transmission as the speedometer climbed to seventy, then eighty. He blew by other cars on the highway, ignoring the blaring horns as he kept right on Krauss's tail. The shoulder was narrow, barely more than the width of the car; at this speed, a bump to the guard rail or another car could be fatal.

Without warning or even slowing, the sports car skirted left, crossing two lanes of traffic in a heartbeat. Zero cursed and stayed on the shoulder. His speed climbed to eighty-five. He dared to take his eyes from the road for a half-second, just long enough to see that Krauss was keeping pace with him in the far left lane.

The sports car vanished for a moment as a tractor trailer passed between them. Then Krauss swerved again, in front of it, coming up right alongside Zero.

*He wouldn't...*

He did. Krauss swerved again, only slightly, and the sports car sidled into the sedan. His passenger side scraped against the guard rail as he struggled to keep the car straight. The grating sound was shrill; sparks flew past the window. The sports car leaned in again. Metal groaned as Krauss pinned the sedan between the black car and the guardrail.

Zero grimaced and held the wheel tightly. By the time he saw what Krauss aimed to do, it was too late. He tried to hit the brakes but Krauss leaned in again as the guardrail ended. The sedan was too small, too light to counter the heavier car.

Zero swerved as the sedan left the road. The back end swung out, around, as it careened down an embankment. Zero took his foot off the brake and braced himself.

Mrs. Gorman's sedan bounced at the bottom, hard enough for two tires to leave the ground. Hard enough for the hood to unlatch and fly up. Hard enough for Zero's head to hit the ceiling, even with his seatbelt on.

The car rolled unsteadily for a few more yards and finally came to a gentle stop. Zero rubbed his head and quickly checked himself in the rearview. He wasn't bleeding that he could see, though his face was still streaked with gray soot from the explosion.

He shoved the door open and rolled out of the car, his legs shaky. Above and behind him, the embankment was empty. He didn't see the black car.

But then a figure stepped into view. Krauss. He held something in both hands, and brought it to his shoulder.

Zero leapt, rolling over the trunk of the car and landing on the other side as an automatic rifle rattled. Bullets pounded the car. Windows shattered and tires blew out as Zero covered his head with both hands, keenly aware that he was one penetrated gas tank away from getting caught up in another explosion.

The gunshots stopped as the magazine ran out. Zero didn't wait around to see if Krauss was reloading; he dashed forward, keeping low. He looked left and right for cover; he didn't know where he was, some industrial area, several blocks of long, flat-roofed buildings and warehouses. The sun was setting. Work was out for the day and the place was a ghost town.

He ran in a serpentine pattern toward a narrow alley to the right. Before ducking down it he hazarded a glance behind him. Krauss was pursuing him, sidestepping quickly down the embankment as he pushed a fresh magazine into what looked, from this distance, to be an AR-15.

Zero cut right, down the alley, and toward a two-story drab gray building with splashes of graffiti and several broken windows. He saw a set of doors, or what used to be doors, boarded up with plywood, and bee-lined for them.

He gritted his teeth. He didn't know how secure the plywood was, or if there were doors behind it. This was probably going to hurt.

Zero threw himself forward, leading with a shoulder, forearms up to cover his face. He smashed through the plywood far easier than he would have thought, as if it was cardboard.

He was right. It hurt.

He landed on his shoulder and rolled, coughing. But there was no time for lying around. He leapt to his feet, his left leg in more pain than it had been before, and half-limped across the dusty warehouse floor. The place was filthy, everything covered in a layer of silt, the late sunlight filtering in through grimy second-floor windows and lighting dust motes he'd sent into the air when he disrupted the relative tranquility of an abandoned warehouse.

There were bits of lumber scattered here and there on the floor and he snatched up a piece, a section of two-by-four about as long as his arm. It wasn't much against an automatic rifle but it was the best he could do.

Then he ducked behind three empty oil drums and waited. From the small space between them he had a good view of the broken entranceway. He could see Krauss coming.

But what good would it do him?

*You should have kept running.*

Sticking around felt like a very good way to get killed. But he needed answers. He needed to know why Krauss was here, why he had appeared suddenly just after Zero had discounted him as a suspect.

And once he had information, he needed to kill this man.

A shadow fell over the doorway. A moment later Krauss took a single wide step inside, the gun to his shoulder, quickly sweeping left to right with the barrel.

Zero held his breath, staying still as could be. His palms were sweating around the two-by-four.

Krauss stalked forward, keeping the gun up. His gaze swept over the three oil drums that Zero was hiding behind, and then past them. He turned slowly, his back to Zero, and took a few steps away from him.

He could get the drop on him. He could leave his cover now, sneak up behind him, strike with the two-by-four. A single blow could knock him out. Maybe even kill him.

But if Krauss heard him coming, it would be over in a heartbeat. Automatic gun beat hunk of wood, every time.

Zero dared to rise from his hiding place, just a bit, just enough for his head to be visible if Krauss suddenly whirled around. The round metal lid of one of the oil drums was loose, on an angle, not secured but just lying atop the empty container. Zero held the length of lumber in one hand and reached for the metal lid with the other.

He reeled back, and he hurled the lid like a Frisbee as hard as he could. It sailed over the silt-covered floor, behind Krauss's back, and landed with a crash on the other side of the warehouse.

Krauss spun the instant he heard the clatter. The automatic rifle rattled, bullets tearing at nothing but air and concrete. The deafening blasts echoed through the empty warehouse—and muffled Zero's rapid footfalls.

The instant Krauss pulled the trigger, Zero made his move. He half-sprinted, half-vaulted the span between them. The gun fell silent just before his third stride fell, and his shoe smacked the concrete floor loudly in the silence.

Krauss spun. But Zero was already there, and had momentum. He stopped the swinging barrel with a forearm and swung the two-by-four with one hand. It made a satisfying sound—*tock*—as it connected with Krauss's skull.

The assassin fell, leaving the gun in Zero's hands. His first instinct was to spin it, point it down, and empty the remainder of the magazine into Stefan Krauss. Make short work of it. End him.

But no. He didn't deserve a quick death, and Zero wanted answers. He ejected the magazine, tossed it aside, and threw the rest of the AR-15 in the opposite direction.

Krauss breathed hard, bleeding from his hairline and down the side of his face as he stared up at Zero. But there was no avarice in his eyes; only confusion.

"Will you not kill me?" he asked.

"Oh, I'm going to kill you. But you don't deserve a bullet. And I have questions first." Zero held the two-by-four aloft, ready to deliver a quick blow if he needed to, but Krauss didn't move from his splayed position on the floor. "Did you kill Dr. Guyer?"

Krauss frowned. "I don't know who that is."

Zero scoffed. "What about Howard Bliss, and his wife? In New York? Did you kill them and leave me that note?"

"I left you no note," Krauss told him. His gaze was steely and somber, his brow knitted just slightly in curiosity. There was nothing in his expression to suggest he was lying, but he had to keep in mind that Krauss was a master manipulator.

"And the bomb? Did you deliver that? Did you set it off?"

"No. I was told only to follow you if you survived it."

"Told? Told by who?" Zero demanded.

"The voice."

Zero grunted in frustration. "What voice?"

"The one that calls. The one that tells me what to do next."

Krauss was messing with him. That much was clear. He didn't work for anyone, let alone a "voice." Zero knew all about his lone-wolf, puppet-master shtick. And his speech pattern… Krauss was a natural-born German, but had perfected many accents, could take on almost any alias. Yet his speech now was clipped, like a native German speaker attempting to do an American accent.

He was messing with him.

Zero wasn't going to get any answers out of him.

"I know you, Krauss," he warned, his voice low. "And you know me, so you know this isn't an idle threat. Start talking, or I'll start breaking things of yours."

But Krauss only shook his head, the furrow in his brow deepening. "I don't know you."

That did it. A roar bubbled up inside Zero, starting deep in his belly and rising from his throat as he reared back with the two-by-four and swung with all his might. He didn't just want to hurt him. He wanted to bash his brains in. He wanted Stefan Krauss to be identified by the teeth that lay scattered across a dirty warehouse floor.

But he telegraphed the swing. As the lumber came down, Krauss's forearm came up, and the wood broke in half over it. Krauss grunted, but he was up in an instant and swinging at Zero's torso.

He barely avoided the blow and leapt back before another could come. He tossed the useless hunk of wood aside as Krauss circled him, both fists up in a boxer's stance.

The assassin closed in and threw a left hook. Zero blocked it, and then ducked the right jab that followed. He responded with a jab of his own but he went low, center-mass, striking just below the sternum. Krauss winced and swept with a leg. Zero jumped it and kicked out while in the air, barely missing.

They went blow for blow, and while they did, Zero's head reeled. He was certain that Stefan Krauss was playing at something, but… but there was something wrong here, and not just his speech. He was fast and his blows were solid, but his movements were mechanical. They lacked the style and individuality that came from an experienced fighter. When Zero feigned a kick and instead threw an elbow, Krauss fell for it and caught the blow on the chin, his head snapping back and his body following it to the floor.

"What's wrong with you? Get up!" Zero shouted. He wanted to kill Stefan Krauss, but he didn't want it to be easy. He wanted it to be deserved. He'd dreamed about this a dozen times, delighting in ending this man's life. Yet everything about this felt wrong.

Krauss rolled backward. As he did he loosed a knife from his boot. Silver flashed as he jumped to his feet and swung the blade at Zero's abdomen.

A sloppy swipe. Zero stopped the arm and twisted the wrist. Krauss yelped as the knife fell out of his hand. Zero kicked him back to the ground and grabbed up the knife.

He dropped to one knee and drew the blade back. No more games or tricks. No more questions. He was going to look Maria's killer in the eye, and end his life. Now…

Zero held the knife backhanded, raised just behind his own right ear, but it stayed there.

He stared down at his own would-be murderer, who stared back as passively as if he were waiting for Zero to deliver his morning coffee, not his very timely death.

But he wasn't staring in Krauss's eyes. Instead his gaze was drawn to a place at Krauss's neck. Just behind and a little below the ear was a thin line, red, slightly swollen, and crossed with tiny stitches.

A scar, still healing and professionally sutured, the placement of which was extremely, intimately familiar to Zero—because he had one there too, long since healed.

*It can't be.*

# CHAPTER FIFTEEN

"How did you get that scar?" Zero demanded.

Krauss only stared back.

He grabbed a fistful of the assassin's collar and shook him, the knife still poised to plunge. "That scar, on your neck! How did you get it?"

"I don't know."

This was impossible. Another trick. It must have been.

*Just do it. Kill him.*

The knife stayed in the air, his fist trembling slightly around it. "You said you don't know me."

Krauss shook his head slightly. "I don't."

"Who are you? Your name, tell me your name."

"They call me S," Krauss told him.

"Who does?!"

"The voice, when it calls."

"Who is the voice?"

"I don't know. But if I do as it asks, I'll remember who I am."

Zero shoved himself to a standing position. This was too much. It could have been a ruse, a fake scar to throw him off, to keep him from killing Krauss…

"Stay down," he warned. Krauss didn't move. "You killed a woman on a beach barely more than two weeks ago. What was her name?"

"I don't know."

Zero's face flushed with heat. He wanted to scream, to finish what he'd started, to kill this man that had killed her.

"Maria Johansson," he said forcefully. "That was her name. And you are Stefan Krauss."

He got nothing in return. When Krauss had accidentally killed Maria instead of Zero on their honeymoon, he'd showed genuine remorse. He'd even spared Zero that night for his transgression. But here, now, there was nothing, not even a glimmer of recognition in his eyes.

Not even Krauss could fake that.

And then he knew. It was real. Someone had implanted a memory suppressor at the base of Krauss's head, where his spinal cord met his brain stem. Just like Zero had done to forget the grief of losing Kate. Just like Seth Connors had volunteered for, to avoid the grief of losing his young daughter. Guyer had implanted the device in his head; Bliss had implanted it in Connors'.

He had no doubt that whoever had implanted it in Krauss was dead somewhere as well.

He had been right and wrong at the same time. Krauss was involved. But this wasn't Krauss. This wasn't retaliation, because the assassin had no memory of the offense. Krauss was someone's weapon, their pawn, using him to eliminate anyone who knew about the program.

And as much as he wanted to kill the man who murdered his wife, this was not that man anymore. Instead, Krauss was the only one who might be able to give him a lead.

"You know me," Krauss said. It wasn't a question.

"I do," Zero murmured. "You're a monster. A murderer. An assassin. You've killed innocent people. Men and women alike. You did it for money. For personal gain."

Krauss sat up slowly but didn't try to stand. He stared at the floor as he took a long, measured sigh. "I had a suspicion… that I was not a very good person."

Zero scoffed. He looked down at the knife in his hand. It was likely that Krauss had no answers for him. He'd been a predator before, and he was still one now—the only difference was that he was doing it for someone else. He'd keep doing it.

*End it.*

Memory or not, he still deserved to die. Besides, some might even have considered it a mercy killing.

Krauss stared up at him, his face an unnervingly placid mask. "If I am going to die," he said, as if reading Zero's mind, or at least his expression, "I'd prefer to do it on my feet."

Zero said nothing, but took a small step back, still gripping the blade tightly.

The assassin slowly climbed to his feet.

*Do it.*

Sirens wailed suddenly, not far. Zero turned instinctively toward the source of the sound, just for an instant, but in that instant he realized his mistake.

As he spun back, a fist connected solidly with his jaw. Pain exploded in his face as stars swam in his vision. He heard feet pounding the concrete floor as Krauss ran, fleeing from him. He heard the crash of broken glass as the assassin leapt through a window at the rear of the building.

Zero rose to give chase but his head swam and he staggered on his feet. He fell to one knee again, and only dully realized that he had dropped the knife when he was sucker-punched.

Krauss could have killed him. He could have gotten the drop, grabbed up the knife, and ended it… but he hadn't.

*Because he doesn't know who he is. And I do.*

Zero rubbed his chin as he came back to his senses. Krauss was involved, however involuntarily—but he wasn't the endgame. He knew that now. Someone had gotten to him and stripped him of everything that had made him Stefan Krauss. Not just his memories, but his experience, his style, even his accent. They'd made him into someone else, someone they could mold and warp to do what they wanted him to do.

There was only one possible answer. The agency had never ended the program; they'd merely hidden it. And now they had a successful implant, far more successful than Seth Connors had been. Which meant that the people who could identify what this was had to be removed. Guyer, Bliss, Zero…

His family.

His friends.

He couldn't fight the CIA. Not alone and not without resources.

*But why Krauss?*

Why not a loyal agent? A volunteer, like Connors? Why not someone who was already on their side?

Why the theatrics, the planted bombs? That didn't at all feel like the agency he knew.

He couldn't figure that one either. He was still missing a piece of this puzzle. And, he realized grimly, he couldn't call anyone to warn them. He'd left his phone plugged into the USB cable in Mrs. Gorman's car, on the floor of the driver's side when he fled.

The police would find it. Even if the old busybody said nothing, they'd be able to link him to her stolen car, and by extension, to the explosion at his former home. Maybe even to the murder of Dr. and Mrs. Bliss.

*But why Krauss?*

That question would have to be answered later. Right now, he had nothing, not even a lifeline, while everyone he held dear was in danger. He had to get back to Virginia—which would mean evading more authorities, stealing another car.

The irony of moral ambiguity was not lost on him.

Zero limped out of the old warehouse, the pain in his left leg worse than before, in search of a vehicle to carry him south.

*

S tugged a thin shard of glass from his forearm and wiped it with a piece of gauze.

He was confused. The sensation was not new, but the motivation behind it was indeed strange. That man, the one he had been sent to kill, seemed to know him.

Not just know him—that man seemed to *hate* him. S saw it in his eyes, how badly he wanted to end his life, to plunge the knife into his chest.

He had called him "Krauss." He claimed he had killed a woman.

*Trust no one,* the Voice had told him. *People will take advantage, try to convince you that you are something you're not.*

But still. That man's pain, it seemed so… visceral.

Perhaps that was why S had not killed him. Perhaps it was because he believed the man in the warehouse. He could have grabbed up the knife and ended it right there. But he was weakened, hurt; the man was better than him, could have killed him.

But he didn't. For some reason, despite the pain in his eyes and the obvious desire to kill S, the man had restrained himself, and so S had as well.

He ran. He'd grabbed up the go bag that he'd left in the alley and fled the scene. As night fell he entered a fast-food restaurant and went to the grimy bathroom and locked the door behind him. He opened his bag and found the first aid kit and set about cleaning himself up, pulling the small shards of glass in his arms from jumping through the window.

He dropped the sliver of glass, pink with blood, in the sink. He turned his head slightly to examine the scar on his neck. It was fresh, not more than a week old. Stitched perfectly. Where had it come from? He had no idea.

The last thing he remembered was being on the car lot. Being handed the keys to the black sports car by a short man in stained coveralls. There was a bag in the back seat with essentials, the man had told him. A gun in the trunk—an AR-15. Did he remember how to use that?

S had thought for a moment and nodded. Yes, he remembered that.

Good. There was an address. S would go there but keep his distance. A bomb would go off. There was a target, and if that target escaped the blast, S would follow him and kill him.

And then the Voice would call him.

"And I will remember who I am?" S had asked.

"Of course, pal. Just do this one thing first."

In the grimy bathroom of the fast-food restaurant, S pressed a bandage over a cut on his arm and replaced the first-aid kit in the backpack. He slung it over one shoulder.

He had failed to kill the man, but he was not dead either.

What would the Voice say now?

As if his mind was being read, the cell phone buzzed in his pocket. He pulled it out, already knowing what the screen would say: Unknown Caller. He had almost come to think of it as a name.

"S," he answered flatly.

"Target?" The Voice was male, smooth, unconcerned. Blasé, even.

"The target survived," S told him. There was no use lying or even trying to avoid the truth. "I failed."

"Hmm. So he saw you?"

"He did."

"Tried to kill you too, I imagine." The Voice sounded almost amused.

"He also failed," S reported, though that was obvious.

"I'm guessing he said some things."

"Yes," S confirmed. "He seemed to know me."

"Perfect," said the Voice.

S frowned. "Sorry?"

"You didn't fail, S. This was all part of the plan. If you had killed him, that would have been fine, but I didn't think you would. He knows you're in the game, might have even put together part of what's going on here, which means he'll be looking for you. He'll think you're the key to all this. And while he's looking one way, we'll be moving on to the next target."

The next target. S had failed; he would have to make up for it.

"And then I'll remember who I am?" S asked.

"Of course."

"He called me Krauss. I had the feeling I did things to him."

The Voice chuckled. "Boy, did you ever. How'd he beat you, anyway? You had a machine gun."

"He was just better," S admitted.

"Better how? Faster? Stronger?"

"Just… better. He seemed to know what I would do before I did it."

"I see. Maybe we took too much… say, Weisman," the Voice called to someone else. "Check motor function? Okay. Seems we're having a bit of an improvisation problem. Maybe we can dial that up without giving him too much? Great. S, you still with me?"

"I am."

"Anything else to report before we do this?" the Voice asked.

S looked in the streaked mirror of the restroom. He looked at the scar that he couldn't remember getting, at the face he barely knew as his own. "Did I kill a woman?"

"You did. But look, no use beating yourself up about that right now. In a few seconds, it's not going to matter. Now I need you to hold real still for a moment, got it?"

S did as he was told.

He felt a tingling in his neck. The foreign scar prickled, and then felt as if it was buzzing, and for the briefest of moments an electric shock seared through it, down his spine, up into his skull. His teeth gritted; the muscles in his neck went taut.

And then they relaxed.

"S? You still there?"

He looked around. He was standing in a public restroom, an unclean one, with the scent of grease and fried food in his nostrils. He was holding the phone. The Voice was in his ear.

"You with me, S?"

“Yes,” he said. “I’m here. But… I don’t know where I am. Or how I got here.”

“What’s the last thing you remember?” the Voice asked.

S thought hard for a moment. “Manhattan. I woke in an empty room. There were clothes, and a phone. You called. You told me I was S, and that I had lost my memory, but you would help me recover it.”

“Good. That’s right. And I will help you. But I need something from you in return, S. There’s a person we need eliminated. Just one person. A very bad person who deserves it. And once that’s done, I’ll help you. I promise. Will you help me first, S?”

“Yes,” he murmured. He looked in the streaked mirror of the restroom. There was a scar on his neck, red and slightly swollen, perfectly stitched, though he had never seen it before. “I will.”

## CHAPTER SIXTEEN

*Wait. Watch. Listen.*

"It's beautiful here," Maya noted. Through the window it was a stunning afternoon in Paris.

*Wait.*

"Too bad this is going to be the only view we're going to get," Trent replied sourly.

*Watch.*

"Nature of the job, I guess," she said with a sigh.

*Listen.*

There were twenty arrondissements, or administrative subdivisions, of France's capital city. They were in the 11th arrondissement, a diverse district that brought young locals and tourists to hip bars, just a stone's throw from Notre Dame, the Seine, the Louvre.

They, of course, would see none of that.

The two of them were holed up in a vacant apartment on the fourth floor of a building across the street from their target. The view through the wide picture window, if it could even be called a view, was entirely comprised of the apartment building across the street, including two of their target's windows. The curtains were closed over one of them.

So far they had seen him only twice, passing by the one visible window, seemingly minding his own business. On the flight over, Maya had read and reread the NSA report that had prompted their presence—and frankly, it looked like gibberish to her.

*Ninety-nine times out of a hundred, it's nothing*. That's what Walsh had said, and now more than ever she was inclined to believe that this "op," if it could be called that, was just an excuse to get Maya out of his way.

Still—this was the job. Wait, watch, and listen. So they did. She and Trent set up shop in front of the window, keeping low and as hidden as they could, with binoculars and a sonic ear and a camera on a tripod.

They waited, but nothing was happening. They watched and saw nothing. They listened and heard almost nothing; the only sounds they'd been able to pick up at this distance were the vague, rapid-fire dialogue of a French comedy series, and they couldn't even be certain it was coming from his apartment.

This man wasn't a sleeper cell. This man had no idea that the CIA was watching him. He was, it appeared, utterly ordinary.

Still, this was the job. Wait and watch and listen, because one time out of a hundred a seemingly ordinary man could be something more.

"Keep watch," she told Trent as she stood, stretched, and paced a few times across the empty apartment. Every now and then she had to move about a bit. Not just so her limbs didn't cramp up, but equally so as an outlet for her nervous energy.

She wished desperately that she knew what was happening back home. She hadn't forgotten about Alan's call. It could have been something, could have been nothing. But she had no way to contact anyone; agents didn't bring their personal cell phones on operations. Hers was powered off and stowed in a locker back at Langley. Her only lifeline to the outside world was a satellite phone that had been programmed with a single number that would connect to a technician (who was not, unfortunately, Penelope León) in the event they had a status update or needed resources.

She wished she knew what was happening back home. But as Alan had said, being on the job was probably the safest place she could be if something was up.

"How long do we have to do this?" Trent moaned as he lowered the binoculars and rubbed his eyes.

"Long as it takes to either confirm the NSA's suspicions or disprove them."

He blinked. "So, we'll have to *sleep* here?"

"Had that thought not crossed your mind before this moment?" It certainly had crossed hers. The idea of shacking up in a Parisian apartment with Trent Coleman for even one night, let alone more than one, was… well, it wasn't exactly an unwelcome thought, but it was still one that frightened her more than a little.

"And if the guy goes to work tomorrow?" he asked.

"Then we follow him."

He groaned again and stretched his arms. "God, this sucks. I'm starving. And we'll need some supplies anyway. I saw a department store down the street; what do you say I grab us some things, and maybe pick up some crepes on the way back?"

"Crepes?" She couldn't suppress her smirk.

"We're in France, so yeah. Crepes. Or how about some escargot? Perhaps some ratatouille? Or foie gras…"

She raised an eyebrow. "That's the extent of your knowledge of French cuisine, isn't it?"

He frowned, but then snapped his fingers and added, "Croissants."

Maya snorted. But all the same, her stomach rumbled. "Sure. Food sounds good. But *not* foie gras. That's duck liver."

"No kidding? Huh." Trent sat on the floor to pull his shoes on. "So food, for sure, but if we're going to be playing house we'll need a few other things. Something to sleep on, at least. How much of a princess are you, anyway? On a scale of sleeping bag to Egyptian cotton."

"A sleeping bag would be fine." Then she quickly added, "Two of them."

Trent Coleman looked up at her quizzically. "Yeah, of course two. Jeez, keep your pants on, Lawson."

Her cheeks turned pink and her ears burned.

Trent grinned, clearly enjoying her discomfort. "I'll be back in a flash. Keep an eye on our boy."

He was headed across the empty apartment toward the front door when a flat tone sounded. He paused, cocking his head slightly like an inquisitive dog. It took Maya a moment to realize that the tone was the satellite phone in her bag. She quickly pulled it out. The number, of course, was listed as "restricted."

"Agent Lawson," she answered.

"Maya, it's me."

"Penny?" Maya frowned. Penny wasn't the tech assigned to their op.

"Don't say anything, just listen. Everyone is safe, but some new information has come to light. It's possible that someone might have access to CIA intel, and both you and I would be on their list, if you catch my drift. It's imperative that you're extremely careful. Do not let your guard down. Understand?"

"Yes," she said, though she didn't, not fully.

"I'm sorry I can't say any more than that on this line," she said quickly. "But everyone is safe. Just take care of yourself."

"I will," Maya confirmed. She didn't like the way Penny felt the need to repeat that everyone was safe, without elaborating on who "everyone" was.

The call ended just as abruptly.

"What was that about?" Trent asked, standing just before the door.

"Um…"

*Someone might have access to CIA intel. Both you and I would be on their list.*

That would mean they might know where she was. Where *they* were.

"Just an NSA update," she lied. "No new chatter."

Trent looked her over. "You said 'Penny.'"

"Yeah. Penny made the call."

He took a small step away from the door. "Is there something you're not telling me? Because we're supposed to be partners. If there's something I should know—"

Maya jumped at a sudden, thunderous bang.

Something slammed against the door of the apartment. Trent spun as the jamb splintered and the wooden door flew open. The edge of it struck him right in the forehead and he reeled, flopping to the floor.

Behind him, a figure in a black ski mask took a single stride into the apartment and raised a pistol.

Maya threw herself forward as the gun chirped twice. Suppressed shots. One round struck the window, breaking a pane of glass. The second hit the wall, sending chunks of plaster skittering across the floor.

Maya rolled, or tried to, but there wasn't enough runway and she hit the wall. She righted herself and hurled the sat phone, sending it end over end and smacking into the assailant's face. He grunted and staggered, giving her just enough time to reach for the nearest makeshift weapon she had—the camera and tripod setup.

The man in the ski mask raised the pistol again as Maya brought the tripod over her head and down. The camera broke over his wrist and he howled. The pistol fell from his hand. She swung again, upward this time, and caught him just under the chin, sending him flat onto his back.

She dropped the tripod and twisted the stunned gunman's arm in a painful lock. He hissed through gritted teeth.

"Trent! You okay?"

He groaned and sat up. "Yeah. Think so." Trent gingerly touched his hairline and his hand came away with a small amount of blood.

"Dammit. Got me good." He crawled over to her and grabbed the silenced pistol from the floor.

Maya turned her attention back to the gunman. She held the arm lock tightly with one hand and tugged his ski mask off with the other.

In the moment, she was half-expecting—or maybe half-wishing—that she would find Stefan Krauss beneath it. But this man was bald, his head shaved, a snarling brown moustache on his lip. She didn't recognize him.

"Who are you?" she demanded.

"Go to hell," he grimaced.

"I'll break your arm," she warned.

"She'll do it," Trent chimed in, holding the gun on the downed man.

"How did you know about this place? Who sent you here?" She twisted the arm a centimeter further and the man yelped.

"Wait! Wait," he panted. "Don't break it. I was paid. All I had to do was—"

*Thwip!*

A bullet entered the man's forehead before Maya even knew what was happening. His head jerked with the impact. Maya leapt back in shock.

Trent's eyes were wide, even as he continued to point the gun downward at the dead assailant.

"What did you do that for?!" Maya demanded, incredulous.

"His hand!" Trent insisted. "He was going for something on his belt with his other hand! I-I panicked. I thought he had a knife or something…"

Maya glanced from Trent to the body on the floor. The man's other hand had been pinned beneath him while Maya had him in the lock. He couldn't have been going for a knife.

*Someone might have access to CIA intel. Both you and I would be on their list.*

That would mean they might know where she was. And she couldn't help but think of how easy it had been to convince Walsh to send them together.

"Give me the gun, Trent." She held out her hand.

His throat flexed. "Why?"

"Because I asked for it." She kept her tone calm, measured. "Please. Give me the gun."

No one else was supposed to know they were here.

Trent Coleman had volunteered to leave. Had Maya not gotten the call from Penny, he would have been gone a full minute before the gunman arrived.

When the door hit him, Trent fell to the floor. The gunman could have easily and quickly put a single bullet in him. But he didn't. He was gunning for Maya.

All of these facts whirled through her head and told her one thing.

"Give me the gun, Trent."

He shook his head a little. "Not until you tell me who was really on the phone, and why."

He looked terrified.

Perhaps because his cover had been blown. Perhaps because she knew, and he knew, that he wasn't to be trusted.

She took a small step toward the door. "If you won't give me the gun, then I'm leaving."

"Maya, wait!" he pleaded. "Please, I don't know what's going on."

"I can't stay here. I have to go. You have a choice here, Trent. You can shoot me, or you can let me leave, but you can't follow me." She took another slow step backward.

"I'm not going to shoot you," he said softly, still staring down at the body.

She reached the open doorway, the broken jamb, and made a run for it. She sprinted down the hall to the stairs, and took them three at a time, glancing over her shoulder every few seconds to see if Trent was following her.

He wasn't.

If he was part of it, the attempt on her life had failed.

If he wasn't, he was in far less danger without her than with her.

If someone knew where she was, and was trying to kill her, she'd be better on her own.

# CHAPTER SEVENTEEN

"I'm sure she's safe," Alan told him for what must have been the twentieth time.

"I know," Zero said, more for his own benefit than Alan's. He rubbed his face. He was exhausted. To sleep for even just a short while, to catch a catnap, would be a small mercy, but he couldn't do that. Not yet.

After his encounter with Krauss he'd fled from the warehouse and hotwired a delivery truck he found on the next block. They wouldn't even know it was missing until morning. Then he'd driven as fast as he dared, due south from New York back to Virginia, under the cover of night.

He knew his home was compromised and Third Street Garage was rubble, so process of elimination dictated where he headed next. Alan had told him about the safe house two months prior when he'd set it up, so he headed there, ditching the delivery truck in a parking lot and jogging the rest of the way.

While he was relieved to find Alan and Mischa alive and well, he was as dismayed as he was alarmed to find that Sara had not made it there with them. Alan explained the situation, bolstered by Penny's previous reassurances that Sara had had the foresight to turn her phone off, and was making sure she wouldn't be found, and had likely holed up with a friend.

"I'm sure she's safe," Zero parroted quietly, because he had no choice but to believe it. As much as he wanted to go out there and find her, to see her safe with his own two eyes, he'd only be putting her at greater potential risk.

Because if he found her, and Krauss found *him*, he'd likely try to kill them both.

Meanwhile, Penny had promised that she would contact Maya in Paris and issue a warning. After all, if Zero's hunch was correct, then the very same people who had sent her there were the ones behind the newest revelation.

"Tell me again," Mischa asked. She'd been mildly concussed when Third Street Garage had exploded, so Alan had dutifully kept her awake, but now she seemed clear-headed and cogent. "You fought with Krauss? You saw him?"

"Yeah," Zero confirmed. "But he wasn't Krauss anymore. They—someone—put a memory suppressor in his head. He didn't know me, or who he was. He didn't even know what he did."

Mischa shook her head. "He still deserves to die."

"You're right," Alan agreed. "And he will. But right now he might be the only one that can lead us to whoever is behind this."

"That… might not be entirely true." Zero had a lot of time to think on the frantic drive south. "I may have an idea. Though it might be sleep-deprived insanity talking…"

"That sounds about status quo," Alan quipped. "What are you thinking?"

Zero hesitated. His logic was simple; Krauss had a memory suppressor in his head. The only people who knew about it that weren't actively being killed or pursued were in the CIA. Therefore, they needed answers from the CIA, answers that not even Penny had or could get.

"I think we should kidnap and interrogate CIA Director Shaw," he said at last.

"I'm in," Alan said instantly.

"Same," Mischa agreed.

"This isn't something to take lightly," he reminded them. As pleased as he was at their zeal (and that they hadn't immediately dismissed it as insane), he couldn't help but feel that it was more than a little personal for both of them.

All of them, if he was being honest. Shaw had tried to get rid of Zero from the first day they'd worked together, and had tried to get him sent to prison on the last day they'd worked together. The former NSA-turned-CIA director had kept Mischa locked in a Langley holding cell for more than three months with no visitors other than Maria. And Alan—well, Alan had his reasons, though he didn't really need anything further than the man's job title to have immense disdain for him.

"We have no protection, no immunity, and few resources," he said. "If we're going to do this, we have to plan carefully and execute perfectly. One misstep and we'll be facing severe criminal charges. There won't be anyone or anything to hide behind."

"Still in," Alan told him.

"As am I," Mischa nodded.

"All right," Zero relented, half-wishing that at least one of them would attempt to talk him out of it. "Mischa, grab us some paper and a pen so we can get started on a plan."

She hurried from the room. Almost as soon as she was gone, Zero turned to Alan.

"Look," he said, "I'm sorry about the last couple of weeks. I've been distant—"

Alan held up a hand. "There are more important things going on. We're good."

"We're good?"

Alan nodded. "Now, what's *really* on your mind?"

Zero almost chuckled. No one could read him like Alan Reidigger could. Despite his best attempts to hide it, he may as well have been grimacing.

"Just between you and me," Zero began. He'd had a lot of time to think on the frantic drive south. Try as he might, there was one thing he simply could not get off his mind. "When I was in New York, at the old house, I had a… I don't know. A memory? A flashback. Some kind of intense déjà vu. It was about Kate. It had happened there."

Alan lowered his voice. "What did?"

"At some point before she died," he explained, "I… I heard her talking on the phone to someone. Checking in, like a status report on an op. Talking about changes in behavior, speech… and memory."

Alan shook his head. "What are you saying, Zero?"

He almost rolled his eyes. Did he need to spell it out so plainly? "I'm saying I had a memory of Kate that wasn't there before, and she was talking to someone. Like an operative. Like she was undercover."

Reidigger stared at him for a moment, his eyes narrow, as if trying to determine whether Zero was being genuine or not. Then he chuckled slightly. "Zero, come on…"

"Don't laugh. This is serious."

Alan's expression straightened. "I'm sorry. It's just—come on. Kate was… she was Kate. She restored paintings for the Met. She was the mother of your kids. She wasn't a spy."

He'd told himself as much no fewer than fifty times. Yet somehow, coming from Reidigger it was far more assuring. "Yeah. You're right."

"Look. Didn't the doctor say this sort of thing would happen? That more false memories might come up as you get closer…" Alan trailed off. He looked away.

He didn't need to finish the statement.

*As you get closer to the end.* It was a stark reminder that Guyer was dead, and with him, Zero's best hope of a successful treatment for his deteriorating brain.

Alan looked past him and cleared his throat. Mischa had returned. She spread a few sheets of paper on the chipped kitchen table between them and laid out pens.

Zero nodded his thanks. "Okay. Let's figure out how to kidnap the director of the CIA."

# CHAPTER EIGHTEEN

They left the safe house just before dawn broke.

With the time it took to form a plan, Zero had about an hour to relax and try to doze. Try as he might, even fully relaxing eluded him. There was simply too much on his mind.

Krauss. Kate. Sara. Guyer. Names and faces haunted him, the dead and alive alike.

Then Reidigger was there, in the doorway of one of the safe house's small bedroom, the wallpaper peeling and the floorboards bowing underfoot, and it was time.

Though Zero had never been anything anyone would describe as close to his former boss, there were some things he knew about Edward Shaw. First, that he had come up in the NSA and had gained a reputation that approached paranoia. His home, Zero assumed, would have a state-of-the-art security system and likely cameras. His car would have GPS tracking. His phone would be a way to find him at any time deemed necessary.

So they simply had to separate him from those elements until they had only the man, no way to trace him, and no eyewitnesses.

If Zero's long career had taught him anything, it was that the best and most effective plans were simple ones. It didn't matter how smart or capable one's team was; a plan too complicated could go haywire from a single misstep. A complex plan left little room to improvise. It got people killed.

So they kept their plan simple.

They left the safe house just before dawn broke. Reidigger drove the Buick the hour drive back toward Langley. Zero sat in the passenger seat and Mischa behind the driver's.

"Seat belt," he reminded her, and she clicked it into place.

Zero also knew that Shaw was an early riser. He was one of those corporate types that believed the boss should be in before anyone else—though Zero suspected that was more so he could watch them come, see their routines, rebuke them for tardiness if need be.

As the sun rose they came to Salona Village, an admittedly beautiful neighborhood of McLean, Virginia, that looked more like Martha's Vineyard than only twenty minutes removed from the Capitol Building. Zero was a little surprised that someone like Shaw would choose to settle here over the ritzier neighborhoods like Georgetown or even Capitol Hill. Salona Village had a quaint charm to it, as if time moved a little slower there.

It was almost a shame they were there for an abduction.

They were only three minutes from Shaw's home when Alan slowed the car and dropped Mischa off first to get into position, along a stretch of tree-lined road in view of only two homes. About a quarter mile's distance up the same road Alan stopped again, and this time Zero got out.

"Good luck," Alan called to him.

"See you shortly." He watched as the Buick pulled away, and adjusted his radio earpiece. "Mischa, do you copy? Over."

"I copy. Over."

"Just testing. Maintain silence until Alan gives the signal. Over."

He waited for a reply, and then realized she'd taken his request for radio silence very seriously, and suppressed a smile. Most fathers took their preteen daughters shopping, or to lunch, or to the movies. Not tracking deadly assassins and kidnapped high-ranking CIA members.

*Just another bonding experience.*

Then he put his hands in his pockets, and as casually as possible he began to walk back toward Mischa's position. He didn't walk too quickly, to avoid getting there before it was time; he didn't walk too slowly to make anyone suspicious. He just walked as if he was out for a morning stroll.

The trees were still full and lush and green. In another few weeks they would start to change color as the weather cooled. He couldn't help but hope he got to see that, instead of being in a prison cell, or dead from one thing or another. If it wasn't Krauss or the CIA it would be his own brain.

He didn't even have the slightest clue of how much time he had. And given how often he found himself in spots like this one, it hardly seemed to matter anyhow.

The radio crackled in his ear. "The eagle has left the building," Reidigger said. "Over."

"You're mixing metaphors," Zero said flatly.

“He left the house, okay? Silver Cadillac. Bright and shiny and obnoxious. Can’t miss it. Over.”

“Confirmed,” Mischa said through the radio.

At that same moment, Alan was in the Buick, parked a block away from Shaw’s house and facing the opposite direction. Mischa was hidden up the road a short ways, waiting to spring. And Zero, he was just walking. Complex plans got people killed.

There was one more thing that he knew about Shaw. Despite claiming to be such a stickler for the rules—the main reason that Zero had been such a thorn in his side—the director would do just about anything to keep himself out of hot water.

*

Mischa hid behind a particularly wide oak tree and waited. She was confident no one could see her; there was just a field behind her that eventually segued into thin woods. The nearest house was cater-corner to her position by at least eighty yards (a term that Sara insisted was “catty-corner” until Mischa pointed out that it was based on the French word *quatre*, meaning “four,” and that Americans had so bastardized their own language that none of them even knew why they would call something diagonally across from them “catty”). Trees on the opposite side of the road further obscured any would-be viewers; it would be difficult to spot someone from there.

She waited. She was, as Alan put it, the “bait” in this plan. She would have much preferred being called the decoy, but it seemed that she was democratically outvoted by her elders who insisted bait was more appropriate in this situation.

An engine was approaching. She peered out from behind her tree to see a dark red SUV pass by. Not her target.

Her position was between two and three minutes from his home. Alan had given the signal. Any time now…

Mischa heard another sound and peered out, and this time she saw it. A silver car with boxy headlights approached. The car meandered, going seemingly under the speed limit. Casual, taking its time.

She waited. This had to be timed just right.

The car neared her position. Almost there…

Mischa darted out from between the trees and into the street. If anyone had been watching, they would have seen the Cadillac hit her right around the left hip. They would have seen the small girl roll up the hood, strike the windshield with a shoulder, and then roll off the car and onto the pavement.

It hurt. But no more than a good body slam would. She'd jumped at the last second; the car had never actually struck her, but the act of rolling up and over it while it was doing at least thirty miles an hour was still painful.

And she couldn't imagine how it would have looked to Shaw when a small body suddenly flew over his hood and off his car.

The tires squealed to a stop. The door of the Cadillac flew open and a tall man stepped out in one quick stride. Director Shaw was lanky, and moved as if his spine was a steel rod. His mouth, it seemed, was good only for grimacing, but at least his eyes were wide and alert in concern.

Mischa rolled onto her back and faked a groan of pain.

"My god," Shaw breathed. "I-I didn't even see you… came out of nowhere…" He took a cautious step toward her, as if she was a wounded animal. "Are you all right?"

"Hurts," Mischa murmured.

For a moment she worried that Shaw would recognize her. But they had met only once ever, when she'd first been arrested at the Calvert Cliffs reactor, just after Samara had been killed.

This man had only kept her imprisoned in underground isolation for three months. Why should he recognize her?

"Can you… can you stand?" he asked. As he did he looked all around. Looking for witnesses.

She slowly and melodramatically got to her feet, making sure to grunt and wince appropriately.

The director was visibly relieved. "Good. Good. Nothing broken? You're okay?"

"Think so," Mischa said. "But I should probably go to the hospital…" She trailed off and looked past him.

He turned, following her gaze, and saw a man trotting toward them at a slow clip about a hundred yards out. "Oh god," he murmured. When he turned back to Mischa, Shaw's face was noticeably paler.

At this distance, he couldn't see that the man approaching them was Zero. All he saw was a possible eyewitness to a CIA director hitting a kid with his car.

"The hospital," Shaw said suddenly. "Yes, come, get in the car and I'll take you, and we can talk on the way about what you might say when we get there…"

Mischa resisted the urge to scowl and instead stuck out her bottom lip. "I'm not supposed to get in cars with strangers."

"Right. Of course not. Good girl." Shaw's teeth were gritted as he said it. "Um, where are your parents? Do you live close?"

"Yes. Can I use your phone? I'll call them. They can come get me."

"Phone. Yes." Shaw pulled his cell from his pocket and handed it to her. "Just… let's maybe keep names out of this, yeah?"

"You should probably get your car off the street," she suggested.

"Right. Yes. Good idea." Shaw didn't even seem to question the suggestion, stunned as he was. He got back in the car, and for a moment Mischa realized the fatal flaw in the plan; he could have sped off, right then. And for a moment it seemed like he might, as the Cadillac lurched suddenly forward. But then he swerved to the shoulder and parked it. He jumped out again and trotted back to her.

"There. Now, we can agree this was an accident, yes? I wasn't speeding, or—or texting, or any such thing, and you came out of nowhere, I imagine you didn't even look both ways, if we're being honest…"

"Shaw," she snapped. "Shut up."

"Excuse me?" He frowned deeply. "Hey—what is that you're doing?!"

Mischa already had the phone open, two halves in her hands. She slid out the SIM card and snapped it in half. They'd separated him from his home, his car, and his phone; now they just needed the man himself.

"What on earth—" Shaw started, but by that time Zero had reached them. He didn't break his stride, but simply linked his arm in Shaw's and tugged him forward, as if they were going for a pleasant walk.

"Hi, Shaw," said Zero. "We're going to need you to come with us."

"You!" The director's jaw dropped. He spun to look at Mischa even as Zero forced him forward. "And you… you're that *girl*… this was a setup!"

"Come on, we don't want to hurt you," Zero told him. The Buick rolled past them and pulled over to the side of the road. "I mean, we *do* want to hurt you, but we won't if you come quietly."

"Do you have any idea how many crimes you're committing right now?!" Shaw protested.

Mischa thought for a moment. “Four? Unless we’re also counting misdemeanors.”

They reached the Buick and Zero opened the door for Shaw. It was clear the director did not want to get in (and for good reason) but Zero leaned forward and whispered something in his ear. The blood drained from Shaw’s face, and his throat flexed with a gulp, and then he climbed into the backseat.

With any luck, there were no witnesses, no prying eyes from nearby homes. If there was, it would look like there had been an accident, but everyone was okay, and the driver was helped by a good Samaritan to take him and the girl to the hospital.

Zero sat in back with Shaw and Mischa slid into the passenger seat. Alan nodded to the director in the rearview as Zero searched his pockets, finding only his wallet and car keys. The wallet he passed to Mischa, who stowed it in the glove box. About a quarter-mile up the road, Zero threw the keys out the window.

“What are you going to do to me?” Shaw demanded, though his voice was tremulous. “What do you want?”

“We just want to talk, Shaw,” Zero said. “And you *will* talk.”

# CHAPTER NINETEEN

Zero knew they couldn't go back to the safe house. Not just because of its distance from Langley, but also because they wanted to keep it safe, to have a place to go if need be, and bringing a kidnapped CIA director to it would make it decidedly unsafe.

But in typical fashion, Alan had a place.

They drove in silence toward the location—relative silence, since twice Shaw tried to protest. The first time it was an overt threat about the charges they would face for their actions. The second was a piteous plea for clemency in return for letting him go now, no questions asked.

After the second protest went ignored, Shaw opened his mouth a third time, but then shut it again just as quickly when Mischa calmly and quietly pulled a paring knife from her pocket and passed it over the seat to Zero.

Stunned as Zero was by the presence of the weapon, he couldn't show it in the moment, so he took it and held it as unthreateningly as a knife could be while still being visible. He assumed she took it from the kitchen of the safe house.

The location Alan had in mind used to be a pharmacy but had gone out of business. The vacant building had been up for lease for seven months; Alan knew the owner and also knew that no one had been by to look at it in more than a month, so it was a safe bet they'd be undisturbed there for a little while.

Zero wouldn't need long with the CIA director.

Alan parked the Buick in the back. Zero guarded Shaw while Mischa picked the lock on the steel rear door. It took her about forty seconds to get in. No alarm went off; there was nothing to steal anyway and no reason for the owner to pay for the security.

The shelving units were still there, five long rows of gray steel forming the ghosts of aisles, empty and gathering dust. Aside from that there were vacant counters at the front, an area in the rear for filling prescriptions, a lot of floor space. The windows had brown paper taped up over them; likely to deter looters or vandals, he imagined, though

Zero didn't see how that would be very effective against either. It did, however, make it an effective place for an interrogation.

The whole place had a silent, eerie, post-apocalyptic sort of vibe. If he was being honest, it probably creeped him out just as much as it did Shaw.

"Bring him up front," Alan told them. "I'll be right back."

Zero frowned but didn't ask. He and Mischa marched the director of the CIA to the front of the former store, to the counter where registers would be if there had been any registers.

"Sit," Zero commanded.

Shaw did so, lowering himself slowly to the counter's surface. He was tall enough that his feet still reached the floor. He stared at the thin blade in Zero's hand.

"You're going to go to jail for a very long time for this," he muttered.

"Maybe," Zero conceded. "But by the time we're done here, you might be joining me."

Shaw frowned at that, but didn't get the chance to ask. Reidigger returned, pushing something into Zero's hands.

It was a black Glock 17.

"Got it from the garage before it exploded," he said. "Almost forgot I had 'em."

"Thanks." Zero tucked the pistol into the back of his pants. He wouldn't need it to interrogate Shaw.

"And now guns?" The director scoffed. "Hey, girl, how many felonies are we up to now?"

"Don't talk to her," Zero told him. "Talk to me. We have questions, and you're going to answer. As the director of the CIA, you're privy to certain information that not even the president knows."

"Like certain research and development projects," Alan chimed in.

"Like what?" Shaw asked caustically.

"Like an experimental memory suppressor," Zero told him outright. "A tiny chip, the size of a grain of rice, implanted near the base of the skull that affects the limbic system, the amygdala, parts of the hypothalamus…"

"Hinders the regulation of endocrine function in response to familiar stimuli," Reidigger added, regurgitating things they'd learned from the late Dr. Guyer.

"An agent named Seth Connors volunteered to test it, to be the first to have it implanted," Zero said. "But it failed. Memories of his former life started coming back. Leaking through. He went insane and eventually committed suicide."

"A few years ago," Alan picked up, "someone stole the latest suppressor prototype from R&D. The program was supposedly shut down, deleted."

"Or so we thought. Until today. When I came face-to-face with the assassin who killed Maria, and he had no idea who he was. He had one implanted recently. No more than a few days ago, it would seem. A week, tops." Zero leaned toward the director, who stared wide-eyed between the two of them. Despite how dangerous it was for them to know what they knew, he was enjoying the look of shock on Shaw's face at just how much they knew. "So, Director. Why did the CIA implant a suppressor in Stefan Krauss, and why is he helping to kill people who knew about the program? Dr. Guyer in Switzerland. Bliss, in New York." Zero leaned in and added, in a low voice, "Their wives."

Despite his obvious fear, Shaw shook his head. "I have no idea what you're talking about! We didn't implant anything into anyone. And even if I did know something, I won't divulge information that could jeopardize national security."

Zero had hoped it wouldn't come down to anything more than threats. But he also hadn't expected the director of the CIA to just roll over, either. "You will."

"Or what?" Shaw dared to challenge. "You'll hurt me? Torture me, like you would some insurgent at H-6? No. You're the good guys. It's not your style."

Zero exchanged a glance with Alan. "He's right. Not our style."

"We're the good guys," Alan admitted.

"That's why we brought her." Zero handed the small knife to Mischa.

Quick as a flash, she swiped out at Shaw's face, faster than he could pull away. He yelped as a thin red line opened on his cheek. It was a small cut, superficial, shallow, but cheeks had the habit of bleeding a lot. Both of Shaw's hands flew to his face and came back with blood on them.

"You—you cut me!" he gasped. "Do you have any idea what's going to happen to you?! Mark my words—"

“Mark mine,” Zero grabbed Shaw’s lapels in both fists and shook him. “My life, and the lives of my family and friends are in jeopardy right now, all because of that chip. You’d better start talking, and fast, because she’s quick with a knife and is just itching to cut some small pieces off of you. Understand?”

Shaw’s gaze flitted from Zero to Mischa, who played with the thin knife between her small fingers. He nodded quickly.

“I-I don’t know much. But—yes. The CIA never stopped working on the program. We moved it, to a facility in New Mexico. Destroyed all evidence of it at Langley. They developed a new one. I don’t know the details, just that the trials were successful, and that it can be controlled remotely…”

Mischa scoffed, evidently dismayed by how easily Shaw folded, but Zero wasn’t surprised. The man had never served in the field, had probably never been threatened like this before.

“Controlled?” Zero demanded. “How do you mean, controlled?”

“Meaning that the subject’s brain can be continuously manipulated,” Shaw said rapidly. “New things they learn or discover can be erased. Old memories, skills, experiences can be returned. Uh, given back, I suppose.”

Zero scoffed. The suppressor had been dangerous enough; they had to go and make it worse? “So why Krauss?”

“We didn’t!” Shaw insisted. “It was stolen. The facility was compromised—”

“Don’t lie to me!” Zero shouted in his face. “You expect me to believe that the suppressor was stolen and then just happened to end up in the brain of the assassin that killed Maria? Try again.” He pulled Shaw close, so their faces were only a few inches apart. “And do better.”

The director trembled, but still he shook his head. “I can’t,” he said quietly, almost a whimper. “I can’t. There are people out there more dangerous than you.”

“Currently? There’s not.” He let go of Shaw, and nodded to Mischa.

Her free left hand darted out and clamped onto Shaw’s ear. Her right hand readied the knife for a quick slice. Zero’s stomach turned; he was certain she would do it, and he was certain he’d let her, and equally certain he didn’t want to watch.

"Wait!" Shaw screeched. "Wait, please! It was given to an asset. A CIA asset—"

"A name, Shaw!" Zero warned. "We need a name, or you lose the ear."

"Bright! He's called Bright!"

He didn't have to wave Mischa off. At the shout of the name, she released Shaw and looked over at Zero in alarm.

Even he wasn't sure he'd heard Shaw right.

"Bright?" Zero repeated. "The CIA gave the memory suppressor technology to Mr. Bright?"

Shaw panted, his narrow chest heaving up and down, but he nodded. "You... know him?"

"Christ," Alan sighed.

"Let me get this straight," Zero said slowly. "The CIA gave some of the most dangerous technology on the planet to a man that funds terrorism? You call him an 'asset'? What sort of counterintuitive, backwards thinking is that?"

"You wouldn't understand..."

"Try me."

Shaw wiped blood from his cheek. "Look, it's simple math. We deal with hundreds of potential threats every single day. Sometimes, strategic alliances are necessary—"

"Strategic alliances? The man is a criminal!" Zero argued.

"So is half of Washington!" Shaw countered. "Grow up. This isn't high school. This is how the world works. Bright has resources that are occasionally loaned to the CIA, and in return, he gets some preferential treatment. Some looking the other way. It's happened a thousand times before. Murderers, politicians, the mafia... we make deals all the time. Hell, just look at the people that our own president is trying to make peace with right now. We've armed or bombed just about all of them in the last twenty years."

"That's different." Zero shook his head. "I know what these men have done. What they can do. I don't need to remind you that I was the one that brought in Mr. Shade."

'Yes," Shaw agreed quietly, "you were. And if Mr. Bright were here, I'm sure he'd thank you himself."

Zero frowned at that. "What are you talking about?"

"Don't you see? There's a reason Shade is a permanent resident of H-6 and Bright isn't."

There were few things Zero knew about the figure that went by the *nom de guerre* Mr. Bright. He knew that he funded terrorist cells all over the world. He knew he was a war profiteer, and now that he was apparently a CIA asset with his hands on the suppressor technology.

He also knew that Bright was a master puppeteer. He'd been pulling Stefan Krauss's strings for years without the assassin knowing it—and that was when Krauss still had his memories.

And now, it seemed, he'd done the same to Zero. If Shaw's vague remark was to be believed, Bright wanted his "business partner" gone, and Zero had taken care of it for him.

If there was one thing he didn't need, it was another thing in common with Stefan Krauss.

"I don't believe you," he murmured. "But it doesn't matter. If Bright's behind this, he will go down for it. Where is he?"

"I don't know," Shaw replied with a short scoff. "It's not like we do lunch. I've never met him, no idea what he looks like. He could be a she, for all I know."

"He is a he," said Mischa. "And he is headquartered in New York."

Shaw scoffed. "How would you know?"

"I spoke to him once," she said simply. "I'll find him again."

"Please. You have no way of knowing it was actually him. Even if you found him, you'd be dead before you got within a hundred yards of him," Shaw said. "We've tried. He wasn't always on our good side."

"So you're saying he's harder to get to than a CIA director?" Alan mused.

Shaw glared.

But Zero was barely listening. He was thinking. Even if he was an asset, even if the CIA looked the other way on Bright's "dealings," there was simply no reason to give him something like the memory suppressor—unless it had been a trade, and it would have to be something significant they got in return.

"What did he give you?" Zero demanded.

"What?" Shaw frowned.

"You gave Bright the suppressor. So you must have needed something from him. Something you couldn't do yourselves. Something that couldn't be linked back to the CIA in any way…" It dawned on him then, as he worked it out aloud. "You needed him to get rid of anyone connected to the memory program. In return for the tech, he'd make sure no one knew it ever existed."

*Including the thieves from four years earlier.* Him and Reidigger.

Whoever had killed Guyer—Krauss or Bright's people—they knew it now. They knew about Zero and Reidigger being a part of it. But had they shared that with the CIA? If they hadn't, Zero had just showed Shaw their full hand.

"Is that what it was?" Zero demanded. "Kill off anyone who knew?"

The director shook his head. "I'm not saying another word."

"Mischa." Zero nodded to her.

"Wait!" Shaw cried, but her small hand was already grabbing for his ear. He tried to pull away but she held fast. The blade sang in the air. Zero looked away. The director howled.

When he dared to look again, blood ran down the side of Shaw's neck. His eyes were squeezed closed tightly, tears streaming from them as he breathed ragged breaths.

Alan craned his neck for a peek. "Buck up, Shaw, she only took off about a quarter inch."

"Take more," Zero said flatly.

"Wait," Shaw gasped. "It was a whistle… a whistleblower."

*Whistleblower?*

"Someone was going to spill about the memory program?" he demanded. "Who?"

"You… you know who."

He did. As soon as Shaw said it, he understood immediately. The one person he knew was involved but hadn't yet considered. It wasn't Guyer, or Bliss, or Dillard. Not anyone in EOT, past or present. Not John Watson, and certainly not Zero's own daughters. It wasn't Penny León.

"Bixby."

The eccentric inventor and engineer who had served for years as the CIA's R&D head. The man who had been mentor and father-figure to Penny. He'd been a friend to Zero, Alan, and Maria. He'd been on the lam ever since destroying the CIA supercomputer called OMNI. Zero had found him once, and Bixby had pointed him in the direction of Seth Connors. He'd vowed then that Zero would never find him again.

Bixby would need damn good reason to poke his head out of the hole. Learning that the memory suppressor program was still ongoing would be a damn good reason.

Which meant that Bixby was on the list of targets—if he was even still alive now.

"Did they kill him yet?" Zero demanded. "Shaw, did they get to him?"

The director shook his head. "No. Can't find him."

"We have to go," Zero said to Alan and Mischa. "Let's get out of here. Leave him, let them find him like this. He can't prove anything."

"Wait," Shaw said. "There's one more thing you should know."

Zero frowned. "What is it?"

Shaw gingerly touched his mangled ear and winced. "I wouldn't be telling you any of this… if I thought for a second you'd leave here alive."

Mischa looked up suddenly, tensing. "I hear something. We're not alone."

Alan hurried to the front windows, carefully tearing a small corner of the brown paper away. "Oh, shit."

Now Zero understood why Shaw had tried to stall, even under the threat of torture. And why he'd suddenly been so willing to talk. He was the paranoid director of the CIA.

Just like Zero's own daughters once had, Shaw had a tracking chip implanted in his shoulder.

# CHAPTER TWENTY

Zero rushed to the window and looked out through the thin hole that Alan had torn away. Two black cars had pulled into the parking lot, parking at angles in the empty lot a safe distance from the entrance, about twenty-five yards. Behind them, a black SWAT van rolled in, and a four-man team in full tactical gear jumped out.

"He's being tracked," Zero murmured.

"Four agents, four SWAT," Alan noted. "More on the way, I'm sure."

He recognized one of the men who emerged from the black cars, a senior agent with a bald spot named Mulligan who had to be near retirement. They'd met only a few times in passing. Mulligan motioned with a hand and the SWAT team moved in single-file around the side of the building.

"Is the back door secure?" Zero asked.

"It's locked, but it's not all that sturdy," Alan said. "A few good swings with a battering ram would knock it right off the hinges."

"They won't try that; at least not right away. They don't know who they're dealing with or how many, and we have a hostage."

They also had only two handguns and a kitchen knife between them. But above all, these men were just doing their job. They were innocent in this; he refused to kill anyone over Shaw or his secrets.

"Even with a hostage," Alan said, "every minute we wait is another minute for reinforcements to show up. Any ideas?"

"Yeah," Zero admitted. "Just one. But it's crazy."

"When is it not?" Alan asked, and there was no jest in his tone.

Zero marched back to Shaw. The director held his damaged ear but managed a smile. "I can hear the gears turning in your head," he said snidely. "You can try to shoot your way out of this and they'll shoot you dead. Or, you can give yourselves up. And if we can strike a deal about the nature of our conversation today, and how much it never happened, maybe you'll find yourself in a nice cell with a cot and a toilet, instead of a hole at H-6."

"I have another idea," Zero told him. "One way or another, you're walking out of here with me. If you do it on your own, and you admit the truth about what's happening, no one else gets hurt today."

Shaw scoffed. "I don't know if you noticed, but the only person who's going to get hurt today is y—"

Zero swung. His right fist connected with Shaw's jaw. It was a solid, satisfying smack, even though it sent pain shooting through his hand and up his arm. The director's head jerked, and his body tumbled backward, off the counter and crashing to the floor.

He shook out his aching hand as he rushed around the counter to scoop up the unconscious director.

"Zero," Alan said slowly, "please tell me you're not thinking of doing what I think you're thinking of doing."

"What is he thinking of doing?" Mischa asked.

Zero didn't answer. He scooped up the limp Shaw, slinging one arm over his own shoulders, and hefted him with a grunt. He was heavier than he looked. "Find someplace to hide for a minute," he told Mischa. "A closet or something. Come out when you hear the signal."

"What's the signal?" she asked.

"You'll know it. And hey—no killing."

"But what if—"

"No buts," he said sternly. "No killing, young lady."

"Fine." She stalked off to find a place to lie low.

"You too," Zero told Alan.

He grunted. "I'm not hiding."

"Don't think of it as hiding. Think of it as… finding cover."

Alan raised an eyebrow. "I don't know what you're planning, but can I remind you that a friend owns this building?"

"Hope he's insured." Zero dragged Shaw with him to the front entrance. The glass doors were covered with the brown paper, and he couldn't hear what might be going on outside at that moment. He had no idea what he was about to walk out to.

But still he twisted the lock, and he pushed the sliding doors apart.

He winced in the morning sun as he took a single step out into daylight.

"Stop right there!" a stern voice shouted. The four agents had guns drawn, and on him, three of them partially hidden behind open car doors, except for Mulligan, who stood closest to the pharmacy.

"Don't shoot!" Zero shouted. "I've got him. I've got Shaw!"

"...Zero?" The barrel of Mulligan's pistol wavered. "Is that you?"

"Help me with him!" Zero half-dragged the unconscious Shaw toward the cars as Mulligan holstered his gun and rushed forward.

"Hostiles?" he asked as he reached Zero.

"Gone," Zero reported. "Out the back. I would've pursued, but he's hurt."

Mulligan spoke quickly into a radio. "Hostiles escaped through the rear."

The radio crackled. "There's no activity here, sir."

"Then do a sweep of the area!" Mulligan shouted. He took Shaw's other arm and asked, "Zero, what the hell happened? How are you here? Thought you retired."

Zero flashed a grin. "Is that what they're telling you?"

"Should've known," the senior agent muttered. Together they carried Shaw toward the two black cars. "Put your guns down!" Mulligan barked at the other three agents. "Don't you know who this is? And someone call an ambulance!"

They set Shaw down gently on the asphalt and leaned him against one of the cars. The director's head lolled as Mulligan knelt to check him over. "Jesus. Look at his ear. What were they doing to him?"

"Trying to get some information, I imagine," Zero said. "I didn't ask and they didn't stick around to tell me."

"How many?"

"Three of them, all male, in black. Possibly former Division, or at least they looked like it."

Shaw groaned slightly and tried to keep his head straight. Zero tensed; he wasn't sure if he'd hit him hard enough to break his jaw, and if he hadn't, Shaw was moments away from talking.

"You three, sweep the inside," Mulligan ordered the younger agents. "Find me something that tells us who or why they did this." As the three agents pushed forward toward the pharmacy the senior agent muttered to Zero, "They stick me with these kids. One of them's younger than my son. You okay?"

"I'm okay. Thanks." Zero took a few steps backward, towards the SWAT van.

Shaw groaned again, and tried to move his jaw.

"Sir, just sit still, ambulance is on the way. Don't try to speak; looks like your jaw might be cracked," he heard Mulligan say.

The radio crackled. "No sign of anyone," said a voice. The SWAT team, he was sure. "Are we sure the inside is secure?"

"My guys are on it," Mulligan replied. No sooner did he say it than there was a shout, and two gunshots from inside the pharmacy. "What the hell—?"

Zero jammed the stun baton between Mulligan's ribs. Standard-issue for SWAT, easily accessible in an unguarded truck. Twelve million volts surged through the senior agent's body. His mouth opened wide but silent. His body jerked, and then he slumped to the side.

"Sorry," Zero said quickly.

Shaw stared up at him, eyes wide, making unintelligible grunts as he was unable to shout for help. He could have zapped him, but the director wasn't a threat. And he still had to rescue his daughter and best friend.

Zero jumped behind the wheel of the SWAT truck and started it up. He shifted into gear, pulled the wide steering wheel, and gunned the engine.

Then he drove straight into the front doors of the pharmacy.

They gave easily, like driving through paper, though the explosion of glass and twisting of steel was like a bomb going off. He saw someone leap out of the way, diving to the floor and covering their head; one of the young agents.

Mischa was there in an instant, jumping into the open passenger door. "I take it that was the signal?" she said breathlessly.

"Where's Alan?"

"Move over, I'm driving!" Reidigger climbed up to the driver's seat as Zero scooted over, crouching between the two bucket seats as Alan shifted into reverse and slammed the gas. The truck lurched backward, groaning as it scraped the broken entranceway. Zero lurched a second time as the rear bumper smacked one of the CIA sedans.

"Sorry, sorry!" Alan shifted again, and the truck shot forward. He twisted the wheel with a grunt. "Thing barely has power steering, for Christ's sake…"

Gunshots split the air and they ducked low. Bullets pounded the side of the truck but didn't penetrate the siding as one of the agents fired at them from the vestibule. Zero clambered into the rear of the truck, where two long bench seats sat against either side of the truck, and an unlocked rack of weapons beckoned.

Through the small square window at the back, he saw a SWAT member sprinting, trying to chase down the truck, but they'd reached the street and he was quickly growing smaller behind them.

"So this was your big plan?" Alan shouted from the front. "Steal the second-most conspicuous vehicle possible and make our getaway?"

"I wasn't hearing any suggestions from you!" Zero shouted back. "Wait, what's the first?"

"The Wienermobile. Obviously."

"What's a Wienermobile?" Mischa asked.

Sirens blared behind them. Zero looked through the window again to find two police cars gaining quickly, no doubt en route to the scene and now pursuing the stolen SWAT van.

"Company!" he shouted. "Mischa, with me!"

She climbed into the back as he reached for the rack. He took a Colt M4 carbine for himself, and handed her the smaller MP5 submachine gun.

"Tires. Not people. Got it?"

"Got it." She expertly checked the magazine, pushed it back in, and cocked it.

Zero shook his head; for just the briefest of moments he felt a pang of remorse for the girl. Maria had wanted nothing more than to give her a normal life. She should have been in school at that moment. She should be watching cartoons on the weekends and hanging with friends. Not kidnapping CIA directors and stealing SWAT vans.

Mischa threw open one of the rear doors, crouched in a firing stance, and opened fire on the police cars behind them. Bullets bounced off of pavement and headlights shattered.

"Keep it steady!" she shouted at Alan.

"Sorry, this thing handles like a barge on wheels!"

She fired another burst. One of her rounds found a home in rubber; a front tire exploded, shredding in an instant, and one of the cruisers fishtailed sideways.

"I'm out, switch!" She stepped aside to reload as Zero stepped forward and brought the carbine to his shoulder. The kickback was powerful, and the gun roared like a lion, but the truck bounced and his shots went wild.

"Intersection!" Alan warned. Zero reached up and grabbed onto a canvas loop hanging from the ceiling. The truck swerved. Tires screeched. Mischa's feet left the ground for a moment, and Zero reached for her. He let go of the M4 and it slid out the open back of the truck, his free arm catching the girl around the waist.

"Thanks," she said tightly, seeming to realize how close she'd come to bouncing out instead of the gun. While Zero maintained his grip on her, she aimed again and fired another burst out the open back door.

The MP5 pounded large holes in the hood of the police car. Smoke billowed from beneath it, and the distance between them grew as the cruiser lost power. Alan cut the wheel left and the truck leaned again. The last thing Zero saw of the second cruiser was orange flames erupting from the hood and the two officers inside leaping out.

Zero pulled the rear door closed. "I figure we have less than five minutes before there's a chopper on us. Alan, you have someplace for us to go?"

He hesitated. "I do… but you're not going to like it much."

"Anything is better than this."

"Sure," said Reidigger. "Just remember you said that."

*

"I don't like this much," Zero muttered.

"Told you so," Alan retorted quietly. "Let's just get it done and move on."

The place he'd taken them looked like a fairly ordinary garage, but it was nothing short of a chop shop. More than that, Zero recognized the tattoos of the two young men who were currently doing inventory of the SWAT van in one of the bays (with the door securely closed behind it, of course) and knew who they were. Members of a local gang, the Imps, if he recalled correctly. This was the kind of place they brought stolen cars to get stripped down and sold for parts.

*Which is exactly what we're doing here,* he reminded himself. Well—it was half of what they were doing there. The other half was arming known gang members.

"All right, old man." One of the kids hopped out of the truck. He wore a black tank top and jeans that hung far too low from his hips. He had a silver stud in his chin, of all places, and kept his head shaved. "The truck and everything in it for a car."

"What have you got?" Alan asked.

"Got a 2004 Civic with about a hundred twenty K on it. The VIN is scratched off but the plates are legit."

Alan folded his arms. "Stolen?"

The kid shook his head. "Not this one. We just use it for cruising. Used to be a digger, back in the day, so lots of aftermarket parts. She can handle herself just fine."

"Digger?" Zero asked.

"Drag racing," Alan replied.

"We should keep a couple of the guns," Zero noted.

"No way," the kid said immediately. "The truck and everything in it, or no deal."

Mischa stepped forward slightly, as if to intimidate the kid, but he merely grinned at her.

Alan put out a hand and gently touched her shoulder. "We'll take it," he told the kid.

Five minutes later the three of them were in a car older than Mischa and on their way to put some distance between them and Washington.

"You know they'll probably just sell them, right?" said Alan. "The guns? Either that or they'll do something stupid and get busted with them, and end up in jail anyway."

"Right," Zero agreed quietly. Even so, Shaw's words rang in his head: *Sometimes, strategic alliances are necessary*. The CIA had aligned with Bright out of perceived necessity. Zero had tased an agent, stolen a SWAT truck, and traded guns to gang members for the same reason.

*And we're the good guys.*

"Once we're clear of DC, I want to find a payphone and try to call Sara," he said. "I need to know she's all right."

"Absolutely," Alan agreed. "Until then—we need a heading."

"New York," said Mischa. "We need to find Bright and cut the head from the snake."

Zero shook his head. "I don't think that's the play here. Shaw is going to make it known that it was us. Considering what they've asked of Bright, I'm sure he'll share what he now knows about us. We were already targets before, now we're just targets to more people." Not just Bright, but the CIA, the police, and Krauss would all be looking for them. "We know Bright operates out of New York. There's no way we'll get the drop on him, even if we could find him."

"So we're on our own," said Alan. "And we can't get close to the one person who we know is behind this."

“There might be someone else we could get close to.” Zero rubbed his chin. “We should find Bixby.”

Alan scoffed. “Last time you found him it took six weeks and he was in a remote cabin in the Canadian tundra. What makes you think you can find him again?”

“A hunch,” said Zero with a shrug. “Head to Bethesda. There’s someone we need to have a heart-to-heart with.”

# CHAPTER TWENTY ONE

Sara awoke. The dark curtain over the only window in the basement kept any outside light from filtering in. Was it day? Was it night? Her phone was still off. She had no idea what time it was. Or what day it was. She felt like she'd slept for a week.

At last she rose from the bed and trudged up the stairs from the basement. She didn't bring the gun. She didn't try to muffle her footsteps. If someone was in the house and they wanted her dead, they could have shot her in her sleep.

It was silent in the kitchen. She took a jug of orange juice out of the refrigerator, unscrewed the cap, and took a long drink. To her right, the soles of the dead man's boots stared back at her from the short hall just outside the bathroom.

For better or worse, no one had come for her. Not assassins or commandos or her family or friends.

Were they even alive?

*Do you care?*

Yes—on some level, she did. Of course she did. She would prefer them be alive than not. But if they weren't… well, it was out of her hands, wasn't it?

*What's wrong with me?*

She was tired. That's what was wrong. Not tired in the sense of physical exhaustion; just tired. Mentally, emotionally, bone-tired. She felt as if her soul itself had been dredged of anything that might have made her feel something.

Sara stalked through the house slowly, checked each room to make sure she was alone. Satisfied, she returned to the basement and dressed in jeans, sneakers, a sensible black top, and a light jacket. She didn't need it for the weather but wanted the pockets. The small black pistol she'd taken from Alan went into the left pocket. Her phone, into the right.

She emptied her shoulder bag of art supplies and brought it with her upstairs. She relieved the dead man of his gun, a silver pistol that felt too big and bulky for her hand. There was a hammerless revolver in the coat closet; she took that too. She pulled out the utensil drawer in the kitchen, which was a few inches shorter than it should have been, by design. She reached into the empty space and groped in the darkness for the Glock that she knew was secured to the rear of the cabinet behind the drawer.

There were others in the house, she was certain, but she wasn't about to waste time searching for them. She had enough.

*Enough for what, though?*

*Enough to feel safe?*

*When was the last time you actually felt safe?*

If she really thought about it, it probably hadn't been since her mother was still alive. She could barely recall what life was like back then. Of course she remembered being a child, and things that happened, but how she actually felt… that eluded her.

She'd felt—secure, she supposed was a good word for it. And then her mother was gone, and her dad did his best, but that sudden loss of her mom had shaken her. She had been only twelve at the time. Twelve years old when she learned just how quickly someone could be taken, or how quickly she could be taken from them.

She hadn't truly felt safe since.

A strange chime suddenly broke the silence of the house. Sara sucked in a breath at the sound of it, foreign and intrusive as it was on her thoughts. It took her a moment to realize it was a phone ringtone, and then it took another moment to recognize that it was not her own, which was still powered down in her pocket.

It was coming from the dead man.

She knelt beside him, not looking at his face as she reached into a pocket and pulled out a cell in a durable black rubber case.

And then she answered it. At least, she pressed the button to answer the call, but she said nothing, just breathing into the phone.

"You didn't check in," said a gruff male voice.

"He's dead," Sara told him.

"Who is this?!"

"You don't know?" She chuckled mirthlessly. "You people tried to kill me, and failed, and I've been home all night. How embarrassing that must be."

"Garfield is dead?" the man asked.

Sara wrinkled her nose. "Garfield? That was his name?" She dared herself to look at the man's face, which had bloated a bit in the night. Still, he didn't look like a Garfield to her.

"When we find you..." the man threatened.

"Get to it," Sara interrupted. She ended the call and tossed the phone down. She knew she probably shouldn't have done that—shouldn't have answered the call at all, much less taunted the people who were actively trying to kill her—but she simply didn't care. She felt as if she'd been scraped clean of the ability to give a shit.

But she couldn't stay in the house. That would be suicide now. She powered up her phone—they already knew where she was at the moment anyway—and saw that she had a single voicemail waiting for her, though she didn't recognize the number.

"Sara, it's Dad," he said on the recording. He sounded frazzled and worn. "Listen, I'm with Alan and Mischa, and we're... well, we're trying to get to the bottom of all this. I just want to know that you're safe, okay? So please, if you get this, contact Penny. She'll get the message to me. I love you."

They hadn't come for her. He was with Alan and Mischa, and she was in the most obvious place she could think of to be found, and they hadn't come for her.

Sara sighed, and she leaned a hip against the counter as she did her daughterly duty and sent a text to the number she had saved for Penny. It was a secure line that her dad had made her put in her phone in case of emergencies. She kept the text simple and clear.

*It's Sara. I'm safe. Keeping the phone off.*

And before Penny could reply, if she was even going to reply, she shut the phone down again. She slung the shoulder bag across her chest and retrieved her bike from the garage, walking it through the foyer to the front door.

*Where do I go now?* she wondered as she pedaled quickly down the street. She could go to Camilla's place. Her former roommate from Florida had come north for rehab and decided to stay. But Camilla's current roommate was kind of a bitch, and Sara couldn't rely on her not posting something to Instagram. She could go to Maddie, the founder of the trauma support group Common Bonds. But anyone who knew Sara would know Maddie and check for her there.

But there was a place she could go. A place she could hole up without disturbing anyone. Last time she'd checked, it was still closed due to a lice outbreak in one of the daycare classes. It was still closed, it would be an ideal spot to lie low for a bit.

Sara increased her speed, enjoying the sunshine and the wind in her hair, as she pedaled toward the community center.

# CHAPTER TWENTY TWO

Todd Strickland was uncomfortable in the Oval Office. There seemed to be something sacred about the place that kept his spine straight and tension in his shoulders. Not to mention that any visit to the Oval Office also warranted a suit, which he just couldn't relax in. He was a jeans and T-shirt sort of guy. Even his dress blues, his ASU from when he was still an active Ranger, had always felt stuffy and overly formal.

So he was glad that this particular meeting was being held in the Situation Room, the president's command center-slash-conference room in the West Wing basement, rather than the office. It was informal enough that he could get away with jeans as long as he wore a shirt with a collar. At least that's what Penny had told him.

But then again, she'd shown up in a hot pink V-neck and lime-green pants.

Penny sat across from him at the long, polished table as she manipulated the screen at the far wall with her open laptop in front of her, reviewing the details of their final security briefing before the Cairo Accord.

"As you can see," she was saying, "we not only referenced the CIA database, but we ran all names through the FBI's system, as well as consulting third-party background check software. This is the partial list of those who have been fully vetted thus far."

*Thus far?* Todd suppressed a smile at her proper British accent, despite how improperly she usually spoke. Her personality was a strange one, like someone had stuffed a Cambridge professor into the body and mind of a feisty Latina.

He had absolutely no idea why she found him interesting in the slightest. They'd only been dating for a couple of months, but half of that time he spent feeling like the high school quarterback was dating the president of the chess club.

"Let's talk security personnel," said Vice President Barkley. She sat at the right-hand side of President Rutledge, who had spoken very little so far in the meeting and seemed content to let Barkley take point on it.

He'd already made it very clear that the Cairo Accord was the VP's show more than his own, and wasn't taking any credit where it wasn't due.

That was one of a long list of things to like about Rutledge. Another was that he too had opted to forgo a tie and jacket, and had even rolled up the sleeves of his white shirt. Todd took it as a sign that he felt at ease around his new lead agent on EOT.

Strickland cleared his throat. "Well, Madam Vice President, aside from EOT—"

Joanna Barkley held up a hand to stop him. "Please, let's dispense with the 'madam' while we're able." A thin smile passed her lips. "I'm not even married and it makes me feel like a grandmother."

"Certainly, ma'am." Todd frowned. "Then… what should I call you?"

"Well, 'Joanna' feels a bit too informal. How about, Ms. Barkley?"

"All right, ma—um, Ms. Barkley."

Across from him, Penny bit her lip to keep from grinning.

"Aside from EOT," he continued, "we'll have four teams of Secret Service agents available, all of them with top clearance and vetted by both myself and Dr. León. We're also calling in some support from Agent Mendel and the Is-Pal joint task force…"

Rutledge winced. "Good grief, is that really what they're calling it?"

"Uh, for now, sir," Todd confirmed. He couldn't disagree; it was a terrible name, and he doubted Talia Mendel had much to do with it. "They'll be sending a dozen of their people to assist, which we'll use primarily for external security and perimeter sweeps."

"And what about attachés?" Barkley asked.

"Penny?" Todd gestured to her with a hand. "I mean, Dr. León."

Penny flashed him a smirk. "Each administration has been notified that their maximum permissible attaché is six. We've been provided names, photographs, fingerprints, medical histories, records, the works. All of that has been cross-reference with the CIA database, and we've only had to discount three people—all in all, a pretty positive note, if I may say so."

"On what grounds were they discounted?" Barkley asked.

"Nothing serious, just incomplete information," Penny replied. "We're being as thorough as possible to avoid any potential…"

She trailed off as one of the double doors to the Situation Room opened. Todd twisted slightly in his seat to see a tall agent in a black suit enter. Agent Clark, if he wasn't mistaken.

"Mr. President, Madam Vice President," said the agent. "Director Barren would like to see you. It's urgent."

Rutledge beckoned with a hand. "Send him in."

A moment later DNI Barren swept into the room. He nodded quickly to Rutledge and Barkley, without so much as a glance toward Strickland or Penny.

"Sir, there's a situation," he said tersely.

"Well, we're in the right room for it, aren't we?" Rutledge leaned back in his chair.

Now Barren cast a glance at Strickland as he said, "It's a… security concern, sir."

"Then you're in good company," the president noted.

The DNI hesitated, but when it became clear that Rutledge was not going to dismiss Todd or Penny, Barren continued. "It's about Agent Zero."

*Zero?*

Todd leaned forward in his seat. So did Rutledge.

"Go on," the president said cautiously.

"CIA Director Edward Shaw was abducted during the commute from his home to Langley this morning," Barren reported. "After his car was found abandoned, agents tracked him to a vacant commercial property, where they found Shaw with Zero. According to agents on the scene, Zero pretended as if he had rescued Shaw from captors, just before stealing a SWAT van and evading capture."

Rutledge held up a hand. "I'm sorry, David, that is quite a bit to process."

Todd frowned at Penny in a way that he hoped was saying, *What has he gotten himself into?*

She gave him a small shrug in return.

"What did he want with Shaw?" Rutledge asked. "Did he mention?"

"No, sir. Director Shaw is currently under anesthesia, getting his jaw wired shut."

"Christ," the president murmured.

"There's more," the DNI said. "Zero is also wanted in connection to the recent bombing of his former home in New York, two stolen vehicles, and the homicide of five people in Zurich."

"Okay, that's enough," the president said shortly. He rubbed his temples. "David, we get on a plane to Egypt in less than three hours. What do you want me to do with this information?"

"Send me," Todd heard himself saying. Penny looked up at him in alarm as all eyes were suddenly on him. He cleared his throat. "Sir. You can send me. I've tracked him down before; I can do it again. I'll bring him in."

"Absolutely not." Rutledge shook his head. "I need you, both of you, on that plane with me. You've been working on this tirelessly; I won't compromise security by letting you run off after him again." He sighed and murmured, "Retirement just does not suit that man, does it?"

"Are we certain he's still in the country?" Barkley asked.

"Fairly so," Barren replied. "We couldn't get too much out of Shaw, but there's reason to believe that Zero might be headed back to New York as we speak."

"Then the FBI can handle it," Rutledge said. "And notify NYPD."

"Both already done," Barren told him. "I merely wanted to apprise you of the situation, given your affinity for Zero and his former affiliation with EOT."

Strickland couldn't help but wonder if Barren always spoke like a robot. So mechanically, almost crassly, about a man who, for two whole days, had been his son-in-law.

"Director," said the vice president, "is there any reason to believe that whatever is… motivating Zero's action might have anything to do with our efforts here?"

Barren shook his head. "None, ma'am. I don't believe the information Zero was after had anything to do with the accord, nor do I think he knows anything about it. However… if that is a legitimate concern, there is an asset that we can employ."

"What asset?" Strickland blurted out.

The DNI regarded him as if he was a child demanding answers from an adult. "Classified."

Strickland gritted his teeth to keep his mouth from opening again out of turn. He and Zero had not been on speaking terms since Maria's murder—and since Zero had bested him in a fight and left him behind in Morocco—but still, if they were sending someone after him, Todd wanted to know. Especially if it was going to be some trigger-happy goon squad like the Division had been.

Rutledge drew in and released a long sigh. "Fine. Send whoever you can. But let's not make a big mess of this. I want him brought in to answer for all of this. That means *alive*, and make sure your people know it."

"Yes sir. Thank you, Mr. President."

Rutledge suddenly looked drained. "You two. Anything more to add from your report?"

"No sir," said Penny. "We just have to finish a handful of clearances before we depart."

"Get on it, then. Dismissed."

Strickland rose from the seat and collected the file folders in front of him as Penny shut the laptop lid and scooped it up. They left the Situation Room, remaining silent as they were escorted down a corridor by a pair of Secret Service agents. It wasn't until they were outside again that either of them spoke. And even when they did, they kept their voices low.

"Did you know anything about that?" Strickland asked.

She shook her head. "Not a thing. Any idea what it's about?"

"No," he admitted. "But I really don't like how the DNI came running straight to the president with it."

"What are you thinking?" Penny asked.

"I'm thinking that it was a lot less about EOT and a lot more about letting the president know that Zero's gotten into some trouble…" He didn't want to say it aloud. "So that it's not all that surprising if he ends up dead. And whatever this asset is, Barren clearly wanted permission from the top."

Penny nodded, furrowing her brow, thinking, when her phone rang. She pulled it out and glanced at the screen. "One moment." Then she answered. "Hello?"

She rolled her eyes slightly at Todd as she said to the caller, "Uh-huh… Yes. Okay… I will."

She ended the call. "Mrs. Carmichael says I forgot to give her Bathsheba's eye drops." She groaned. "Do you think you can run those remaining clearances while I dash home and fix this quick?"

He nodded. "Not a problem, as long as you're back by wheels-up."

"Of course I will." She leaned in and gave him a quick kiss.

“And what about the Zero situation?” he asked as she turned.

“Todd, I don’t think there’s much we can do about that. We have a job here, a serious one. It’s not like he reached out to us. There’s going to come a time when he does, and we’ll have to decide then whether we put ourselves on the line to help him, or move on. But right now… it quite seems like he’s on his own.”

“Yeah,” Todd agreed quietly. “You’re right. Go, do what you gotta do. See you soon.”

He watched as she hurried toward the White House parking garage and her car. She was right; Zero hadn’t come to them, and they couldn’t jeopardize all their work to go looking for him. They had been tasked with international security. There was nothing more important at the moment.

## CHAPTER TWENTY THREE

Zero had reached out to her, and she was jeopardizing all their work to go looking for him.

Penny drove as quickly as she could without breaking any major traffic laws back toward Bethesda. She hated lying to Todd. But for all his charm and innocence, he was entirely too honest to trust with something like this.

She hadn't even told him about the possibility that someone was tracking down and killing anyone who knew about the memory suppressor program. For one, she was afraid he'd tell someone else, try to escalate it to someone like Shaw or Barren or even Rutledge. He might even tell the others on EOT and endanger their lives. And two, no one outside of their little clique even knew that Todd knew Zero's secret—so as long as he didn't talk about it, he was safe. Or as relatively safe as he could be given his position.

Todd had heard only one side of the phone call. How it had actually gone was:

"Hello?"

"Penny. It's me. I'm nearby."

"Uh-huh."

"Can we meet? It won't take long."

"Yes. Okay."

"Make up an excuse and meet at your place."

"I will."

And instead of telling Todd the truth, she'd instantly invented a lie about her cat. It wasn't entirely a lie—her neighbor Mrs. Carmichael really was watching Bathsheba while Penny was in Cairo, and her surly British Shorthair really did have a mild infection in her eye. But she certainly had not forgotten to give Mrs. Carmichael the eye drops.

It took her twenty-five minutes to get to Bethesda in her hybrid hatchback. She pulled around to the rear of her building and let out a groan of frustration; someone had parked an ancient Civic in her dedicated parking spot. So she pulled into a visitors' spot and hurried up to the second floor.

She liked her building; it had a lot of character. The exterior was more than a hundred years old, but the apartments had been renovated only three years prior, updated and modern. They'd knocked a wall down in her unit to make it more spacious. And the first floor housed a flower shop, so it always smelled like springtime.

Penny took her keys from her purse as she reached the second-floor landing. As she searched for the house key, Zero came around the corner and startled her so badly she dropped the key ring.

"Jesus! Do your shoes ever make noise?" she scolded. "And calling my personal cell? What were you thinking? I gave you a special number for situations like these!"

"I tried it," Zero told her. "It went to voicemail."

"Oh." Her cheeks flushed as she realized she'd left the second cell in the apartment. "It's… inside." She scooped up the keys and unlocked the door. "Well, come on."

He followed her inside. She locked the door behind him. Then she started shouting.

"Just what the hell is going on out there?! You kidnapped Shaw?"

"Yes, but—"

"And what happened in Zurich?"

"Guyer is dead."

"New York?"

"More people are dead." Zero rubbed his face. He looked exhausted, like he'd aged five years since the last time she saw him. "Penny, just listen a minute. I was right. The CIA never ended the memory suppressor program; they just moved it out of Langley. Krauss has one implanted in him, because Shaw gave the tech to Bright, who in return is eliminating anyone who worked on it or knows about it so that the agency can wash their hands of it."

Penny blinked a few times. "I… *what?*" She felt like her head was spinning.

"It's all true, and we have zero evidence. But there may be someone who does," Zero explained. "I think you know who that person is."

She did. "Bixby."

"Right. Shaw said someone was going to blow the whistle on the suppressor tech. It was him. They haven't found him yet. If he has hard evidence of it that he was going to go public with, he's our best shot at keeping anyone else from dying—and to bring down Shaw, Bright, and the whole thing."

Penny reached out and grabbed the back of a chair. She knew that her mentor wasn't just going to vanish, that he'd be keeping tabs on things as best he could—and though he hadn't been specific, she also knew that the memory suppressor tech was certainly one of those things.

Being involved in that was one of Bixby's biggest regrets. If he discovered that the research had continued, he certainly would have wanted to put a stop to it.

"It's not just about evidence," Zero said gently. "He's my friend. But he was closer to you than any of us."

She nodded. Bixby had been more than just a mentor; he'd been a father figure. He'd taught her how to have a sense of humor. His eccentric wardrobe had inspired her own colorful choices.

"His life is in danger," Zero told her. "He didn't dare give any of us a clue about where he would go, or where he could be found if it was absolutely necessary. But something tells me that maybe, just maybe, he gave you one. Did he, Penny? Did he leave you a clue?"

She sighed. Her chin came to rest near her collarbones. "Yes."

"What was it?"

"It was… it was just a word. He left me one word. I don't know what it means. It could mean a thousand different things. Or it could even be a code, or a cypher. You know how he was." She'd thought about that word innumerable times since Bixby had left. She tortured herself over it, wondering what it could mean and coming up with nothing.

"What was the word, Penny?" She felt his hand gentle on her shoulder. "What was it?"

"Turtles."

"Turtles?" Zero repeated.

"Yes. That was it. Just the word 'turtles.'" She turned to him, not even attempting to hide the hope in her eyes. "Does that mean anything to you?"

Zero looked at the floor and shook his head. "No. I'm sorry."

"Me too. Wish I could help more. What will you do now?"

He shrugged. "Try to find him through other means. If he really was the whistleblower, he might make it a little easier on me." Zero chuckled. "Though I doubt it."

"Yeah. Sorry." She crossed the dining room to the attached kitchen and pulled open a junk drawer, atop which was the secure cell she kept for emergencies. "There, got it now. If you need me…" She trailed off. There was a text.

From Sara.

"Zero, look!" She waved the phone in his face.

*It's Sara. I'm safe. Keeping the phone off.*

He put a hand over his heart and let out a sigh of relief. "Thank god. That's her cell number, too. When was that sent?"

"Little more than an hour ago. She must have turned it back on just long enough to send a message." They were both silent for a long moment, sharing in the relief of knowing that their hopes had been confirmed and Sara had gotten somewhere safe. "Are Alan and Mischa with you?"

Zero nodded. "They're close. But I should go. And you should keep yourself safe."

"Actually…" She knew she shouldn't be telling him this, but it was Zero. No one kept secrets like he could. "I'm getting on Air Force One in about two hours."

"Oh? Heading where?"

"Can't tell you that." She smiled.

"Right." He smiled too. "I'm not part of the club anymore."

"Nothing personal. But the only CIA around will be Todd and EOT. I'll be fine." Her smile faded. "You're sure you don't know what 'turtles' means?"

He shook his head. "Wish I did. Sorry."

"Me too. I'll have the secure line with me, but this is where we part ways. For now. Take care of yourself, Zero."

"I will, Penny. You too."

*

As Zero got back into the old Honda he realized he'd parked in a numbered spot that was probably reserved for one of its residents. No matter; it wasn't like he'd been there long. He circled the block and double-parked outside a coffee shop where Alan and Mischa joined him. Reidigger handed him a coffee. Mischa sucked happily on some frozen caramel-colored drink in the backseat.

"How much sugar is in that?" he asked her.

She shrugged. "I don't know. But judging by the flavor, I would say 'a lot.'"

“Terrific.” Zero pulled the old car out onto the street.

“Well?” Alan asked him. “How’d it go? Did she know about Bixby?”

“Yes and no. He’d left her a clue, but she had no idea what it meant. She thinks it’s a cypher or something.”

Alan frowned. “Then why leave her the clue?”

“Because it wasn’t meant for her. It was meant for her to give to me.”

He knew exactly what it meant the moment she said it. But he wouldn’t put Penny in any further danger.

“So? What was the clue?” Alan prodded.

“Turtles.”

“Ah.” Reidigger chuckled and shook his head. “So I guess we’re going to Rome.”

# CHAPTER TWENTY FOUR

Maya didn't know where she was. By the light of a streetlamp she knew she was on Rue Quatre, but she had no idea how far she'd gone from the vacant apartment, from the dead gunman, and from Trent Coleman.

She had nothing. No gun, no phone, no money, not even an ID. All of it had been left behind when she fled. She had found a working payphone and attempted to make a collect call to Penny's emergency line but the call wouldn't go through to the States.

Twice she'd stopped and tried to ask a stranger if she could use their phone, but her French was rusty, a bit clunky, and they hurried away from her.

There was hardly anyone on the streets now. She imagined it would be dawn soon. Every now and then someone would pass by with their hands in their pockets and their head low, the international signal for not being bothered.

She stopped at a bench across the street from a small park and sat. She needed a plan. Come dawn, she would navigate her way out of Paris. Perhaps hitchhike, put some distance between her and the city. Then she would only have to hope that the generosity of the French countryside was in more abundance than here, that some stranger would let her use a phone.

*Or*, she reasoned, *you could steal one.*

Maya didn't much like the thought, committing a crime for the sake of avoiding one, but desperate times and whatnot. The irony of moral ambiguity was not lost on her.

She didn't want to believe that Trent Coleman had anything to do with the attempt on her life. The more she thought about it, replaying the events in her head, she realized that if the gunman was only after her, then perhaps Trent had just panicked in the moment. Maybe he was just as freaked out and alone as she was at the moment.

One thing was certain: their op was a sham. The man in the apartment was no sleeper cell. This was a setup to get her in the right place at the right time, to make it look like an accident had occurred on the job.

Maybe even to frame Trent as the shooter.

*Assuming he isn't involved.*

Had Walsh predicted that she would argue against splitting them up? Was she that easy to read? Or… was she that much like her dad?

Now wasn't the time to worry about all that. Now was the time to get the hell out of Paris.

Maya heard footfalls from nearby and went on alert. A man approached, walking casually toward her bench. His hands were at his sides and appeared empty. She stood to cross the street to the park.

"*Pardon?*" The man was close now, and speaking to her. "*Est-ce que ça va?*"

Excuse me. Are you all right?

She glanced him over. He'd paused about fifteen feet away, his hands still at his sides but his fingers spread unthreateningly, as if showing his hands were empty. He smiled at her; his face was clean-shaven and angular, his hair long, nearly to his neck.

"Um… *parlez vous* English?" she asked sheepishly.

His smile broadened. "Yes, I do." His accent was thick. He was, admittedly, quite handsome. Maya imagined that under different circumstances she might have felt a little flutter at the way he spoke. But currently she only felt an icy distrust.

"Are you lost?" he asked.

"Yes," she told him. "I am. Do you have a phone I could use?"

"I am afraid not." He looked remorseful. "I was just out for a stroll to help sleep. How do you say, cannot sleep? *Insomnie*."

"Well… thank you anyway. I should be going." She stepped into the street.

"Do not go that way," he warned.

She paused.

"The park," he said, "lovely in the day. But at night, sometimes, uh, not so nice people are about." He frowned for a moment, as if thinking. "I live close. My phone is there. You can come, use it, if you like."

Maya bit her lip. Despite her situation, she wasn't about to follow a stranger home. "Thank you, but I think I'll be okay."

"Of course. I understand; you do not know me." He chuckled. "I do not think my wife would be very pleased if I brought a young girl home anyhow. Can I help you find your way?"

Maya almost laughed at that. "I don't think you can. Thanks though."

He nodded. "All right then. Be safe. *Au revoir.*"

He turned and headed back the way he'd come. Maya stood there for a long moment, wondering if she was being paranoid or smart. Hadn't she been thinking about stealing a phone just a minute earlier? Hadn't she already asked strangers on the street, and now one was offering her help, and she was denying it?

"Wait."

He paused and glanced over a shoulder.

"Um… actually, a phone would be nice. Assuming you won't get in trouble with your wife."

He smiled. "She will understand. Come, it's this way."

Maya caught up with him and walked alongside him, or mostly so, lagging just a half-stride and keeping an eye on his hands. Just because she might be paranoid didn't mean she couldn't also be streetwise.

"So," the man said. "You are tourist? Or, maybe student?"

"Tourist."

"Ah. And may I ask what happened? Were you, separated, from your… friends? Family?"

"Yeah. Separated from family. I tried to ask around, but…"

The Frenchman chuckled. "But French hospitality towards Americans is traditionally lacking, yes?" He turned off the main street and headed up an alley.

"It would seem." She paused. The alley was narrow, barely more than a car width, and had no streetlights. An alarm blared in her head. "I never said I was American."

"Oh. My apology. I assumed." He paused as well, turning to her with an eyebrow raised. "It is just up here, come along. There is nothing to be afraid of."

But she didn't move. Nothing about this seemed right. "I need you to empty your pockets."

The Frenchman took a small step back, his brow creasing into a frown. "*Pardon?* Are you… robbing me?"

"No. I just need to see that you're not carrying any weapons."

"Weapons? *Merde.* Is this what I get for trying to help—"

The Frenchman's body jerked twice, and with it came the familiar sound of a chirping gun. As he fell forward, Maya threw herself to the right. There wasn't enough space to roll so she hit the ground hard and slid behind a metal trash can as two more shots rang out. Small chunks of brick exploded just above her head.

The Frenchman looked at her from his spot on the ground, facing her, his eyes open wide in terror. He blinked once, and then didn't again.

He really had just been trying to help her. Now he was dead for it.

Maya stayed entirely still, listening, waiting, but no more shots came. Instead she heard footsteps, heavy and deliberate, stalking closer to her position.

She could try to make a run for it, down the mouth of the alley. But she'd be an open target; a single well-placed shot could end her. Even if she made it to the street, there was nowhere to hide. She didn't know the area.

The footsteps ceased. "Come on out," said a gruff voice. American, by the sound of it. "I promise I'll make it quick."

Her heart pounded in her chest. She did not want to die at all, much less alone in a dirty alley in Paris.

*Think, Maya!*

The only thing she had was her cover, the metal garbage can she was hiding behind.

"The longer you wait, the harder this gets," the gunman warned.

Maya pushed against the metal can, tipping it forward slightly, just enough to get her fingers under it. Her other hand reached up and wrapped around the top lip of it.

Then she stood, and she hefted the can, holding it in front of her like a shield. She couldn't see where she was going, but still she charged forward anyhow.

"What the hell…?" Two shots thwipped. She felt them strike the front of the can, no doubt penetrating one side but not through.

She surged forward in the narrow alley, hoping to ram into him, to knock him off balance, just long enough to get the gun away…

Something struck her ankle. A foot. She stumbled forward, landing on top of the garbage can with a clatter. It rolled away from her as she rolled onto her back.

The gunman stood over her. She could see his grin in the moonlight. "Nice try," he admitted. "But you brought a garbage can to a gunfight." He raised the pistol.

Maya winced.

There was a shout, and for an instant it looked like the gunman had grown a second head. No—there was someone behind him, someone taller, someone jumping at him. The new figure grabbed him by the shoulders and pulled him down in a full-body tackle. Maya rolled out of the way as they crashed down in a tangle of limbs. The gun was loose; she reached for it.

The new figure regained his footing first. He kicked the gunman in the chin before he could stand. Then he grabbed the gunman by the back of his pants and his collar, and heaved him into the brick façade with a grunt.

The gunman staggered, dazed, bleeding from his head and chin as Maya pointed the pistol at him.

"Thanks, Trent," she murmured. She wanted to be relieved, to be happy to see him, but she was still uncertain about his role in all this. Still—he had saved her life just now.

Trent Coleman breathed hard and showed her his empty hands. "I didn't shoot him this time."

"You still have that gun?"

"I'll give it to you if you want."

She took her eyes from the gunman for just a second. Trent's gaze was apologetic, remorseful. And also a little scared.

"Keep it." She turned her attention back to the gunman. "You. Are you CIA?"

The man touched his forehead gingerly and inspected the blood on his fingers. "Is that a joke?"

"Then who are you?" she demanded.

"Name's Mick. And that's all I'm telling you."

"You'll tell me who sent you or you'll get a bullet in an uncomfortable place."

Mick—if that was his real name—laughed derisively. "Look at you; you're just a girl. You ever shot anyone before? You don't have the nads—literally."

Maya shot him in the kneecap.

The bullet tore through flesh and muscle and lodged in bone. Mick screamed and grabbed at the leg with both hands.

"Now I've shot someone," she said. She pointed the gun at his other knee. "Who do you work for?"

"Wait, don't!" Mick wheezed. "I-I'm a contractor. Out of New York…"

A contractor? He meant a contract killer. An assassin. But not a real pro, like Krauss or Rais. Mick was just a thug with a gun.

"Who hired you, Mick?" she demanded.

"Clients are… anonymous." He grimaced. "God, I think I'm gonna bleed to death. Please, call an ambulance!"

"Information, Mick," Maya said as calmly as she could. "Who did they tell you I was?"

"They didn't tell me anything! Just a photo. And to… follow you, take you out." He gritted his teeth. "I lost you when you… ran off. But saw you… from the park…"

His head slumped.

"Mick." Maya knelt and slapped him twice. He tried to open his eyes again, and murmured something groggily, but his head lolled again and he passed out. "Dammit."

"We should go," Trent said gently behind her.

But she didn't move. She was thinking. She believed Mick when he said he wasn't CIA; he fought dirty and lacked formal training. He'd killed the Frenchman to get to her. He'd tripped her like they were in a schoolyard scrap. His gun was a reliable one, a 9mm Browning, but it was at least a decade old.

Yet he'd known things that only the CIA was supposed to know. He'd been provided with information. Mick had been a failsafe in case the first gunman failed—whoever wanted her dead had sent two after her.

*Maybe more*, she realized suddenly. Trent's idea seemed like a good one.

She stood, tucked the Browning in the back of her pants, and turned to face Trent Coleman. "Someone is out to kill me. There might be others. So I'm only going to ask this once. Can I trust you?"

Trent nodded solemnly. There were no jokes, no smirks, no gentle ribbing, and nothing in his gaze that betrayed him. "Yes. Of course you can, Maya. I'd never hurt you. I panicked earlier. That guy… and this guy… they wanted you dead." He looked down at the toppled trash can. "I won't let that happen if I can help it."

"Okay. Then let's go. You got our things?"

"This way." He trotted back to the mouth of the alley and grabbed up a black nylon bag he'd left there.

"The sat phone?"

He dug in the bag and handed it to her.

She dropped it to the ground and stomped it until it was in a dozen pieces.

"What did the phone do to you?" Trent asked, wide-eyed.

"Who knew where we were?" she asked pointedly. "Who knew exactly where to find us?"

"Walsh," he answered, with some venom in his tone.

"Yes. But more broadly, the CIA. And who's on the other end of that phone?"

"The CIA," he murmured.

"Right. So we're on our own now." As much as Maya would have liked to put a call in to Penny, or even her dad, she couldn't count on the phone not being tracked or recorded. "We need to get on a plane and back home, now."

*Before anyone else shows up to kill me.*

# CHAPTER TWENTY FIVE

"We're running low on favors," Alan grumbled as they disembarked the Cessna at Rome-Fiumicino Airport. There were far worse ways to travel than private jet—Zero knew it firsthand, having flown internationally while being bound and hooded in the back of a cargo plane, and yet another time cramped for hours inside a wooden crate.

But Alan was right. Their resources were already scarce; they couldn't go burning every bridge. To get to Rome, Zero had enlisted the aid of Ryan Scott, a pilot who had once illegally flown him to Ankara, Turkey, when he had no one else. Scott owed him nothing—less than nothing, since he'd been a friend of Chip Foxworth, who had died to save Zero.

Still, Scott came through and got them aboard a plane with a manifest to Rome under the pretense of a corporate scout scoping Italian properties for expansion.

Zero was far from well rested, but at least he had managed to get some sleep on the flight. He'd stolen only snatches of slumber, his unconscious thoughts plagued by the memory he had of Kate, her strange words, her outright lie that it had been work.

*Not real*, he reminded himself. He had to believe that. There were too many other things going on at the moment to concern himself with it.

Mischa had been wide awake and alert the entire time, thanks to the overly caffeinated and sugar-saturated beverage Alan had bought for her, and though she should have been crashing from the high she seemed just as alert as ever.

She didn't say it, but he couldn't help but imagine she was enjoying this. As well as she'd acclimated to a (somewhat) ordinary American life, espionage and combat were what she'd been trained for most of her life.

Strange as it was, he was glad to have her. He'd spent so much time trying to keep his daughters out of harm's way, to save them from one horror or another, that it felt like an outright betrayal to have her along.

Still, having her at his side meant she was safe, and he felt a little safer for it too.

They hailed a cab at the airport and asked him to take them to the Piazza Mattei. The driver popped the trunk, expecting luggage, and raised an eyebrow at the lack of it, but he didn't ask any questions and drove without a word.

The street signs they passed, the sights and structures of Rome, were all familiar to him, like seeing the face of a long-lost friend. It was here that he and his team, years prior, had established an off-the-books safe house in an Italian apartment. It was here, after the suppressor had been torn from his head, that he found himself returning—only to find Maria holed up in the apartment. It was here that the rogue Agent Morris showed his true colors and tried to kill Zero.

The cab dropped them off and Alan paid the fare, and then the three of them stood in the Piazza Mattei. It was a lovely plaza, paved in cobblestones, arranged with small planters, and surrounded by colorful apartment buildings. The centerpiece of the piazza, however, was what tended to draw tourists there. The Fontana delle Tartarughe, or simply Fountain of Turtles, was not particularly large in relation to other Roman fountains, or even all that grand in comparison, but it was stunning.

At the fountain's center, four men cast in bronze held up a vasque, each with a hand raised up as if they were reaching for the very realistic turtles around the edge of the marble basin. The Fontana delle Tartarughe was more than four hundred and twenty years old. It had survived since the days of Pope Gregory XIII, originally built to provide citizens of Rome with drinking water from an aqueduct supplied by the Tiber.

It was a beautiful spot. In fact, its beauty had been the impetus for establishing a safe house there in the first place. Zero's former team—Reidigger, Johansson, and Morris—had planned an operation there, in a hotel across from the piazza. Years earlier, they had reconned the area and found a vacant apartment that provided the perfect view of the entire plaza. When the operation was finished, none of them wanted to give the place up, so they had leased it for ten years, paid in full on the dime of the Central Intelligence Agency, and had the cost hidden in an expense report as payment for collateral damages while apprehending insurgents.

It was Bixby who had helped them hide the expense, with some clever computer work, making five people in the world that knew about the place. At least as far as Zero knew.

Zero looked past the fountain, at the tall, white-bricked building behind it. It was the former manor house of the Mattei family, long since renovated into luxury apartments. The entrance was through a stone archway, which opened onto a small courtyard, across which was a set of exterior stairs leading up to a covered corridor, which ended at a door, which opened on the smallest unit on the second floor. That unit had two windows that faced the piazza, both of which afforded a magnificent view of the Fountain of Turtles.

He glanced up at those windows. With the time difference it was morning in Rome, and the eastern sun glared on the glass. He couldn't see anything that might tell him what was going on inside.

And anyone who might be in there would need only to take a look out one of the two windows and recognize him standing there. But there was no other way in.

"You two should wait here, just in case," he told them.

Alan snorted. "Like hell."

"What he said," Mischa added.

Zero scoffed lightly, but he wasn't going to change their minds. They were stubborn, just like him. Just like his other two daughters, and just like Maria had been. Headstrong, every one of them. "Then let's go."

He crossed the piazza and walked under the domed stone archway of the apartment building and into the courtyard. The gardens were well tended; even in early fall the impeccable rows of vibrant flowers were carefully cultivated. He followed a paved walkway to the stone stairs that led upward. Mischa stuck close behind him and Alan brought up the rear.

Zero reached the top and the corridor with two doors on each side. The walls were rough and uneven, decades-old plaster over centuries-old stone. There was a history to these walls, an artisanal beauty to their asymmetry. He'd been a small part of that history, an almost negligible part, but a part all the same. Like humanity, in the scope of the age of the earth.

He paused just before the last door on the left and stowed away sentimentalities as he slid the Glock from its place, tucked in the inner pocket of his light jacket.

He motioned for Alan and Mischa to stay put. Then he reached out with his left hand and tried the knob, gripping it with only two fingers and turning it slowly, very slowly.

It twisted easily in his grasp. Not locked.

He pushed the door just a few inches, putting the barrel of the Glock in the opening as he carefully glanced into the apartment. He was looking into a small living room. A dark-stained coffee table. A secondhand sofa with a few colorful throw pillows on it. Exposed wooden beams overhead.

It was exactly as he remembered it. It also appeared empty.

He took a breath and pushed the door open a bit further, taking a cautious step across the threshold by turning his body sideways and slipping inside.

From his vantage point he could see only the edge of the small, corridor-like kitchenette, around the corner from the living room. With the Glock in both hands, he whirled around the corner.

There was someone there, and it was just the person he'd hoped to find there, but not at all how he hoped to find them.

"Jesus... Bixby!" He dropped the gun and knelt beside the body.

Alan and Mischa were inside in an instant, but stopped at the threshold to the kitchen when they saw the state of him.

The time away hadn't been terribly kind to the old engineer; though he was pushing sixty he'd always looked good for his age, dressed in colorful bow ties and vests, kept his face shaved and his hair neatly parted.

But the Bixby on the floor was disheveled, his hair a mess, a few days' worth of gray stubble on his chin, and several stab wounds to his abdomen.

Zero's fingers trembled as he examined the wounds. The blood was fresh; this had happened recently. If he wasn't mistaken, it was still flowing, still leaving his body.

He realized sourly that they may have walked right past the killer when they arrived at the Piazza Mattei.

"Bixby... I'm so sorry," he murmured. "You didn't deserve this. I should have gotten here in time. I shouldn't have hesitated." He felt Alan's hand on his shoulder.

And then Bixby coughed.

# CHAPTER TWENTY SIX

"Bixby!" Zero carefully cradled the engineer's head with one arm, propping it up as gently as he could. He didn't dare try to sit him up, but he reached up with his free hand and grabbed a hand towel from the narrow counter of the kitchenette.

Bixby winced as Zero pressed it softly to his abdomen. "Zero." His voice was hoarse, croaking. "You came?"

"I did." *A few minutes too late.* "Just hang tight. We'll call an ambulance." He looked up at Alan and Mischa, neither of whom had moved from their positions. "Call someone!"

He felt Bixby's weak grip close around his arm. "Zero… look at me. We both know… what this means."

The hand towel was already saturated in blood. It was incredible that Bixby was still alive now, let alone speaking. Of course Zero knew what it meant, but he didn't want to acknowledge it, much less say it.

He'd be dead inside a minute.

"How?" Zero demanded. "How'd they find you here?"

"I got greedy." Bixby tried to chuckle, but instead coughed again. Blood bubbled from his lips. "Stealing… files. They tracked me."

"Files. You have them? Evidence of what they were doing?"

Bixby groaned. "Had." His eyes rolled. Zero held his breath, thinking this was the end. But no; Bixby was looking at something. He hadn't noticed it when he'd first entered the kitchen, but there was something else on the floor, just barely touching the puddle of blood that had flown from the engineer.

It was a tiny USB drive. Or it had been. Someone had stomped it into pieces.

Zero hung his head. He'd come here for evidence to put away Bright and Shaw and Krauss and expose them to the world. Instead he found a dead end and a dying friend.

"Tell me what to do," Zero implored him. "I don't have anywhere to go from here. You must have found something. Please."

"Bright," Bixby rasped. "Mr. Bright…"

"We know about Bright. We know he put a suppressor in Stefan Krauss—"

"Listen, please." Bixby's grip on his arm tightened. Zero was surprised he still had that much strength left in him. The engineer lifted his head off of Zero's arm, and in a moment of lucidity he said, "Zero, I found something. Something I wasn't meant to see. A classified file, about the Cairo Accord. He'll try to stop it. He'll *need* to stop it."

"What is it? What's the Cairo Accord?" Zero's mind raced but it didn't jog anything. He glanced up at Alan, who merely shook his head. Clearly he hadn't heard anything about it either.

He felt Bixby's head upon his arm again. When he turned back, his old friend let out a long sigh. The tension left his neck and shoulders. The grip on Zero's arm waned; the hand fell away. His eyes were already closed.

Zero slowly slid his arm out from beneath Bixby and rose to his feet. "We can't leave him here like this. We'll have to call someone."

"I understand how you feel," Alan said carefully, "but we'd be compromising this location—"

"I don't care about that."

He'd lost yet another. Kate, Sean Cartwright, Karina Pavlov, Chip Foxworth, Guyer, Seth Connors, Maria, Bixby… their names lived in his head, their faces swam in his vision.

When would it end?

Would it ever end?

Or was this his fate, to keep losing those close to him, to watch friends and family and lovers die while he was forced to keep going?

A phone rang.

All three of them glanced at each other in alarm. It rang again. It took Zero a moment to realize that the ringing was coming from Bixby's shirt pocket. He pulled out an old flip phone, a burner, the bottom edge of it stained with blood.

*Unknown caller.*

He answered it, but said nothing.

"Hi, Zero." The voice was male, deep, didn't sound like it was much older than he was. "Do you know who this is?"

"I can guess."

There was authority to the voice. It wasn't threatening but it wasn't casual either. This was the puppeteer. The asset. The Voice.

"Mr. Bright."

"That's right," said Bright. "Listen, I'm sorry about your friend, but he was sticking his nose where it didn't belong."

"I'm going to kill you," Zero promised. His hand trembled around the phone.

"Come on now," said Bright. He sounded a little impatient. "I was expecting more interesting conversation from you. Let's not be a stereotype."

"Zero," Alan whispered harshly. "We need to get out of here."

"You know about Krauss," Bright said, "and you know about me. That makes you a liability. But if I wanted you dead, you'd be dead by now. Hell, I could have just bombed that apartment and ended it here."

Zero tensed. Bright was, unfortunately, right; he'd been so concerned finding Bixby that he hadn't even considered they could be walking right into a death trap.

"But I don't want that," Bright continued. "See, I have the doctor's files on you. I know what's going on in your head. Personally, I think it's a much more fitting death than a bullet or a bomb. Still, personal feelings aside… I could help you. We could come to an arrangement."

Zero scoffed. "I'd never accept anything from you. You're a terrorist."

Bright sighed. "I thought someone as smart as you would have a more evolved perspective. The world isn't black and white, Zero. It's gray. You want to think of me as this villain, like I'm the big bad wolf. But how many lives have you taken for the people that signed your paychecks? How many families have you broken up? How many homes destroyed?"

"That's different," Zero murmured. "I stop killers. You make them."

Bright scoffed. "Make them. Right. Are we going to ignore how you started your own career? I know all about the CIA's dark agent program. I don't *make* killers, Zero. I control them. What do you think the world would be like if people like Krauss, or Amun, or the Brotherhood were allowed to operate unchecked? I provide order to chaos. I give them structure. If you really think about it… I've given you purpose. You're a living legend. But—and let's be honest with ourselves here—you're not getting any younger. Your own brain is melting down. The FBI, CIA, and Interpol want to bring you in. Not to mention a half-dozen police departments. Tell me: what's going to happen to your daughters if they get to you?"

"Zero," Reidigger warned uneasily. "Hang up. Let's move."

But he ignored it. A red-hot fury ignited within him at the sound of a man so callously, so cavalierly threatening the lives of his family. "No deal. Krauss can come find me. I'll kill him first. And then I'm coming for you."

Bright chuckled. "Krauss isn't going to come find you, Zero. The ego on you! He doesn't even know who you are. He's moved on to… well, let's just say 'others.' Of a less conspicuous nature."

"Who?" Zero demanded.

"Please. I'm not going to make it that easy on you."

"Then why are we even talking?"

"Honestly? I wanted the chance to speak with you, in case you get yourself caught or killed," Bright said. "But… I'm also stalling you. Speaking of, tell your friend I like his hat."

Zero turned. "Alan, down!"

Reidigger spun. A shot cracked. The window broke.

Alan grunted, and he fell to the floor.

Zero dropped the phone and leapt forward, tackling Mischa. The two of them crashed into the coffee table, splintering it. He rolled away with a groan.

"You okay?" he asked her.

She nodded. "I am. See to him."

"Stay down." Zero crawled over to Alan and rolled him over with some effort. Reidigger winced and held his shoulder. Blood ran between his fingers. "Let me see. Move your hand, let me see."

"We should have just left." Alan grimaced as he pulled his hand away from the shoulder.

"I know. I'm sorry." Zero took a look at the wound. The bullet had hit not two inches from his heart, no more than a half-inch from a lung. He was lucky. If he hadn't moved in the instant before the shot went off, he would be dead.

"A shooter on an adjacent roof," he said to Mischa. They could have fired from a window, but the angle of impact and ease of accessibility suggested one of the surrounding low-slung roofs. "Can you draw his fire without getting shot?"

Mischa nodded. "I'll have to use your friend. The dead one."

Zero opened his mouth to protest, but closed it in favor of having a conversation later about tact. "Do what you have to. Give me a ten-second lead."

"Got it."

He crawled toward the door of the apartment. It wasn't until he was in the corridor again that he stood, and then he dashed across it, down the stairs, and through the courtyard and its vibrant flowers. At the stone archway he paused, pulling the Glock from his jacket.

*Eight... nine... ten.*

He heard two shots, accompanied by breaking glass. The short scream of a bystander. He dared to peek out from the archway and quickly scanned the rooftops. The sun being behind them made the glint of a barrel all the more evident.

Zero raised the Glock, and he fired at the sniper twice. The shots were loud, louder than the suppressed rifle. He wasn't expecting to hit anything. But he also wasn't trying to.

The barrel pulled back. The sniper was fleeing.

Zero dashed out into the open piazza in pursuit.

# CHAPTER TWENTY SEVEN

Zero tucked the gun away as he sprinted the span of the Piazza Mattei. He turned the corner at Via dei Funari to get around the building before the shooter could reach street level. There were quite a few people out on the street, many of them running for cover at the sound of the gunshots, others searching frantically for a source. There were cell phones in hands everywhere he looked. Too many of them taking videos when they should have been calling the police or just getting clear.

He reached the entrance of the apartment building, a heavy outer door of black wrought iron rungs with a solid wooden one behind it. As he pulled open the outer door, the wooden door opened inward, and Zero suddenly found himself face to face with an equally startled man with a square jaw, wearing a black skullcap, a bag slung over his shoulder.

The shooter. There was no doubt.

Zero lurched forward to tackle him, and the shooter had the same idea. Their skulls knocked together hard. Zero's vision went hazy for a moment, brown and fuzzy at the edges, as he reeled backward. The shooter seemed to recover first, as he shoved Zero back, sending him toppling to the paved sidewalk, and made a run for it down the avenue.

He staggered to his feet and went after him. The shooter was bigger than him, stockier, but slower too. Zero shook the fogginess from his skull and upped his pace, gaining quickly. The block had emptied fairly quickly, but up ahead the sidewalks were more crowded.

Until the shooter turned in what looked like a glance backward. He raised his arm, a pistol in his hand, and fired off two shots.

Pedestrians screamed. Zero instinctively crouched and covered his head. A bullet smacked the street sign two feet to his right.

The shooter took off running again, shoving people aside. Zero broke into a sprint, reaching into his jacket as he did.

*Son of a bitch!* The Glock was gone. It must have tumbled out of his jacket when the two men had collided. He was unarmed.

But he did have an advantage; he knew these streets. As the shooter ran down the next block ahead, Zero hung a left at Via di Ambrogio, headed south toward the library, then swept to the right and dashed down a narrow walkway between two buildings. He cut right again as he came out the other side—just as the shooter was reaching the corner.

The man was looking behind him, glancing back for Zero. Instead he came at him from the shooter's left, throwing himself into him and sending them both tumbling into the street.

He braced himself for the impact but it still hurt as they hit the pavement and rolled. Cars honked; brakes screeched. Zero leapt to his feet in time to see a red Fiat coming straight for him. He skirted out of the way a second before being run over, the driver's profanity-laced Italian shouts Doppler-effecting past him.

The shooter scrambled on his hands and knees for the pistol that had fallen from his grip. Zero rushed forward, kicking out toward his chin, but the man saw him coming and stopped the foot with both hands. He twisted, and Zero twisted with it to avoid getting his ankle broken. He hit pavement again, this time on his shoulder, and grimaced.

But the pistol was close. The shooter reached for it. Zero wasn't fast enough to grab it first, so instead he swatted at it. The gun slid away from both their grasps, and slid into a sewer grate.

The shooter wasted no time grieving the lost weapon. He clambered to his feet and took off across the street, jumping to avoid an oncoming car. Zero staggered after him, across the avenue, down the block, into another intersection. Drivers honked as they slammed their brakes and swore loudly in Italian, but Zero paid them no mind. He kept his eyes on the shooter ahead.

He already had a feeling where the man would try to go.

The shooter's cap came loose and fell from his head as he ran cater-corner across the intersection and toward the entrance to the Rome Metro tunnel. His shock of messy black hair vanished as he barreled down the stairs.

Zero followed. He knew these stairs. He knew this station. He'd been there before, pursuing Agent Morris after he'd taken a shot at him in the Italian apartment.

He vaulted the turnstile, ignoring the wide-eyed Italians who shouted scornfully after him. There was no train at the platform, and no sign of the shooter.

*Restroom.* Just a short distance down the platform was the white door to a men's room. He had no gun. The shooter had a rifle. But it would be close quarters. He'd have to hit hard, fast, and avoid getting shot.

Zero shouldered the door open and dropped into a roll. He ignored the wet, dirty floor of the bathroom and came up on his feet near two faucets, a fist raised, as the man before him jumped back in bewilderment.

It wasn't the shooter. A portly man in a brown blazer gaped at Zero, backing toward the door, his fly still open as he retreated from the urinals.

Not him. Which meant…

He tried to spin toward the two stall doors behind him when he felt the blow land. Something like a fist, but more solid slamming into him—into his shoulder, and not the back of his neck and spine, as he'd turned just enough to avoid what might have been fatal. Still it sent a shock of pain up his neck and down his arm, and he dropped to a knee.

The shooter had the rifle out of the bag but it was turned around in his hands. He'd struck Zero with the stock of it like a club. He must not have had enough time to reload it before Zero barged into the restroom.

The onlooker fled the bathroom as the shooter reared back for another strike, this time aiming the rifle's butt at Zero's forehead. He swung his good arm as it came toward him, knocking the stock aside, and pushed off from his kneeling position.

Zero's skull, right where his hairline began, connected with the shooter's nose at an upward angle. The only force it took was the strength to stand, pushing his entire body weight behind it. He felt the shooter's face give way under his head, heard the crunch of bone. The shooter staggered back, bleeding profusely from his smashed nose, and collapsed to a seated position on the toilet.

His head slumped, and he didn't move.

"Dammit." Zero wanted answers, but he'd gone and knocked the man out cold—at least he hoped that was all he'd done. But he couldn't wait around and find out. There had been a witness, and soon there'd be police.

Zero took the rifle, stowing it back in the canvas bag, and hurried out of the restroom.

*

"How is he?" Zero asked as soon as he was back at the safe house.

Mischa knelt beside the couch. Alan was lying on it, his eyes closed.

"Alive. Are you all right?" she asked him.

"I'm fine. But our shooter's not. And I didn't get any answers out of him." He sighed. "We can't stay here. Bright knows about it. We shouldn't even be here now." He had passed by the police on his way back to Piazza Mattei, who were on their way to the subway station where they'd find the shooter. Zero had rubbernecked with the passersby—keeping one's head low in a situation like that was a great way to look guilty—and eventually found his way back to the piazza, where he'd done a quick sweep for any other surprises before heading back inside.

"I managed to remove the bullet," Mischa reported.

Zero was impressed; he wasn't aware that field medicine was among her talents. "With what?"

She showed him the paring knife in her pocket, the same one she'd sliced Shaw's ear with.

"Sorry I asked. Is he going to be okay?"

"He's lost a lot of blood, but the site is clean and I believe it has mostly stopped," she told him. She'd cut the collar and part of the sleeve of Alan's shirt open and cleaned the wound with a first-aid kit that had been hiding somewhere—likely in the bathroom, the same place where Maria had once tended to Zero's injuries. Still, the white compress over his shoulder was mostly red. "He'll need painkillers. And a sling. He won't be able to use this arm if the wound is to heal properly."

"We should take him to a hospital."

"Like hell," Alan murmured. His eyes were still closed.

"Alan, this is a serious injury—" Zero tried to argue.

"I've had worse," he interrupted. His voice wasn't strong but there was conviction behind it. "No hospital. Too easy to find me there. Might as well shoot me now."

"You can't travel," Mischa told him. "And you cannot stay here."

"I know." Alan grimaced. "Where's that burner? The one Bixby had."

Zero had dropped the phone in the kitchenette. He retrieved it, noting not only that Bixby's body had been moved out of the way but that Mischa had covered it with a sheet.

He gave the phone to Alan, who didn't make any calls, not right away, but gripped it in his fist. "You two go. Find whatever this Cairo Accord is, save the day, all that jazz. I'm gonna call in a favor. I'll get an extraction from here and lay low. I'll call Penny if I need anything."

Zero shook his head. "I don't like leaving you here. It feels like we're abandoning you."

"No worries." Reidigger grunted in pain as he dug into his pants pocket and pulled out a wad of bills. "Take this, you'll probably need it more than me. Mischa, grab my gun, yeah?"

He rolled onto his side as best he could, with another grunt of pain, and Mischa loosed the Sig Sauer he had stowed in the back of his pants.

"Thanks." He set the gun and the phone on his belly and sighed. "Much better. That thing was poking me. Take that too—"

"You might need it," Zero protested.

"I won't," Alan promised. "Take it."

"Stupid fat man," Mischa murmured in Russian. Zero blinked, about to rebuke her, but she briefly held Reidigger's hand and he smiled up at her.

"I'll be fine, kid. Get out of here, both of you."

Zero took the gun, and then he gave his best friend's shoulder a squeeze—his good shoulder, of course. "We'll see you soon."

"Course you will."

It took a lot of effort to get his feet moving toward the door. Zero didn't want to go, but Alan was right; he couldn't come with them. He would only be a liability at this point. Still he found himself lingering at the threshold, unable to cross it, unable to leave a friend behind when he'd lost so many.

He felt fingers wrap around his own. Mischa took his hand, nodded once to him, and together they walked wordlessly down the corridor, down the stairs, across the courtyard. At the Piazza Mattei they went the opposite direction as the Metro station and the cops.

"What now?" she asked him.

"First? We get a cab back to the airport. Get back to the Cessna."

"Can you fly it?"

"I can… *mostly* fly it."

"That instills confidence."

He ignored that. "We need a phone too. A burner. Shouldn't be hard to find."

"I will steal one."

"We'll buy one. No stealing unless it's necessary."

*Father of the Year, right here.*

"And then?"

"And then... we're going to find out just what's going on in Cairo."

*

Alan Reidigger waited a full ten minutes after Zero and Mischa had left before he made the call. A part of him thought that Zero might change his mind, might come back and stick a finger in his face and demand that he get his ass up and come along.

Zero didn't come back. Alan was glad for it. Mostly glad for it.

He knew the number by heart. He'd memorized every important number in his contacts, every number he might someday need in a pinch.

Alan had run out of favors. He'd called in just about every one that he'd accrued; the few he still had out there were ones that couldn't possibly help him now.

When the operator answered, he said, "Vicente Baraf's office, please."

He'd lied about the favor. He wasn't calling one in; he was doing one.

His shoulder burned. What he wouldn't give for a couple of hydrocodone.

"Baraf," said the Italian-accented voice.

"Vicente. It's Alan Reidigger."

A pause. "It has been a while, Agent Reidigger."

"It has. And it's not agent anymore."

"To what do I owe the pleasure?"

Baraf was a former Interpol agent, now a director, who had been more than a colleague in the past when they'd needed it. He'd been a friend.

Alan had not been a friend. He'd lied about the favor.

He'd lied about Kate too, when the memory came back. It was only a matter of time before Zero realized it. Alan was pretty certain that the déjà vu that Zero had back in New York hadn't been real. But it was a reminder, and it would only be a matter of time before some actual memory returned that betrayed the secret.

"I'm at an address in Rome," Alan said. "There was recently a shooting here. And a number of other crimes that have been wrongly attributed to Agent Zero. They weren't him. They were me. I'm here, now, and I'll give myself up. But only to you, and you personally. I need that assurance. There are too many people that want me dead."

Baraf was silent for a long moment, save for the sound of his breathing. "That is… quite the confession. This is no trick?"

"No trick, Vicente. I'm injured. I'm unarmed. I won't resist—unless someone other than you comes through that door. And then we'll talk. Will you come?"

"I'll come," Baraf promised. "Give me the address."

# CHAPTER TWENTY EIGHT

In Todd Strickland's experience, five people could keep a secret. No more than that. Add a sixth, and suddenly everyone knew. In his line of work, that could mean lives lost.

He paced near the south entrance of the convention center, his tie loose around his neck and his jacket off. It was hot in Cairo, ninety-two degrees today, and he feared he might sweat through his shirt as he oversaw security admitting entrance to heads of state and their attachés.

Five people could keep a secret. No more than that, at least in his experience.

So to him it was no less than a marvel, perhaps even a miracle, that it appeared the Cairo Accord would go off without a hitch. There would be a total of eighty-six people in attendance, every single one of them thoroughly cleared and vetted by Strickland and his team, not one person armed, not one cell phone allowed, not one exempt from search.

The accord was being signed at the Cairo International Convention Centre, a sprawling white property dotted with palm trees that housed dozens of halls and rooms, adjacent to Cairo's International Stadium. Strange, despite being in a city with thousands of years of history, the place looked as if it could have been in South Florida.

Everything from El-Nasr Road to the far side of the stadium was locked down. Police barricades and sentries kept anyone from entering who wasn't supposed to be there. Staff had the day off, with pay, courtesy of the Egyptian government. All entrances, save for one on the south end of the convention center, were locked and guarded. The accord itself would be signed in a round hall with a dais that bore a remarkable resemblance to a larger version of the US Senate chamber. Police and members of the Egyptian armed forces patrolled the perimeter of the center and the stadium. Agents on loan from the Is-Pal joint task force covered entrances and interior halls. And EOT oversaw it all.

This was going to go off without a hitch, he told himself. His job was to see to that, and he would.

The cat was nearly out of the bag anyway. Air Force One couldn't fly from Andrews to Dulles without the public knowing; it was no secret that President Rutledge was in Cairo. The same applied for several other world leaders, and if Strickland was a social media type of person he would probably see plenty of buzz about what was afoot. But it was all hearsay for now; no press was allowed. The White House Press Secretary had arranged for two cameras to be present, only two, and a crew of four operators who would patch the signing of the accord via satellite and stream it online for the world to see.

Within an hour, the world would know what was happening here. The formal announcement would come only when everyone was present and accounted for. This was history in the making, and he was a part of it.

Strickland touched the earpiece radio in his left ear. "O'Neill, copy?"

"I copy," said the familiar female voice. O'Neill was an eight-year Army veteran and helicopter pilot, now his second-in-command on EOT, tough as they came and unflappable. She was currently covering the eastern side of the convention center with a team of six Is-Pal members. "All clear here, over."

"Copy that. Hauser?"

"You worry too much, chief." Hauser's voice came through the radio, an affable former Louisianan who'd spent five years and change with the Secret Service. "Security here is tighter than a nun's—"

"Hey now," Strickland interrupted. "Let's keep it professional."

"Of course, boss. All clear here, over."

"McMahon, copy?"

"I copy," said Preston McMahon from his position between the convention center and the stadium. The newest member of EOT was also its youngest at twenty-eight, but McMahon had proven himself more than capable. It certainly didn't hurt that he was the grandson of former President William McMahon. "We had a tourist couple slip past the barricades and try to get close, they're being questioned now."

Strickland's jaw tensed. "American?"

"British."

"Detain them," Todd ordered.

"You serious? They're like sixty. I think they were just curious…"

"We're taking no chances," Strickland said firmly. "Have local PD hold them for a few hours. If they have nothing to hide they'll be fine, and maybe they'll learn a lesson about crossing police barricades."

"Ice cold, boss," Hauser chuckled in the radio.

"Stay alert," he reminded them. "We're taking *no* chances. Anything goes down today, it is directly on us. Understand?"

"Yes sir."

"Yes sir."

"Yeah, boss."

*Boss.* It was still strange to be leading EOT. But he'd led platoons before. He'd led squads into hostile territory, into firefights, into uncertainty. He could do this; he was made for it.

A familiar sight approached him from the south lawn and he couldn't help but smile. Penny almost looked like a stranger in a black pantsuit, a white shirt with a collar crisper than his own, her dark hair pulled up into a neat bun. Before today he hadn't even been aware she'd owned any such outfit, but apparently the situation called for it.

"Christ, it's hot out here."

"What are you doing out here? You should be inside," he told her.

"Security has it handled. I've done my part." She smiled, but there was something in the smile that seemed… sad? No, that wasn't right. Remorseful.

"What is it? Is something up?"

She nodded once, and then she slipped her arms around his waist in a hug. At least he thought it was a hug, until he heard the click. Penny had reached around him, to the radio clipped at the back of his belt, and she'd switched it off.

Now he was concerned. "Penny… what's going on?"

"I'm sorry, Todd. I really am." Penny reached into the inner pocket of her blazer and produced a phone. "There's a call for you, and I really need you to take it."

Strickland's throat ran dry. He recognized that phone; it was a secure burner that she kept for emergencies, in the event someone needed to contact her without the CIA tracing them.

He had a very strong suspicion about who would be on the other end of the call.

And if he was right, it would mean she had lied to him. That she knew exactly what was going on, what he was involved in. She'd lied to the president, the vice president, and the DNI.

But most importantly, she'd lied to *him*.

His expression must have given him away, because she shook her head and said again, "I'm sorry, Todd. Later we're obviously going to have a long talk. But right now, I need you to take this call."

Strickland sighed, and he took the phone.

"Zero?"

"Todd," the voice said through the phone. Zero spoke quickly, with urgency. "I know we haven't spoken, but I really need you to listen now—"

"I can't be talking to you," Strickland interjected. "You're wanted in… what, three countries now? In connection to nine murders? Maybe more? What the hell have you done?"

"Todd, please. I can explain all of that, but not now. I have reason to believe that something is going to happen at the Cairo Accord."

Strickland's blood ran cold despite the Egyptian heat. "What did you just say?" he asked, his voice a hoarse whisper. "How do you know about that?"

"Through a friend," Zero said quickly. "A friend who's dead now, because he found out about it. I'll admit I don't know exactly what's going on, but I'm guessing it's the top-secret deal you and Penny have been working on…"

Todd scoffed and shot Penny a look. She looked away. It wasn't bad enough she'd known about Zero's antics, but she'd told him about their work? She'd betrayed national security?

He'd been wrong. Four people could keep a secret. Apparently no more than that. Add a fifth, particularly Penelope León, and suddenly everyone knew.

"Zero," Todd snapped. "You'd better get to your point extremely quick. I've got a job to do here, and I could lose it just by having this conversation."

"Fine. Then just listen. Remember Mr. Shade, the guy at H-6 that was funding the Palestinian terrorists? He has a partner, goes by the name Mr. Bright. The CIA gave Bright the memory suppressor technology, the same tech I used after Kate died. He put a chip in Krauss's head—"

"Hang on," Todd stopped him. "Just hang on." Zero was ranting; this sounded insane.

"I'm not done. He's out there somewhere, Krauss is, with no idea who he is. The only thing in his mind is the target Bright set him on.

I've got a hunch that this Cairo Accord is an effort on Rutledge's part to secure peace, which is very bad for business if you're Bright. See where I'm going with this? I think Krauss's target is there. In Cairo. I think he's going to show up. I think he's going to try something."

Strickland pinched the bridge of his nose. He'd trusted Zero in the past, but this… this sounded like he'd lost his mind.

*Maybe he has.* Maybe the condition in his brain had finally cracked him.

Or—maybe he was right. They'd operated on Zero's hunches before and it had worked out. Not always. But sometimes.

"I know how this sounds," Zero said. "But please. Believe me on this."

"Look," said Strickland. "Whether I do or I don't doesn't matter. Security is tight as a drum here. No one, not even Stefan Krauss, is getting into that chamber without my say-so. If you're right and he tries something, we'll get him. But no one knows about this. We've kept the lid on it this long, not even this Bright character could know—"

"I know about it," Zero countered. "Bixby knew about it!"

"Bixby?" Strickland said aloud.

Penny snapped to attention at the sound of her mentor's name.

*Through a friend*, Zero had said. *A friend who's dead now.*

"What about him?" Penny demanded. "What about Bixby?"

Strickland opened his mouth to speak, but words didn't come.

"Don't tell her," Zero said in the phone. "Not now. Not like this."

But there was no keeping it from her. Penny's gaze darted left and right, as if searching his face for some sign that it wasn't true.

"Is he…?" she asked. "He's not…?"

"I'm sorry," Todd said quietly.

Tears welled in her eyes. He hadn't known Bixby all that well himself, but Penny had spoken of him fondly and often. He had been like a father to her.

She nodded slowly. "I see." She wiped her eyes before a single tear could run down a cheek. "I… I have to go."

"Penny, wait—"

She jogged away from him, toward the convention center. Strickland wanted to go after her, but then he heard the voice in his ear again, almost forgot that he was still holding the phone.

"I didn't want her to find out like that," Zero said softly.

Too much. This was too much. Strickland had worked too hard for this to have Zero swoop in and unravel it. And he didn't mean just the job; Zero was singlehandedly ruining his relationship, possibly his life, just by being a voice through a phone.

"Where are you?" he demanded.

"On a plane," Zero said vaguely.

"Listen to me," Todd warned him. "You stay away from this place, you understand? Or you *will* be arrested, and you will be charged for every possible crime you've committed. This isn't the Zero Show anymore. If Krauss wants to come, he can come and get himself killed. I'll shoot him myself. But if I see you, and I have even the slightest hint that you're trying to disrupt this based on a hunch… I'll shoot you too. You've run out of chances. Do you understand?"

Zero was silent.

"Tell me you understand!" Strickland nearly shouted into the phone.

"I understand, Todd. Thanks. For hearing me out. Be safe." The call ended.

Strickland stood there for a long moment, holding the phone and trying to process the last minute of his life. Penny had lied. Zero had either lost it or stumbled onto something big that could get him killed. Bixby was dead.

"Sir?"

He turned to find a Secret Service agent there, sweating from the forehead under a black suit. "King Basheer of Saudi Arabia has arrived. I assume you would like to see him in personally."

"Yes," Todd murmured. "Thank you. I'll be right there."

He still had a job to do. Everything else had to wait.

Strickland turned his radio back on. "Team? Let's do another sweep. Tighten things down if we can. I know we've taken every precaution, but let's take them again."

He heard the echoes of "yes sir" in his ear. They'd prepared for this.

Nothing was going to happen here. He would see to that.

# CHAPTER TWENTY NINE

Zero guided the Cessna southeast over the Mediterranean Sea. He'd managed to take off with little difficulty, and keeping it steady wasn't an issue. Landing—now that would be another thing entirely, but he'd worry about that later.

"Did you get it?" he asked his copilot.

"I did." Mischa sat beside him in the small cockpit, the headset comically large on her small head. She navigated the touch screen of a burner they'd picked up just outside the airport in Rome. "The signal came from the Cairo International Convention Centre."

Penny had put herself on the line once again for them. Just before handing the phone off to Strickland, she'd turning on location sharing and pinged them.

He felt a deep pang of remorse at her finding out about Bixby in such a callous fashion. He wanted to tell her himself, in person, to explain that he was with him at the end, to justify the cause Bixby had died for. He could still try, assuming he ever saw Penny again—assuming he lived long enough to see her again—but the damage had been done.

"You know it?" Mischa asked.

He nodded. "A few miles east of the Nile, next to the stadium."

"We are not seriously going to go there?"

"No choice," he answered. "Bixby was right; Rutledge's efforts to bring peace to the Middle East are a direct assault on Bright's business. An accord threatens him far more than me or Krauss or anyone else ever could, and he's got the perfect patsy in his new assassin. He'll try something there. I just know he will."

"This is suicide," Mischa said as she settled back in her chair, seemingly unperturbed by the notion but merely remarking it aloud. She'd heard Strickland's end of the call; Zero had patched it into their headsets. "He said it himself; security is tight as can be. Perhaps Krauss could have found a way, but he is not Krauss anymore."

"Exactly," said Zero. "That's why we don't need to think like Krauss. We need to think like Bright. Now, we have a small advantage here in that Bright doesn't know that we know about the accord. Problem is, we know almost nothing about what's going down. Who would the possible players be?"

"Israel and Palestine," Mischa noted. "They already have a treaty in place with each other, and with the United States."

"Right. Plus Iran and Saudi Arabia," he added.

"Syria, Lebanon, Jordan, Iraq, Kuwait," Mischa counted off on her fingers.

Zero was impressed. "Been watching the news?"

"Reading the paper," she admitted.

"That entire region is Bright's bread and butter," Zero said. "Just about every faction he's funded comes out of there or attacks there or both. So he'd have very good reason to disrupt the accord. What's the best way to do that?"

"He's proven to be partial to bombs."

That was true; Bright's people had already blown up Third Street Garage and Zero's former home in New York, presumably on his orders.

Yet he had to trust that Strickland and his new team had a strong handle on the situation at the signing of the accord. Someone like Krauss wouldn't be able to get within a hundred yards of them without being arrested—or shot, as Todd had made very clear. They would have thoroughly swept the area, the buildings. As Mischa noted, it would be suicide.

*Unless that's his intention? Sacrifice Krauss to stop the accord? Send him in as a suicide bomber?*

No—that didn't quite fit. Bright had taken a sickening delight in his new pet, "S." He doubted Bright would just blow him up. In fact, if he had to guess, he would assume Bright had big plans for mind-controlled Krauss, even after this was done.

*I don't* make *killers*, Bright had said on the phone. *I control them.*

*I provide order to chaos.*

They couldn't strike while the accord was happening. At least not *where* it was happening.

What would Bright do if he couldn't get to them where they are?

*What would you do?* he asked himself.

"Get to them where they will be," he murmured.

"What's that?" Mischa asked.

He didn't answer, not at first. *Get to them where they* will *be.* And he was pretty sure he knew where that was. The more he rolled it around in his head, the more it made sense.

"I… I think I know where he might strike," Zero said. "Not where they are. Where they will be."

*He's moved on to… "others."*

That's what Bright had said when Zero demanded to know who Krauss's next target was.

*Others. Of a less conspicuous nature.*

Others. More than one.

"And where will they be?" Mischa asked.

"Ever been to Cairo?" he asked her as he adjusted their heading.

"No, I have not."

"There's only one place visiting heads of state would be invited to stay after the accord is signed." And if he wasn't mistaken, it was less than ten minutes from the current location at the Cairo International Convention Centre.

"And if you're wrong?" she asked.

"Well… then at least you'll be able to say you've seen a real palace."

# CHAPTER THIRTY

Sara sat atop a stack of folded green mats against a far wall of a wide, high-ceilinged room. She knew that this particular room was sometimes used for a gymnastics class on Tuesdays and Thursdays, or used to be. On Wednesdays there was a women's self-defense course taught there. She snacked on some crackers; she'd raided the cabinet in the daycare room and found some food and a bottle of water and then she'd climbed up the stack of thick green mats, the kind they'd unfold for high school wrestling matches, and she sat up there swinging her feet as she ate for the first time in more than a day.

She wasn't even really hungry. But she knew she needed to eat.

She was feeling better, much better than she had earlier, when the shock of the explosion had gripped her mind. Going back to the house had been insane; it barely felt like it had been her decision, looking back.

So she'd left there, and without any other place to go and not wanting to put anyone in unnecessary harm, she'd come here, to the community center.

The first time she'd ever stepped foot in this place was for an art class. Painting landscapes in watercolor and bowls of fruit in oil. It had been something to take her mind off of all the terror and the drugs and her escape from rehab and dropping out of school and… well, everything. Then she'd met Maddie, the queen-bee soccer mom who organized Common Bonds, and she'd started attending the women's trauma group.

Then she'd stopped attending, because Maddie started catching on to the fact that Sara was beating the hell out of guys who assaulted the group's members.

The community center had been closed for two weeks now after a lice outbreak required a complete fumigation, cleaning, and replacing of furniture. When Sara had arrived the night before she'd found a cleaning crew there. They'd left a single entrance unlocked. It had been easy enough to slip in, hide in a closet, and wait for them to leave. Once she was sure they were gone she crept to the front desk and turned on the computer. She saw that the cameras in the place were closed-circuit and she was able to shut them off pretty easily. As long as she didn't leave, she wouldn't trip the alarm.

And she had no intention of leaving.

She wasn't the least bit tired. In fact, just the opposite, she felt well rested. She roamed the community center's halls, rifling through cabinets, peeking in on rooms. She went into the familiar art room and took a seat at an easel, but no inspiration came. She snuck crackers and water from the daycare room and climbed the stacks of mats.

Eventually she dared herself to go into the room with the door that had a single piece of white paper taped to it with some words printed in black ink. The paper said:

*Common Bonds*

*Sharing Trauma, Sharing Hope*

She stood there for a long time in the empty room. Then she took a metal chair from the rack in the corner and she unfolded it and set it near the center of the floor. She grabbed another chair, and another, until she had about ten chairs in a semicircle facing the windows.

Sara sat in the one farthest from the door and closest to the windows. She eyed up the empty chairs and visualized the women who used to sit in them, and maybe still did sometimes.

She reached into her pocket for her phone and powered it on. But she didn't try to make any calls or send any texts or even check her voicemails. Instead she put it on silent and slid it under her chair face-down.

Then she sighed, and she began.

"My name is Sara Lawson," she told the empty chairs. "I've been coming here for a while. Or… I used to. And I never shared. Not much, anyway. I sat here, and I listened to the stories that the other girls told. I used their stories, to try to fix myself, I guess. Like it was going to give me some kind of purpose. I guess you could even say I kind of… stole their stories. Or at least tried to make myself a part of them."

She scoffed at herself. "Anyway. Seeing as I might be dead soon, this seemed like as good a time as any. To share."

So she shared. To an empty room, to nine vacant chairs, to the darkness of the community center, she shared. She wasn't sure how long she talked for, but she shared it all. She talked about her mother. She shared the grief of her loss. She opened up about her trauma, her addiction, her attempts to get clean, her overdose. Her trafficking experience, about seeing the girl called Jersey shot before her eyes. About the lies she'd been told and the lies she'd told.

"For a long time, I guess I thought I could get over it. Like, I could just power through it and things would just be okay again. But I'm not okay. The truth is, most of the time I don't really care if I live or die. I've even…" She trailed off, her throat dry. But she had to say it. She had to share it. "I've even thought once or twice that maybe it wouldn't be such a bad thing to die. But I couldn't do that."

Then she heard it, in the silence of the community center, over the dull roar of blood rushing in her own ears, she heard an engine.

"At least not to myself," she said. She stood from the chair and peered out the window to see a black van rolling up to the community center.

It stopped abruptly. A door slid open, and six men climbed out quickly. They wore black vests and boots and carried guns, and they split off into teams of two and separated.

They were here. It was time.

"I'm not just going to sit around and wait anymore," she told the room quietly. "If this is how it happens, then… this is how it happens."

There were people who wanted her dead. There were people who wanted her family dead. Running and hiding was an option, but it wasn't living. It wasn't a life.

But… she certainly wasn't going to give herself up.

She had no intention of making it easy on them.

Sara opened the door and treaded down the hall to the front desk. Behind it, she kicked off her sneakers so she was just in her socks. On the desk there she'd left the small black pistol with the silencer, the one she'd taken from Alan.

She crouched behind the desk and its computer, and she waited.

The auxiliary lights blinked off, throwing her into near-complete darkness. The streetlights in the parking lot were snuffed out a moment later. They were cutting the power. No alarm would trip.

She squeezed her eyes shut for several seconds and then opened them again, let them adjust to the darkness. She wasn't worried. She knew the center's layout well.

Then she heard it—the high-pitched crack of a single pane of glass. From where? Not the main entrance. The single-doored side hall, past the daycare room.

She heard the footfalls of their boots as they approached. Always boots with men like them. Why boots?

Sara crawled forward slightly on her hands and knees beneath the desk. There was a small round hole at the back of it, for the computer cables that she'd already yanked out. She put an eye to it like a peephole and watched as four dark figures reached the end of the corridor, where it branched in two directions. One of them motioned with two fingers to his left, and two of the men split off that way. The other two turned to the right and stalked forward, their guns up.

She waited, counting in her head. *One-Mississippi, two-Mississippi, three-Mississippi.* Then she crept out from beneath the desk. Sara stayed low, her socks completely silencing her footsteps as she stole after the two men who had gone right, toward Common Bonds. They were maybe fifteen feet ahead of her when she raised the gun and fired.

Sara squeezed off three shots in quick succession. In the otherwise quiet community center, there may not have even been a silencer on the gun; the shots were muffled but loud. Even at this close of a range, it was dark and she'd never been all that great of a shot.

One missed. One hit a man square in the back of his thick black vest. He grunted and stumbled forward a step. The third hit the second man at the base of his neck. He yelped and fell.

"Contact!" The man she'd hit in the back spun, off-balance, and fired. Automatic gunfire split the air, much louder than her shots, louder than she thought anything could be.

But she was already running. Three quick shots and she ran, sprinting down the hall. Her ears rang even after the shooting stopped.

"She went this way!" a voice shouted. Boots pounded the tiled floor.

But Sara was already skirting noiselessly through an open door. She'd spent the night roaming the community center, poking around every room—and making sure every door was unlocked and open just a few inches.

She didn't stay there. This room had a second door that connected to the next room over, the wide, high-ceilinged room that was sometimes used for a gymnastics class and a women's self-defense course.

She scrambled up the stack of folded green mats and laid herself flat.

*One down.* She was pretty certain the man who'd taken a bullet to the neck was dead, or would be soon.

The stomp of boots came closer. A harsh, angry voice ordered, "You, through there. You—clear this room! Radio Sid, tell him she's armed."

She peered over the side of her tall stack of mats as the barrel of a gun pushed through the partially open door. Her dad had showed her how rooms were cleared, and it wasn't typically by looking up.

Sara carefully aimed, and she squeezed the trigger, just once, just as the man stepped through.

The man's head jerked back and he fell.

"Wilson!" a voice screeched.

Sara was already moving, sliding off the mats and running across the room. She shoved through the door and back out into the wide hall but didn't stop. Instead she ran straight across its width and into the men's room on the opposite side.

Then she stopped. It was pitch-black in there, no windows, no auxiliary lights, no moonlight. But she'd spent the night roaming the community center, memorizing its layout.

Out in the hall she heard the harried voices. "Where'd she go?"

"Son of a bitch, she got Wilson!"

*Two down.*

"Nobody said she'd have a gun…"

"Shut up! She's just a kid. She got lucky—"

"She ain't just a kid. This is *Zero's* kid. Pair off, watch your backs. You—head that way. Me and Taggert will check the gymnasium."

The boots faded. Sara caught her breath. She was surprised to find that her heart rate felt… not normal, but not pounding. Not beating out of her chest like she might have expected.

She liked the small black pistol with its long barrel, but she had no idea how many rounds were still in it and it was too dark to check. So she carefully set it on the sink, and then she reached underneath it for the hammerless revolver she'd stowed in the wastepaper basket.

She'd spent the night roaming the community center, poking around every room—not just making sure every door was unlocked and open, but planning a route. Hiding weapons.

The revolver had six shots, was fully loaded, needed no cocking. It was point-and-shoot. Simple. Her kind of gun. It had a bit of a kick to it, more so than the small black pistol, she knew from prior use, but it also had more power behind it.

Sara counted her footsteps in the dark, crossing the bathroom, and then she reached and felt the door. The community center had two pairs of bathroom, and this bathroom had two exits, one that emptied out into the hall and the other that connected to the locker room.

She pushed the door open and listened. She didn't hear anything. The locker room connected to the gymnasium, with its full-size basketball court, but she wouldn't be going there. The angry voice had said they'd be searching it. Besides, it was the largest room in the center, nothing but open space.

Sara stalked forward in her socks. There were three rows of lockers, their doors open, one row against each wall and another in the center, cutting the room in half. The row of lockers was six feet high, too high for her to see over—too high for anyone to see over. Each row had a low wooden bench between it, attached firmly to the concrete floor.

She maneuvered slowly to the second-to-last locker in the center row, and she wedged herself inside it. It was a tight fit, but there was just enough space to move her arm and point the gun, if she kept her elbow tight to her body.

Then she waited.

She didn't have to wait long.

The door to the gymnasium squeaked loudly on its hinges, as she already knew it would.

"Locker room," one of the men whispered.

"No shit," said the other flatly. "We should call Sid in."

"Someone needs to watch the lot. In case she makes a run for it. Go that way."

Sara held her breath. At least one of them would walk right by her. Any moment…

"There's another door here."

"Check it." The voice was close. Right around the corner.

A flashlight beam shined on the wooden bench in front of her.

*Shit.*

She hadn't counted on that.

It was too late to improvise. Leaving her hiding spot would certainly get her killed.

She could hear the man's breathing as he stepped forward.

*If this is how it happens, then… this is how it happens.*

She slowly maneuvered her arm as best she could with the revolver tight in her hand, and she pointed the barrel at the open door of the locker.

The flashlight beam swung.

Sara pulled the trigger. The revolver kicked in her hand. The report was a satisfying pop echoing in her head.

"Gah!" The man made a sound, one of surprise or pain or both. The flashlight beam bounced but didn't fall to the floor. She fired again, through the door, and a third time, punching holes in the thin metal.

Finally the flashlight fell, and Sara clambered out of the locker. The flashlight was attached to his rifle. It, the gun, and he were on the floor.

She dropped to the ground as the door to the bathroom was kicked open. Another flashlight beam bounced off the walls as she rolled beneath the wooden bench.

"Bitch!" the man shouted as his light fell over the dead man. "Where are you?!"

Sara answered by shooting him in the shin.

He screamed. His leg gave out. He pulled the trigger as he went down and bullets tore up the ceiling. Sara rolled again and finished him with one more shot.

She'd used five rounds. She quickly navigated to the far row of lockers, closest to the gymnasium, and traded the hammerless revolver for the Glock she'd hidden in the bottom of one. The last gun, the big silver one she'd taken from the man at her house, was hidden in the cabinet of the daycare room. It might as well have been a mile away.

*Four down. One outside.*

She didn't know where the sixth man was, and she had only two options: backtrack through the bathroom or take a chance across the open gymnasium. Neither was appealing. She chose the gym. In the darkness of the bathroom she wouldn't see if there was someone waiting for her.

Sara pulled open the door. It squeaked loudly on its hinges and she winced. She'd forgotten about that. Too late now; she pushed into the gymnasium.

There was an exit here, a door that would lead outside. But she knew it was locked tight. She hadn't been able to get it open. So she made a run for the far side.

She was more than halfway there when she saw the door swing open. A flash of light. She backpedaled, or tried to, but her socks lost purchase on the waxed floor. She slid, her feet flying out from under her, as the man fired a burst in her direction.

Pain shot through her arm as she raised the Glock. Even as she slid she brought it up in both hands, her arm searing, and pulled the trigger. Once, three times, five, eight—she wasn't sure how many times she shot, but she didn't stop, not even when the gun and flashlight fell. Not until he fell, face-first, to the polished hardwood.

Sara breathed hard and set the gun down. A bullet had caught her right arm, had torn at her bicep. She touched it and sucked a breath through her teeth. Even in the darkness of the gym she could see it was bleeding badly.

And the pain.

God. It hurt so much.

The tears came then, suddenly and powerfully. She couldn't stop them. Her vision blurred, and she drew her knees up on the gym floor, and she cried. Not because of the pain in her arm, but because of the pain in her head and in her heart.

*What am I doing here?*

*Why did I do this?*

*I don't want to die.*

*Not here. Not now. Not alone.*

"I don't want to die." She sniffed, and wiped her eyes.

*And you won't.*

"I won't." Sara forced herself to her feet.

*Five down.*

"Just one more."

They'd called him Sid. He was waiting for her to make a run for it.

Sara left the Glock there. She wiped her face again and pushed through the gymnasium door. She made her way to the daycare room and retrieved the bulky silver pistol from the cabinet. It felt unwieldy in her hand, but powerful.

Then she headed for the main entrance. The van was out there, and the man would likely be too.

She dared to glance out the glass door. He was there all right, standing not twenty-five feet from the door, just in front of the van. The moon hid behind clouds and obscured his features, but not the gun he cradled in both hands.

He was looking right at her. Waiting. There was nothing to hide behind out there. No way to trick him or lead him elsewhere. He looked patient, like he would wait all night for her to come out if need be.

There were other exits. If she could get to one before he could, she could flee. Make a run for it…

The man turned suddenly, awash in headlights. He put one hand up to shield his eyes, and in that moment Sara saw his face, a thin beard, squinting eyes.

In the moment she thought, *He doesn't look like a Sid to me.*

But it was just for a moment, because an instant later a car smashed into Sid. It hit him at the waist, folded him in half over the hood. Then the car hit the brakes, and Sid kept going, tumbling end over end across the parking lot like a stone skipped on a lake.

Sara's breath caught in her throat. The car idled there for a moment, and then the passenger-side door flung open, and someone climbed out. They ran to the entrance of the community center. They had no gun and pressed both their palms flat against the glass.

"Sara!"

She pulled the door open and practically fell into Maya's arms. Her sister hugged her back, tightly but briefly. "You okay?"

"Mostly."

"You're bleeding…"

"I *said* mostly."

"Come on." Maya urged her toward the car. "We have to move, now." She helped Sara into the backseat of the silver sedan. There was a young guy behind the wheel that she didn't recognize.

"Let's go," Maya told the driver. He nodded once and the car lurched forward. "Sara, this is Trent. Trent, this is my sister."

"A pleasure," said the driver.

"Whose car is this?" Sara asked.

"Not sure." Maya shrugged out of her jacket.

"How did you find me?"

"Your phone." Maya passed the jacket back to Sara. "Here, tie this around your arm until we can get it cleaned. We got off a plane from France less than thirty minutes ago. Looks like you turned your phone on about fifteen minutes ago or so."

"My phone," she said. "I left it back there. They'll know… the police, or whoever comes. They'll know I was there."

"I think they're going to know either way." Maya sighed. "There's no easy way to say this, but… we're not safe, not from anyone. I don't know where Dad is, or Mischa, or Alan. Until we hear from someone, it's just us. We're on our own, completely."

Sara eyed up the driver.

Maya noticed. "We can trust Trent. They probably want him dead too, at this point."

"Yay for me," he muttered.

"Trent knows a place we can lay low. We'll clean you up, get some rest—"

All three of them jumped slightly at the sudden, deep boom that shook the car's windows. Sara twisted in her seat to see an orange fireball pluming in the air, black smoke billowing over it.

The van. A bomb. Just like the garage. Another minute of hesitation and Sara would have been caught in that blast. She'd be dead.

Maya must have sensed what she was thinking. She felt her sister's hand on hers. Maya twisted in her seat, reaching back. "We'll keep each other safe. We'll find them."

Sara nodded. She knew now what she had refused to acknowledge for months. For years, even. She couldn't do this on her own. Neither could Maya. Or her dad, or Mischa.

"We will," she promised.

# CHAPTER THIRTY ONE

By the time Zero landed the Cessna, the Cairo Accord was international news—which, oddly, worked in their favor. He knew they'd never get within sniffing distance of Cairo's main airport, so instead he directed the jet toward the small Bijam Airfield, about twelve miles northeast of Egypt's capital, and radioed a distress signal for a loss of cabin pressure.

The landing was a bumpy one—he heard Mischa audibly gasp for the first time that he could ever recall—and they scrambled out of the jet before any help could arrive. The two of them made a run for it in the opposite direction from the low-roofed terminal, across open ground, over a chain-link fence that surrounded the furthest runway, and toward a nearby residential area.

He had Mischa wait on a corner with the burner as he snuck into the small parking garage of an apartment building. He stole quickly along a row, trying door handles until he found one that was unlocked, a late-model Kia. Two minutes later it was hotwired, and Mischa jumped in beside him, poking at the touch-screen of the burner.

"What'd you find?" he asked her.

"This is… impressive," she admitted. "The Cairo Accord was kept completely secret until today. A summit involving nine countries. Their leaders are convened currently at the convention center to sign the accord."

*All of them.* That was the answer to who was involved. All of them were in one place, and that place had been completely locked down. But if Zero's hunch was right, it wasn't the only place they'd be gathered.

He drove as quickly as he dared due southwest, toward central Cairo and the stadium. But that wasn't their destination.

"Would you like to share what you're thinking?" Mischa asked him.

Had the situation not been so dire, he might have laughed at her candor. "The Heliopolis Palace. That's where we're going. It's one of three presidential palaces of Egypt. Not only is it the closest to the accord, but it's also where visiting heads of state stay while they're here. It was built in 1908 as a hotel, actually, the grandest hotel in all of Africa at the time—"

"Zero," Mischa interrupted, "I'm sure you know much about its history, but let's keep it limited to necessity."

"Sorry." He tended to rant when he was nervous—and he was nervous. The heads of nine countries, including the United States, would sign the Cairo Accord, and most likely be the guests of the Egyptian president at the Heliopolis Palace. While he had no doubt security would be tight, the perception would be that the threat had passed, that the endeavor had been successful—that no one would dare strike at them there, not after the accord.

*But Bright would.*

In one fell swoop he could throw half a continent into chaos. And once the finger-pointing began, Bright could manipulate it to his liking, place blame wherever he wanted, even if it was the work of only one man who didn't even fully know what he was doing.

Zero swerved around a truck going too slow for his liking and back into the left lane. "Let's think. If it's Krauss, and it's a bomb, what's the likeliest delivery method?"

"At the garage, it was a van," Mischa pointed out.

"In New York, it was a package." But that seemed unlikely; packages to the presidential palace would be carefully scanned and checked.

But so would delivery vehicles. And Krauss would have no way to personally ensure that the bomb made it inside the building.

*Think, Zero. If you had to get a bomb inside a presidential palace, to take out foreign heads of state, how would you do it?*

It would have to be a powerful bomb.

Or… it would have to be multiple bombs.

But that didn't get him any closer to figuring it out.

He gripped the wheel tightly in frustration as the palace came into view. And for only the second time ever that he could recall, he heard Mischa audibly gasp.

"Wow," she said quietly. "It looks like something out of a storybook."

She wasn't wrong. The Heliopolis Palace had been an architectural marvel when it was built more than a hundred years earlier, and still was one today. The front of the structure featured a wide, round reception hall that resembled a miniature Colosseum; behind that was the Central Hall, the dome of which stretched skyward in a golden spire that peaked above the rest of the palace. The Heliopolis had been designed as a four-hundred-room hotel, in the lavish style of Louis XIV and partially inspired by Italian architecture.

It looked like something out of a storybook—and they would never get even close to within its walls. Zero slowed the stolen Kia as they drew near and he could see that security at the palace was significant. The roads surrounding it had been closed and barricaded; police cars and Egyptian military personnel were in force on the grounds as they rolled past.

Zero took the Al Ahram road to the next block and parked the car in the lot of a post office. They walked briskly back toward the palace and joined a small group of tourists snapping photos across the street from it. The gates that accessed the main entrance to the Heliopolis were closed, military standing guard.

It seemed that was as close as they were going to get.

"We could call someone," Mischa suggested. "Todd Strickland, perhaps. Tell him your theory."

"I don't think he's going to hear me out again." Zero shook his head. They were here, and it appeared there was no way in. Not for him—and not for Stefan Krauss, either.

*What if you're wrong?*

He wanted to be wrong. But it wouldn't mean that anyone was any safer; it would mean only that Bright would attempt something else, something he hadn't considered.

Or what if he was right, and they were too late? What if Krauss had already come and gone?

No—Bright would have his lapdog wait around, watch it happen, make sure it unfolded in the way it was supposed to. He wouldn't leave it to chance.

"Think, Zero," he urged himself. The crowd of onlookers across the road from the palace was growing, people lining the street. It seemed that it had become common knowledge that the members of the Cairo Accord would be coming here, to the Heliopolis Palace, and that these people would soon have a front-row seat to a parade of foreign leaders making history as they entered these gates.

He wasn't wrong. This had to be it.

He turned to Mischa. "How would you do it?" It felt outright wrong to ask, but the girl had some experience in situations like this one. "If it was you, and you were trying to get bombs into the palace, knowing that security would be everywhere, how would you do it?"

"Hmm." Her small face scrunched up in thought. "Luggage, I would imagine."

"Luggage?"

"Yes. The accord is attended by dozens of foreign leaders and diplomats. They do not handle their own luggage; that would have been taken from the planes to the palace by porters. And while I don't know this for sure, I imagine a king or president's bags are not searched."

"I…" He wanted to scoff at the suggestion, but he couldn't bring himself to. "Mischa—you might be a genius."

"Yes," she agreed.

"We need to call someone," he told her. "Todd first. If he won't take it, then we'll have to find someone who will…"

He trailed off as an eager young passerby jostled his shoulder, not watching where they were going. Zero half-spun and regained his balance, threw the pedestrian a glare that they didn't see—and then his face went slack.

Through the growing swarm of people, he caught a glimpse of sandy, disheveled hair. A jaw with a few days' growth on it. Just a glimpse, nothing more.

Krauss.

Zero shook his head roughly and looked again. He wanted so badly for it to be him, but it could have been his brain playing tricks on him. It had happened before.

But the man was gone just as quickly as he'd appeared.

"You still have that knife?" Zero asked quickly. "Give it here."

"I do." Mischa slipped it from her pocket and handed it to him discreetly. "Why?"

He knelt in front of her, looked her in the eye, and spoke urgently. "Listen to me. You stay right here. Do not move from this spot. Not an inch. You call whoever will take it. Todd, Penny, the police, emergency services, whatever you have to do. Put in an anonymous bomb threat to the palace if you have to. Just don't move. Understand?"

The look in her eye suggested she didn't, not fully, but she nodded once. "Where will you go?"

"Just to check on something. I'll be back."

He couldn't tell her the truth, or else she would try to follow, and he wouldn't put her in that kind of harm. They said they would do this together, but Krauss was arguably more dangerous now than he'd been before—and he wasn't the same Krauss that had killed Maria.

Zero would handle this on his own.

He slipped the knife into his pocket and pushed through the crowd in pursuit of the man he was fairly certain was Stefan Krauss.

# CHAPTER THIRTY TWO

Zero shoved his way to the street corner before he could see in any direction over the growing sea of people outside the presidential palace. He scanned quickly left to right, but saw no one that resembled Krauss. His shoulders slumped in disappointment. It was a mirage, nothing more…

Unless it wasn't.

Maybe he was wrong about all of this. Maybe there was no big plot about to happen here in Cairo. Maybe Bright had nothing at all planned. In his career, Zero had been wrong more often than he'd been right. He'd worked as much off of conjecture and educated guesses as he had actual intel, oftentimes under duress and a ticking clock.

He could have been wrong. But maybe he wasn't.

Zero checked for oncoming cars before stepping out into the street. He took a deep breath and as loud as he could over the din of the nearby crowd he shouted, "S!"

He looked around quickly, and he shouted again. "S!"

Halfway up the block, a familiar face spun at the sound of what he thought his name was.

Zero spotted him. For a moment, they merely stared. There was no recognition in Krauss's expression. But there was something else there, and it looked like fear. Fear he had been discovered. In Zero's own chest, a familiar cold fury returned at the sight of Maria's murderer, and he was certain it was apparent on his own face.

Then Stefan Krauss turned and sprinted up the block.

Zero took off after him. There was pain in his legs but he ignored it, sidling past people as he ran. "Stop him!" he shouted, pointing. "Stop that man!" But passersby just looked at him like he was crazy.

Up ahead, Krauss skidded to a stop, nearly falling over, and pushed through a shop door. Zero was there three seconds later. He paused at the door, panting, realizing that Krauss could have a gun, could try to get the drop on him.

Zero pulled the Sig Sauer that Alan had given him. He shoved the door open and, just like the subway bathroom in Rome, he shoulder-rolled into the store, coming up on one knee with the gun level.

It was a clothing store, full of colorful Egyptian fabrics and trends. And Krauss was nowhere to be seen.

Zero climbed to his feet as a female clerk emerged from the rear of the shop. He quickly hid the gun behind his back.

"I am sorry, sir," she told him in Arabic, "but we are closing early. On order of the government."

He glanced left and right. Krauss was here somewhere. "I followed a man in here," he said in her native tongue. "He is dangerous. You need to leave."

She frowned at him. "I saw no one else."

"He's here." Zero took his hand from behind his back. The woman's eyes grew wide at the sight of the gun. "I will not hurt you, but please leave."

She didn't need to be told again. She kept her eyes on the gun as she sidled past him, and then fled onto the street.

He assumed she would go to the police. That was good. He needed only to stall Krauss for a short while.

"Where are you, S?" He stalked forward, keeping the gun level, keeping alert for movement in his periphery. "Krauss. That's your name, your real name. Stefan Krauss. You're a killer. A murderer-for-hire. But you knew that already, right?"

He paused, listening. Krauss might have already made a run for it, through a back door, or a window.

*No.* He was listening. Zero just knew it.

"You can feel it, even if you don't remember. You said it last time we met. You had a suspicion you weren't a very good person. And you're not—"

He heard a rustle and spun. Not fast enough. Krauss leapt out from his hiding spot in a rack of long dresses and reached for Zero. He caught the assassin's body weight and fell with him, landing safely on his back. Krauss rolled backward with the momentum and sprang to his feet an instant before Zero did. A foot shot out and struck the thumb of the hand holding the Sig Sauer. Zero cried out as the gun fell from his wasted grip.

Krauss let out a shout and leapt forward again, both arms swinging. Zero barely got his own up in time to block. He was on the defensive, avoiding every blow that came but giving ground. Soon he'd hit a wall.

There was something different this time. Krauss wasn't faster, or stronger; he was just… different somehow. More like himself, yet not.

The wall was behind him. Zero had no choice. The next swing came and he dropped to one knee, then sprang off his left leg and tackled Krauss into a jewelry display. Glass broke beneath them as trinkets scattered across the floor.

"Where's the bomb?!" Zero demanded. He landed a blow across Krauss's chin and the assassin's head lolled. "I know you planted it! Where is it?"

Zero hit him again. "Is there more than one?"

Zero swung again. "Where?"

Krauss's teeth gritted, blood between them. He put up his forearms and bucked his hips. Zero shifted, off balance, and threw out an arm to steady himself. A blow landed on his own chin and he staggered to the side.

Krauss climbed to his feet, breathing hard. He spat blood on the floor. "I won't tell you a thing. This needs to be done."

"Why?" Zero panted as he stood. "Because a voice told you to do it?"

Surprise flickered across the assassin's face.

"I know about the voice," Zero told him. "His name is Mr. Bright. He's manipulating you. I know who you are. What you've done. How you got that scar on your neck."

Krauss didn't take his eyes from Zero, but his hand instinctively rose and touched the stitched scar.

"And I'll tell you everything. But first—you need to tell me about the bomb."

Krauss's throat flexed. "How can I trust you?"

"How can you trust the voice?" Zero asked him.

Krauss looked away. It seemed like he was considering it.

But then he frowned in confusion. His hand reached up again to the scar.

"What is it?" Zero asked, or tried to ask, but he was cut off by a cry from Krauss.

"Aah!" He fell to a knee, his hand gripping the scar and his neck tightly, his eyes squeezed shut. It was all Zero could do but watch.

Almost just as quickly as the seeming attack had come on, Krauss's features smoothed. He stood again.

Zero tensed as Krauss looked left and right, and then at him.

"Who are you?" His voice was barely a murmur. "Where… where am I?"

*No.*

A chill ran down Zero's spine as Shaw's words echoed in his head.

*It can be controlled remotely.*

Krauss winced and put a finger to one of his cracked lips. His brow furrowed further as it came away with blood. "What's going on here?"

*The subject's brain can be continuously manipulated. New things they learn or discover can be erased.*

"The bomb," Zero demanded. "Where is the bomb?"

"I don't know about any bomb."

They took it. They waited for him to plant it, and then they stole the knowledge away.

No, he realized. Not stole. Merely hid. If his own brain was any indication, the information was still in there, somewhere.

And Zero needed it, before anyone was killed.

Before anyone *else* was killed.

A phone buzzed from somewhere. Krauss, just as confused as he was a moment ago, reached into his jacket and pulled out a cell phone.

"Don't," Zero warned. "Don't answer that."

Krauss directed his attention to the phone. His thumb moved for the button.

Zero sprang. He swatted at the phone and it clattered to the floor. As Krauss grabbed for it, Zero swung with his right and delivering a cracking blow across the assassin's jaw.

His knees buckled. His body swayed, and Krauss hit the floor.

At any other time in their history, he would have ended it there. He would have found the gun and shot Krauss dead on the spot while he was still unconscious. He deserved nothing less.

But he couldn't. Not now. He had information that Zero needed, before anyone was killed. And it was still in there, somewhere.

He worked quickly, pulling the paring knife he'd taken from Mischa from his pocket and kneeling over Krauss. He turned the assassin's head so he had a clear view of his neck and the scar.

He cut the stitches. They popped easily, one by one, until the wound was open. Though it made him queasy to do it, he gritted his teeth, and he dug the tip of the knife into Krauss's neck.

He knew where it was. He knew where it had been in his own neck.

He worked the tip of the knife back and forth gently, prodding. It scraped the surface of something tiny, something rigid.

"There you are, you son of a bitch," he muttered. He angled the knife, getting the blade under the suppressor chip.

"Halt!" a stern voice shouted behind him. But not in English. The command was in Arabic.

Zero glanced over his shoulder to see two Egyptian police officers, pistols out, pointed right at him. Their expressions were a blend of anger and disgust; he couldn't imagine how this looked. He had blood on his hands and a knife in the neck of an unconscious man.

"Wait, it's not what you think," he tried to say, but he said it in English, forgetting the Arabic words in the moment.

"Move away from him!" one of the officers demanded, responding in accented English.

He couldn't do that. He was right here. He was so close.

He twisted the blade. He felt the chip pop free.

"I said move!" the officer shouted, stepping closer. He holstered his gun as the other officer covered him, and reached for handcuffs at his belt. "You are under arrest…"

"Just wait…!" Zero pleaded.

This would work. It had to work. Krauss would wake and know who he was and where the bomb was, and he could clear all this up with the police, and EOT, and Interpol, and everyone.

Krauss's eyes opened as the officer moved in to cuff Zero.

"Hands up," the cop warned. "Do not move."

Zero did as he was told.

Then Krauss screamed.

The officer leapt back. So did Zero.

It was a primal, bubbling scream, a roar of unintelligible pain, and with it his entire body jerked as if he was electrocuted.

Zero could only stare in shock. What had he done?

"Sir!" The officer held up a hand, as if that would somehow calm Krauss. "Please, remain on the floor, we will call for help!"

Krauss rolled onto his stomach. Spittle bubbled between his lips. His eyes were wide, simultaneously terrified and furious.

He opened his mouth as if to speak, but it was as if he couldn't form words.

It was, to Zero, as if the assassin's brain had short-circuited.

*What did I do?*

The cop with the handcuffs ignored Zero and kept his eyes on Krauss. He reached for his gun again, seeming to second-guess who might be in the right or wrong in the situation they'd stumbled upon.

That was when the bomb went off.

The explosion was strong enough to rattle the windows of the clothing shop. It shook the building's foundation. It made all four men in the building cease in their tracks, able to do little more than glance at each other in bewilderment.

But of all of them, Zero had heard such a sound before, and he knew what it meant.

It meant he was wrong.

The cops abandoned the shop and dashed for the exit. Zero hesitated, looking between the door and the seemingly feral Krauss, who was baring his teeth at him.

He ran for the door.

Out in the street, people screamed and ran in every direction. He could see the smoke before he reached the end of the block.

That was when the second bomb went off.

Zero ducked instinctively at the resonant blast and covered his head. The Heliopolis Palace was ablaze. People were fleeing.

Mischa. He needed to get to Mischa.

Krauss. He needed Krauss.

He had been wrong. Not about the location, and not about the culprit. But about the timing. He thought he had time.

*But all Bright had to do was disrupt the accord.*

Zero understood now. Bright didn't have to kill any foreign leaders or diplomats. He didn't have to try to get past the extensive security at the convention center. He didn't need an army or a lot of firepower.

All he had to do was disrupt the Cairo Accord with a terrorist attack, both of which were happening now.

A third bomb went off. Palace windows exploded as military personnel ran for their lives across the expansive front lawn, burning debris falling down around them.

"Mischa!" he shouted. He shoved someone out of the way. Someone ran into him. He pushed forward in the crowd. "Mischa!"

He saw her there, and he breathed a sigh of relief. She hadn't moved an inch from where he'd left her. Even as bombs went off right across the street, even as crowds surged around her, even as there was panic in the streets, she had done as he'd asked and hadn't moved an inch.

She was crying. Her mouth was open a little, staring at the fire, watching the palace burn, and there were tears on her cheeks.

He reached her and scooped her up in his arms and turned right around to go back the way he'd come. "I got you. You okay?"

"Yes," she said softly. "We... we were right."

"In the worst way."

"Don't leave again."

"I won't. I won't," he promised.

He carried her through the crowd, hurrying back toward the clothing store, even though he already knew Krauss would be gone.

# CHAPTER THIRTY THREE

Todd Strickland stood near the wall on the eastern side of the dais of the round chamber in the Cairo International Convention Centre. He was alert, his senses in overdrive. This was the moment they'd built toward. This was the moment he'd worked for.

He'd silenced the phone that Penny had given him when Zero called. He couldn't afford interruptions. He was barely listening as the young King Basheer of Saudi Arabia said a few words to those in attendance and the millions—perhaps even billions—watching around the world. He did not even glance up as the king signed his name to the accord document.

Strickland was scanning those in attendance. Keeping alert, keeping an eye on his periphery. Watching for sudden movements. Watching for anyone who didn't look like they belonged, anyone who looked nervous or tense.

But there were none. This was going off without a hitch. Exactly as planned.

Millions were watching. Perhaps even billions.

That was when the bomb went off.

It was more of a feeling than a sound. The way a strong peal of thunder could make one's knees weak. The walls seemed to quake. Nearly every person in the room froze, suddenly alert.

There were certain sounds that triggered certain responses. Like Pavlov's dog and his bell. Like a mother hearing the cry of an infant. Like a firefighter when the alarm rings. Like Todd Strickland and the sound of a bomb going off.

He was no stranger to it. After tours in Iraq and Afghanistan, and then the CIA, and then EOT, he knew the sound of an explosion when it happened. So when the bomb went off, three things happened almost simultaneously. First, a shiver ran down his spine. That was normal. An explosion was more of a feeling than a sound, and it was one of instant doom, instant fear. If it didn't elicit that response in someone, there was something wrong with that someone.

What wasn't normal was pushing aside the flashbacks that wanted to come, of leveled villages, of people trying to flee while burning. But he was no stranger to that either.

The second thing was the approximation of distance. It sounded less than a mile away; an imminent and absolute threat.

The third thing was pushing himself off the wall and shouting orders as the assembly hall of the Cairo Accord broke into chaos. Diplomats stood, their eyes wide in alarm. Anxious chatter broke out. Heads darted left and right, trying to make sense of what they'd just heard. The feeling of doom and fear surging through them. Searching for some semblance of control.

There was a fourth thing, though he didn't want to acknowledge it: Zero's face conjured in his mind's eye, his words echoing in his head, and the dire sensation that he'd been right.

But Strickland had prepared an emergency protocol for the Cairo Accord, and he put it into action instantly as he shoved his way toward the dais.

He found Agent Clark first, and grabbed him by the shoulder. "Take Alpha Team, secure the president!" Rutledge had been seated upon the dais, beside Vice President Barkley, but he stood at the sound of the explosion. Barkley remained seated, but she gripped the armrests of her chair with both hands.

"Bravo Team, secure the VP and—"

That was when the second bomb went off. It sounded louder, somehow, but no closer. Or maybe it wasn't louder but just more real after the first explosion.

*What's being hit?* It wasn't their location. But it was near.

Strickland shook agents from their stupor and shouted orders and got bodies moving toward the appropriate exits. He radioed the Is-Pal team outside to cover exits.

"Just what the hell is going on out there?" he demanded.

The voice crackled in his earpiece, broken up with static.

"… not… confirmed," was all he caught.

No time for that now. The emergency protocol coordinated by EOT designated specific destinations for each world leader in attendance. It outlined the exit they would take, the vehicle that would be waiting, and the security team that would escort them.

But this was chaos. Personnel ran every which way, toward the wrong exits, with the wrong teams. Strickland saw Clark and half of his unit securing Rutledge. Members of Bravo Team had Barkley. Two Secret Service agents took the astonished King Basheer by the arm and directed him away from the dais.

Across the chamber, O'Neill and Hauser blocked the main exit, directing the flow of foot traffic back toward the two rear exits. At least someone remembered the plan.

A third bomb went off. It sounded as if there was an airstrike on Cairo.

"Emergency protocol!" he shouted, his hands cupped around his mouth. He shoved bodies in one direction or another, reminding them harshly where they were supposed to be. His security personnel were Secret Service, police, military. All trained for this sort of situation, and yet the human instinct was panic.

Slowly the protocol formed. Agents and officers got the leaders out of the building. Is-Pal would help get them into cars and in eleven different directions. A convoy of leaders would be disastrous in the event of an attack.

"Penny?" he said into his earpiece radio. "Penny, you copy?"

"I'm here," she said, her voice strained.

"You okay?"

"I'm fine, just…"

*Scared.* She didn't have to say it.

"Get down here as soon as you can," he told her. Penny was one floor above them, holed up in a small office with an array of three computer screens. Her job during the signing was being patched into the NSA, keeping an eye on digital chatter for any potential threats to the Cairo Accord.

Strickland waved to O'Neill and Hauser. He looked for McMahon and found him across the round hall, ensuring the Ayatollah of Iran and his detail were evacuated.

"Is-Pal," he said into the radio as the hall emptied. "Evacuation is nearly complete. Confirm when everyone is secure and gone, copy?"

"Copy," said a voice in the radio. "But… what the hell happened?"

*I wish I knew.*

The Executive Operations Team converged in the center of the chamber as the last dozen or so attendees were escorted through the rear exit of the hall.

"We should be with the president," O'Neill said firmly.

"That's the Secret Service's job," Strickland told her. In his emergency protocol plan, EOT was the only group he hadn't designated a task for—because at the time, he didn't know what it might be. "Our job is to oversee security of the accord, so we're going to secure the accord. And then we're going to find out what the hell is happening."

"I can tell you." Penny strode into the hall with an open laptop balanced on a forearm. "The Heliopolis Palace has been bombed. The explosion went off inside; the bombs were planted, and there may be more."

As if in response, another explosion rattled the chamber. He winced. They all did. A shiver ran down his spine. That was normal, insofar as bombings went.

"Are they evacuating?" he demanded.

"They'll try," Penny said, "but…"

*But it might be too late for that.* He couldn't imagine the casualties not ten minutes from their current location. Caught off-guard completely. Dozens were dead, at least. Perhaps even hundreds.

It was only the smallest of comforts that the Egyptian president and his wife had been here, in attendance at the accord signing.

"But why?" Hauser shook his head. "Why the palace?"

"Right place, but totally wrong time," O'Neill noted.

"That," said McMahon. He gestured toward the dais, the black leather portfolio, legal-sized and lying open, containing the document that was supposed to become the Cairo Accord. "That's why."

Strickland understood. The bombing of the palace wasn't about killing anyone in particular. It was about disrupting the accord. Todd had been so laser-focused on security here that he had completely overlooked a key fact: whoever was behind this didn't need to attack the accord to stop it.

And now a significant terror attack had been carried out on Egyptian soil while nine world leaders attempted to make peace. This was a message, loud and clear—and he was pretty sure he knew who sent it.

*This Cairo Accord is an effort on Rutledge's part to secure peace,* Zero had said on the phone. *Which is very bad for business if you're Bright.*

"Boss," Hauser said gently. "We need an action plan here."

"Right." Strickland rubbed his eyes. "O'Neill, secure the accord. It's coming with us." Only three member nations had signed before the disruption. They weren't finished here. "Hauser, get on the radio with Is-Pal. Ensure everyone is out safely and en route to secure destinations. McMahon, find out what's going on at the palace. If we can spare anyone to help with efforts there, we will."

They split off as he turned to Penny. "I want you to go back upstairs, lock yourself in there. I'll get someone to come stand guard…"

"Todd…"

"Keep an ear to the ground for anything at all that might tell us who or what—"

"Todd!" she said harshly. "Listen to me. Just a couple of minutes before the first bomb went off, I heard something. A call to local Cairo PD to a clothing shop not a block away from the palace. A woman said that an American man with a gun threatened her. He claimed he was chasing another man, but she only saw one."

He understood immediately. "You think Zero is here in Cairo."

"I don't think so; I know so." She turned the laptop she had propped on her forearm. Displayed on it was a grainy still image, but unmistakable. It was Zero, standing in a street, his mouth open as if mid-shout. "I was pulling up the traffic cam when the explosion happened."

Todd shook his head in dismay. He'd told Zero to stay away from Cairo, and here he was, nearly at ground zero just as the bombs were going off. Of course he didn't think for a moment that Zero had anything to do with it—but clearly he'd known about it, and had done nothing. Instead of alerting authorities, he'd come here, presumably, to try to stop it himself.

*Zero tried to warn you.*

No; Zero had contacted him with a vague hunch, not a discernible threat. What was he supposed to have done—call off the accord?

And now people were dead. The palace was destroyed. The accord was disrupted.

"He has a phone. Find him."

"I can try—"

"*Find* him, Penny. Now."

In his emergency protocol plan, EOT was the only group he hadn't designated a task for—because at the time, he didn't know what it might be. But now he did.

Zero was going to answer for this.

# CHAPTER THIRTY FOUR

Pain. Blood. Confusion.

It was like waking from a sound, dreamless sleep and finding the house on fire around you.

No, that wasn't quite right. It was like waking from a sound, dreamless sleep in a strange house, to find *you* were on fire.

A clothing shop. Where, he didn't know. Pain—searing, in his neck, in his head. Like an electric current passing through his brain.

Men—three of them. Two were dressed alike. Uniforms. He didn't know what the uniforms meant, but he knew he did not like them.

The third—familiar but not.

*Who is he?*

*Where am I?*

*Who am I?*

Blood—on his neck. A gash there. On his lips. He'd bit struck. Perhaps beaten.

*Can't remember.*

The explosion—he'd thought it was thunder at first. Jarring, adding to the confusion. The men in uniforms, they ran first. The third man, he didn't seem to want to leave, but he ran too.

A phone—on the floor. He took it. Standing was hard. He wasn't going to leave the same way the other men did, so he looked for a back door. Found one, as well as a gun on the floor. He took that too.

Outside—sensory overload. Colors, people, screams, running, shoving. There were signs in a language he didn't recognize. Or maybe he couldn't read. He wasn't sure.

The phone buzzed in his pocket. He ignored it and staggered along the street. More thunder. Black smoke, not far. Something was on fire. He ignored that too. Not his problem.

No one seemed to care that he had blood all over him.

He went in the opposite direction from the black, billowing smoke. He saw a sign that he could read. It had the strange, cursive-like writing on it that he didn't understand, but then below that were words he recognized. It said "Banque du Caire."

And then below that it said, "Bank of Cairo."

Cairo.

*Something… grasp it… it's right there… just hold onto it…*

Accord.

Peace.

Target.

Yes. He was in Cairo, and he was supposed to kill someone.

Was it the man from the clothing shop?

Maybe.

No.

The phone buzzed again. He ignored it.

He walked along slowly as people rushed past him. They shoved into him. He ignored them too. This didn't feel real. How had he gotten here? He couldn't remember. Why were there bombs going off?

*Is this Hell?*

*No. You don't believe in Hell.*

*How do you know that?*

The burning in his head subsided, but it still hurt.

A vision flashed suddenly across his mind. It came on so quickly, so powerfully that he put out an arm and steadied himself against a building.

A beach. At night. A knife. A woman.

He killed people.

He was in Cairo, and he was supposed to kill someone.

*Who?*

The phone buzzed again. He pulled it out of his pocket in anger, about to throw it. But then he saw the two words on the screen: Unknown Caller.

He knew that name. Not a name, not really, but he'd seen those words before. Had come to think of it as a name.

"Hello," he answered cautiously.

"S? What's going on? What's the last thing you remember?"

The voice was male, smooth, managing to sound casual and even unconcerned despite its questions.

He knew this voice. A vision flashed through his mind, hazy, not completely formed. A figure, standing in front of him. Men, holding his arms. This voice, chuckling. Laughing at him.

*I'm not going to kill you, Krauss. I enjoy you too much. I'm just going to kill a little part of you.*

"Krauss," he said into the phone.

"What did you just say?" the voice demanded.

"My name… was it Krauss? You called me that."

"Christ," the voice muttered, annoyed. "Weisman, what the hell is happening?"

"We've lost signal," said another voice, behind the first. "Updates aren't going through."

"S? Krauss. Listen to me. What happened?"

His fingers reached for the open wound on his neck. The blood there was sticky as it dried. He felt the jagged edges of it—stitches. "Someone cut my neck. Someone else cut it again."

"Good grief," the voice sighed. "Tell me he didn't…"

"I am in Cairo. I am supposed to kill someone."

"No. You've done what you went there to do. Get your ass back here—"

"You tried to kill me," he murmured. He didn't know how. But he could still hear the voice chuckling in his head.

*I'm just going to kill a little part of you.*

"Who?" the voice demanded. "Who are you supposed to kill?"

"I think we've lost him, boss," said the second voice in the background.

*Who am I supposed to kill?*

Accord. Peace. Target.

A woman on a beach. A knife…

He knew. He knew who he was supposed to kill. The architect. The orchestrator. The one who had brought not only him there, but all of them.

"The mastermind," he said.

"Krauss, hang on—"

He ended the call. He was done talking. He dropped the phone on the sidewalk and left it there. Then he changed direction. He was going the wrong way. He could see the stadium from there, rising above the rooftops, and he started toward it, the black smoke still billowing skyward behind him.

*

Bright stared at the phone for a long moment after Krauss ended the call. He sighed.

"Well. That experiment was short-lived. Fun while it lasted, though."

He spun in his chair on the forty-sixth floor of the Buchanan Building and looked out over Midtown Manhattan as the sun rose. It was early afternoon in Cairo, and he'd been up all night, operating on their time zone. That, and losing his assassin, justified a drink.

"Weisman, get me a scotch, would you?"

Across the wide office, his chief engineer looked up from a laptop. "You want me to stop trying to update?"

Bright nodded. "We lost him."

Weisman pushed his wire-framed glasses up his nose. "I had a feeling that tech was faulty. Like the CIA could actually develop anything lasting like that…"

"Weisman?" Bright held out his empty hand.

"Yes sir." The ponytailed engineer scurried to the oak mini-bar. "Perhaps I could write a patch for it," he said as he dropped a single round ice cube in a rocks glass. He poured two fingers of scotch from a decanter. "It would take some time, but we can get him back—"

"There's no getting him back. It wasn't the tech. Thank you." Bright took a sip and sighed contentedly. "That's good."

"Then what, sir?"

"It was Zero. He tore it out of his head."

Weisman blanched. "He… no. Did he say that?"

"In so many words." Bright sat again, and swirled the glass idly. "I have to hand it to him; it was a hell of a desperate move, knowing what it did to his own head."

But it meant Zero was in Cairo.

Krauss was in Cairo, for now.

Perhaps this was a situation that required putting pride aside.

"What now, sir?" Weisman asked nervously.

"Two things. First—tell Ray to tighten up security." If he made it out of Cairo, Krauss was going to come for him, or try to… again. And if he remembered the mistakes he'd made the first time, he wouldn't make them a second time.

*The mastermind*, Krauss had said. That's who he was supposed to kill. Who else but Bright himself would he mean?

"Second," Bright said, "find me Zero. He's in Cairo, and I'd like to talk to him."

Krauss would come for him, but only if he made it out of Cairo. For once, Bright and Zero had something in common. Neither of them wanted Krauss to leave the city alive.

"Sorry sir, but… how do we find him?"

Bright sighed in disappointment. "He'll have a burner. Access the nearest cell tower to Krauss's last-known location and search foreign, unlisted numbers that made outgoing calls in the last hour. Do I have to do everything?"

"No sir. I'll get on it right now."

"And call Ray," Bright reminded him.

"Yes sir." Weisman scurried out of the office.

Bright set the glass down on the desk. He didn't want the drink anymore. He typically prided himself on being unflappable, collected in even the most chaotic of circumstances. But now he was just… annoyed.

At least he'd stopped the accord. That should have felt like a win. But really all that had done was struck some fear in some hearts in the interest of maintaining the status quo.

These days, it felt like staying on an even keel took too much effort. The ebb and flow between order and chaos wore on him.

Perhaps he should take a page out of Zero's book and retire. Though he chuckled aloud at that thought; look where retirement had gotten him.

"What a mess," he murmured.

He should have just had Zero killed when he had the chance. He regretted it now; if he'd planted a bomb in the apartment in Rome, he'd still have S.

But now they both needed to be eliminated, and ideally, at each other's hand.

## CHAPTER THIRTY FIVE

Zero felt utterly useless.

He hadn't stopped Krauss. He hadn't prevented the bombing of the Heliopolis Palace. After finding Mischa they had returned to the clothing store to find Krauss gone. They'd searched for him, briefly, but found nothing, and it wasn't safe to linger.

He'd come to Cairo on a hunch, and he'd been right, and he'd done nothing about it.

Now the two of them were holed up in a small restaurant a block and a half north of the clothing shop. The streets were nearly vacant; several blocks had been evacuated. The place was empty, half-eaten meals still warm on the tables.

All they had to do was wait until people started returning, and then they could slip out among the foot traffic. But right now they would be too conspicuous out on the streets.

Mischa sat on a stool at the six-seat bar, her feet swinging, the burner phone on the bar in front of her. Penny had tried to call twice, but they hadn't answered.

He couldn't hear her voice right now, not after his failure. Not after Bixby. The next time he spoke to Penny, it would be in person—if he wasn't in jail or dead.

"You're certain you removed it?" Mischa asked him. He'd told her about the suppressor he'd cut from Krauss's neck.

"I'm certain."

"Did he remember who he was?"

Zero shook his head. "Don't know. But I don't think so. If it was anything like what happened to me, his memories will come back bit by bit. Not all at once. Still, it felt different this time. Krauss looked… I don't know. Feral, maybe. Or just really confused and in pain."

"But we can safely assume he is no longer Bright's pawn."

Zero nodded. "Yeah. We can safely assume that." He sighed. "We need a plan. We need to get out of the country."

"No," Mischa argued. "We need to find and kill Krauss. He is here somewhere. He is still a threat."

“We have no idea what he’ll do now or where he’ll go.” Zero had hoped that by yanking out the suppressor, Krauss would remember the bombs. He’d been overzealous. He hadn’t thought it through. And the bombs had gone off anyway.

“What he’ll do now is no concern of ours,” Mischa said forcefully. “Our goal was to find and kill Stefan Krauss. We know he is here, in this city. We haven’t been this close to him since he murdered Maria.”

A flash of anger rose in Zero, but he stifled it. It wasn’t anger at Mischa. It was anger at himself; he’d had the chance twice now to kill Krauss, to just end it, and he hadn’t.

He rubbed his eyes and then gestured to the phone.“Have you checked the news?” he asked her. “Any word on casualties?”

“Don’t do that,” Mischa scolded. “You did not plant those bombs.”

No. Not directly. But people were dead, and Zero felt like it was, at least in some way, his fault.

“We need to get out of the country,” he said again. “Find Sara and Maya. Get somewhere safe, away from everyone.” Away from Bright, and his people…

The phone rang from the bar top. Mischa silenced the tone without a second glance. But Zero leaned over to see if it was Penny again.

It was not. The display read “Unknown Caller.”

Same as it did when he answered Bixby’s phone in Rome.

He picked it up.

“Don’t answer,” Mischa warned.

He had to.

“Hello.”

“Hi, Zero.” The voice was male, deep, didn’t sound like it was much older than he was.

“How did you get this number?” he demanded.

“Please don’t insult your own intelligence by assuming I can’t find you anytime I want to,” Bright said. “Do you have any idea what you’ve done?”

“Yeah. I took away your new toy.”

Bright scoffed. “Hurl all the quips you want, you know just as well as I do that you’ve just created something dangerous. I had him under control—”

“Under *your* control,” Zero corrected. “You had a mindless terrorist at your fingertips.”

“And you unleashed him.”

Zero's jaw clenched. He had no retort to that. "I'm not interested in talking to you. Goodbye—"

"As it happens," Bright said quickly, "our interests find themselves somehow aligned."

Zero had a feeling he was taking bait, but still he asked. "How so?"

"Well, Krauss is dangerous to me. You already want him dead. I happen to know where he'll go."

"And where is that?"

"He's going to leave Cairo. Or try to. He has a new target in mind."

"Who?" Zero demanded.

Bright sighed. "Me."

"He told you that?"

"In so many words."

This conversation was already growing tiresome. "Either you tell me what he said, or I'm hanging up…"

"He said he's supposed to kill someone, and he knows who. Then he said, 'the mastermind.'"

This time Zero scoffed. Bright's hubris knew no bounds. "And that's you?"

"Who else would it be?"

"So you want me to go after him and kill him so that he doesn't come kill you. Why would I do that? Why wouldn't I let him come kill you, and then kill him? He'd be doing me a favor."

"Because," Bright said, "I'll do you a better one. I'll call the whole thing off."

Zero frowned. "What whole thing?"

"Again, you insult my intelligence and your own. I know you kidnapped Shaw. I know Shaw folded and told you things. You know that I was asked to eliminate anyone who knew about the program. You know it was my people that took out your doctors, and your friend in Italy."

Anger rose anew in Zero's chest, heat in his cheeks.

"You kill Krauss before he leaves Cairo and I'll call off my people. No one else needs to die. That includes your family, Zero."

Sara and Maya. His anger was replaced by sudden panic. If Bright could locate him on a burner phone in Cairo, what would keep him from finding them?

"My daughters," Zero said. He glanced at Mischa, who watched the front entrance. "My other two daughters. How do I know they're all right?"

"You have my word."

"Not good enough."

Bright chuckled. "Fine. Just a few hours ago, a team of six men was sent after your daughter's phone signal at a community center not twenty minutes from your home. We recovered six bodies from the aftermath. All male. The girl's cell phone was found, but not her. The older one escaped two assassins in Paris and vanished. Seems your girls are stone-cold killers. Take after their old man, I suppose."

Zero was silent for a long moment. He needed time to process all of that; in the moment, all that mattered was they were safe somewhere and staying off the grid, where Bright couldn't find him… but only if Bright was telling the truth.

"So that's the deal. You take out Krauss, and I call it off. You'll be safe. You can live normal lives. I'll deal with the CIA. What do you say?"

Zero looked at Mischa. He knew that she wanted nothing more in the world than to deliver the death blow to Stefan Krauss. He knew that killing Krauss was a positive move, maybe even a necessary one for the good of people everywhere.

And they would do that anyway. But he wouldn't make a deal with Mr. Bright.

"Here's what I say," Zero told him. "I say that you're not afraid of Krauss coming to kill you. I'm sure you've got plenty of goons to keep you safe, plenty of places to hide if you needed to. I think you're afraid of Krauss because he knows things about you. Maybe he doesn't remember them right now, but the longer he's alive, the more will come back to him. He knows where to find you. He knows what you've done to him."

Bright said nothing in response.

"In fact," Zero continued, "between what I know and what he knows, I bet we have enough information to blow the whole lid on you, Shaw, the program, all of it. I'm a liability, same as him. So you can see how I'm not all that eager to trust your word. I have no reason to believe that if I take out Krauss, and I let my guard down, you won't still send people after me and my family. That's what I say."

"Ah, there it is," Bright said. There was the hint of a smirk in his voice. "There's that intellect I've been waiting to see." He sighed. "You're right, Zero. I'd still send people to kill you, and your kids, in their beds if I had to, and I'd still sleep just fine at night." He clucked his tongue. "Fine. Do what you will and enjoy it while you can. But I hope you'll be looking over your shoulder from now until your soon-to-be untimely death. Goodbye, Zero."

Bright ended the call.

Zero lowered the phone. He'd called a bluff, and he'd been right; Bright would never stop. Zero and his family would never be safe, not until Bright and Shaw and anyone else involved was exposed.

No—exposing wouldn't be enough. Bright needed to die.

And he would… but not today. He was tomorrow's problem. Today's was Krauss.

"We can't kill him," Zero said softly. "I'm sorry, Mischa, but we can't kill Krauss."

Her gaze narrowed. "And why not?"

"You heard what I said on the phone. He knows things, or he will. Bright is the bigger fish here."

They had no choice now. They had to find Krauss before he left Cairo, because Krauss would get himself killed going after Bright, and the information in his head would be lost.

Mischa looked away, her frown deepening. He could tell she was grappling with the same thing. They both wanted him dead. But they had to put personal feelings aside, because there was someone else who deserved it more.

*The mastermind.*

Had Krauss actually said that?

If Bright was actually to be believed, then Krauss hadn't actually threatened him directly. And beating around the bush wasn't exactly his style.

*What if Bright isn't the mastermind?*

*Then who might be?*

He was about to pose the question to Mischa when they heard the squeak of hinges. Someone was entering the small restaurant. Mischa jumped off the stool and tensed. Zero reached for the paring knife in his pocket, his only weapon.

They both relaxed when they saw the familiar face enter.

"Todd," Zero sighed. "Thank god…"

Strickland raised a black Glock and pointed it at Zero. "Drop the knife. Don't move. You're both under arrest."

# CHAPTER THIRTY SIX

Zero did as he was told. He set the small paring knife on the bar, and he slowly raised his hands over his head.

Mischa hesitated. He could see the tension in her shoulders, her small arms. But then she glanced up at him, and he nodded once, and she too lifted her hands until her elbows were right angles.

"Todd," Zero said slowly. "I know what you're probably thinking…"

"Stop," Strickland ordered. "Just stop. I don't want to hear it from you anymore. I told you to stay away from Cairo, and you didn't. You knew about the bombs, and you said nothing. Now people are dead. The accord is ruined."

"I was wrong," Zero admitted. "I had a hunch, and I was wrong about the timing. We tried to contact you—"

"Too little, too late. If that wasn't already clear." Strickland scoffed. "You could have warned the palace guard, or the police, or any number of other people. Admit it, you came here to save the day. To stop it yourself."

"No," Zero denied. "That's not… it wasn't like that…"

"When hasn't it been?" Strickland demanded. "Three years we worked together, and it's always been you against the world. You always had to be the hero. There are a lot of innocent people dead here today." The disgust in his expression chilled Zero to the core. "You feel like a hero?"

"Todd, please. I know how all this must look, but we don't have time. This was done by Stefan Krauss, and he's still here, in Cairo, for now. But we can get him. We can leave now, and together—"

"You're not a part of this anymore!" Strickland shouted. "What about that don't you understand? You can't go flying around the world, committing crimes and killing people, and not expect repercussions. Do you understand that?"

Zero couldn't look him in the eye. Instead he looked at the floor. He saw Mischa's feet shift, just a tiny bit, almost imperceptibly.

*Please don't try anything.*

"Here's what's going to happen," Todd said. "We're going to arrest you—"

"We?" he interrupted.

"We." He turned at the source of the new voice. Preston McMahon emerged from the restaurant's kitchen. He must have come in through the back door, Zero reasoned. Cutting off their exits. McMahon was short but stocky, well-built, his hair still shorn short and face clean-shaven from his Army habits. He held a Glock in both hands but had the barrel directed toward the floor. "Zero. Good to see you again."

"You too, McMahon." Preston was the grandson of William McMahon, a former US president whom Zero had rescued from a hostage situation not two weeks earlier.

"We're going to arrest you," Todd continued. "We're going to bring you somewhere, and we're going to talk. You're going to tell us everything you know, and then EOT is going to catch whoever was behind this. Krauss, Bright, all of them. Then you are going to be put on a plane and sent back to the United States. I'm sorry, Zero, but you have to answer for what's happened here. All of it."

He nodded. "I understand. I'll comply."

But in his mind he knew that they wouldn't catch Stefan Krauss. They wouldn't catch Bright. The CIA would see to that. They'd protect him, or he'd flee, or he'd get off the hook on some bureaucratic loophole or immunity. Shaw and the agency could twist it, make it look however they wanted to. Bright could pin the bombing on someone else.

Strickland was right. Zero wasn't a part of this anymore, and that worked in his favor, because there was no denying it; the situation from here onward was going to require some extrajudicial means, and the type of prejudice that EOT simply could not afford.

"McMahon." Todd kept his aim on Zero. "Cuff him."

Preston stowed his Glock and reached for handcuffs at his belt.

"Zero," Todd commanded, "take two steps away from the bar. Don't try a thing."

He did as he was asked, sidestepping twice slowly so he was standing on open floor, equidistant between the bar and the nearest table.

Behind him, he felt McMahon's fingers close around his left wrist. "Sorry about this, Zero." He twisted the arm behind Zero's back.

"Me too," he admitted.

Strickland's aim was on Zero. McMahon's focus was on him too. They assumed, erroneously, that he was the threat. That the little girl with him wasn't much of one.

Neither of them had really seen her in action, he realized.

"Just one thing," Zero said. "Please… don't shoot her."

Strickland frowned. "Why would I—"

Mischa already had the paring knife in her hand as Todd's gaze flitted her direction. She flicked it, sent it whistling through the air and into his left hand. He howled and dropped the Glock.

Zero dropped to his knees before the cuff could close around his wrist. McMahon still had a firm grip on his arm; the action yanked the former Ranger forward, just off-balance enough for Zero to spin and sweep a leg. McMahon grunted as he fell, and Zero rolled forward.

He snatched up Todd's Glock and had his aim on McMahon while the younger man was still on one knee, a hand on his holster.

"Don't," he warned. "Hands up."

Preston McMahon did as he was told and put his hands up.

"Where's the rest of your team?"

"Nearby," McMahon said. His gaze flickered down and to the left, just for a second. "They'll be here any second, so you should probably drop that."

Zero shook his head. "I've been doing this a long time. I can tell when you're lying."

McMahon rolled his eyes. "It's just us. The other two are at the palace, helping to clear it."

"Mischa, relieve him of that weapon."

She scurried over to take it from him. "Pardon," she said as she pulled the pistol loose.

McMahon moved quickly. As soon as Mischa had the gun out of the holster he reached for her, wrapping both arms around her in a bear hug and lifting her entirely off the ground in front of him.

It happened quickly. Zero hesitated. He didn't want to shoot anyone, let alone McMahon or Strickland.

Mischa's feet kicked at the air. Her arms were pinned at her side. She cursed in Russian.

"You're really going to use a thirteen-year-old girl as a human shield?" Zero asked him.

"You really going to shoot me?" McMahon challenged. "Drop the gun and I drop her."

"You first." Mischa threw her head straight back. The back of her skull connected with his forehead. His grip loosened and she dropped to the floor. McMahon staggered and held his head.

"Oh…" he groaned, blinking as if he was fighting loss of consciousness.

Mischa flipped the Glock around in her hand. She jumped up and smacked him just once, solidly, on the top of the skull with the pistol's grip, and he crumbled.

"Mischa!" Zero scolded. "Was that necessary?"

"What? I didn't shoot him."

He turned his attention back to Strickland, who held his bleeding left hand with his right. He hissed breaths through his teeth; the paring knife had pierced the back of his hand but hadn't broken through to the other side.

Zero knelt beside him. He didn't point the gun at him.

"I'm sorry, Todd. You're right. About almost all of it. I imagine you blame me for this." He could see it in his eyes, the anger and betrayal. "There's going to come a time when I have to answer for all of it. But right now, I'm going to go find and stop Krauss. Call for backup if you want, or follow me if you can, but I have to do this. He's on his way to kill someone, and it's going to get him killed."

"Why do you care," Todd winced, "if he gets himself killed?"

"Because he has information that we need. About this man who calls himself Bright."

*Information about the mastermind.*

He frowned, returning to the thought he'd had just before Strickland had barged in.

*What if Bright isn't the mastermind?*

Bright said there was someone Krauss was supposed to kill.

*What if his target is right here, in Cairo?*

Krauss knew about the accord. It was there, somewhere in his brain. He knew however much Bright had told him. And Bright might have told him plenty, since he could just erase whatever he wanted after the fact.

"The mastermind," Zero murmured.

It wasn't Bright. It was just that Bright's ego wouldn't let him believe Krauss could have meant anyone else.

"The president," Zero said suddenly. "Rutledge. Where is he?"

"He's secure," Todd answered shortly.

"He's the mastermind. The one behind all of this, the Cairo Accord," Zero said quickly. "We need to make sure he's safe. I think Krauss is going to try to get to him…"

"No," Strickland said firmly.

"Todd, this is a matter of life or death—"

"No," said Todd, "he's *not* the mastermind behind the Cairo Accord. Barkley is."

Zero balked. Todd was right. Peace in the Middle East was Rutledge's goal, but it was Joanna Barkley who had largely orchestrated the efforts, arranged the logistics, even drafted the treaties—and he would bet good money that Bright knew that.

Barkley was the mastermind. Krauss didn't believe in peace. He wanted to eliminate the one who had made all this happen. Krauss might have even believed that Barkley had been the root cause of his now-twisted mind.

"Where is she, Todd? Tell me where she is. You know, don't you?"

Strickland grunted. "Yes. Of course I do."

"Call her team. Make sure she's okay."

"Can't do that. Emergency protocol is to go radio-silent until they get a physical all-clear from us." He shook his head. "But you're wrong. Krauss couldn't know where she is. The only people that know are her security detail, EOT, and…"

He trailed off as a look of sheer panic crossed his face. "And Penny."

Todd was up suddenly, on his feet with a groan, reaching for the phone in his pocket. His panicked expression transitioned to horror as he held the phone to his ear. "She's not answering."

Zero felt how he looked. If anything happened to Penny, especially after he'd let Krauss live twice, he would never forgive himself. "Where is she? Where's Penny?"

"She was at the convention center, doing online recon… I have to go. I have to get there."

"Todd." Zero grabbed him by a shoulder. "We have to do this together. Make a choice. If you go to Penny, you need to tell me where to find Barkley."

Strickland's jaw clenched. "Fine." He spoke rapidly as he explained, "Emergency protocol was that each foreign leader would be taken to a unique, inconspicuous location. No embassies, no military bases, no government buildings; nowhere that would be a potential target. Barkley is at an administrative office of Dar El-Salam General Hospital. It's a small building that's been closed for renovations, just off the main campus, behind the emergency room. It's not far. Three miles or so."

"Thank you," Zero told him. "We'll get her."

He tried to pull away, but Strickland grabbed his collar and pulled him in close. "When this is over," he said, "you vanish. You take your family, and you get gone. If I ever see you again, I'll have no choice but to do my job. Understand?"

"Yeah, Todd. I understand."

He doubted he'd have another option anyway.

# CHAPTER THIRTY SEVEN

Zero sprinted up the block, to the right, to the next block over. Mischa was right on his heels, her shorter legs moving double-time to keep up with his stride. They reached the small parking lot of the post office, and their stolen Kia, in under a minute, and thirty seconds later Zero fishtailed out onto the mostly empty street, heading away from the palace and the cavalcade of emergency vehicles still battling the fires and clearing the buildings for any further bombs.

"GPS it," he told Mischa. He was only vaguely aware of where he was heading.

"Turn right up here," she told him.

He tried to, but the road was barricaded with yellow sawhorses to create an emergency route for fire and rescue. He spun the wheel the other way. The tires screeched as he pulled a tight U-turn. "Need another route!"

"Rerouting… ah! Up here, turn by the gas station."

It was no comfort at all that police were busy with the palace fires and fallout thereof, but at least it meant there was no one patrolling the roads. Zero sped up, blowing a red light, and turned sharply when Mischa told him to.

He tightened his hands on the wheel, his knuckles white, his heart pounding, and for more reason than just the safety of the vice president. He could only hope that Penny was alive and well. He couldn't bear to think that anything had happened to her—and he doubted he was going to get so much as a courtesy call from Strickland.

"Listen," he told Mischa. "You understand that there's more at stake here than just our lives?"

"Of course," she answered solemnly.

"Good. That's why I need you to do something for me. When we get there, I want you to secure the vice president. Get her out of there. I can't worry about her, you, and Krauss at the same time."

He expected pushback. He expected her to argue, to want to deal the final blow to the man who had killed her adopted mother, his wife, and had tried to kill both of them.

"Okay," was all she said.

As they came up on Dar El-Salam General Hospital, he saw the glaring error in Strickland's plan of inconspicuous locations, since this location had become anything but.

"Watch out!" Mischa warned. Zero slammed the brakes. The roads outside and leading into the hospital's campus were completely blocked with standstill traffic. Police had all four lanes stopped, attempting to make safe lanes for the myriad screaming ambulances carrying victims of the bombing.

"On foot?" Mischa suggested.

"Looks that way." He pulled the Kia onto the shoulder of the road—right up onto a grassy patch, to avoid blocking the emergency vehicles—and the two of them hit the ground running. They ignored the shout of a nearby police officer and didn't even glance back.

The din was incredible. Cops shouted and drivers shouted back. Horns honked. Sirens screamed. Even the cries of the injured could be heard, and all of that was almost static to the chugging of low-flying helicopters, one of them taking off from the roof above the ER as another came in carrying the worst of the victims.

"…to go?" Mischa shouted, or tried to, but Zero only caught the tail end of it over the noise.

"What?"

"Which way should we go?" she shouted louder as they approached the ER. They darted between two cars waiting to get into the parking lot, and Zero pointed. Todd had said the building was behind the ER, and since they were on foot, they had no choice but to go around.

Zero's lungs burned as their feet pounded the pavement, heading around the side of the wide building and the emergency room entrance. There was a mild incline with a concrete walkway choked with people; nurses and doctors scurrying in on-call, families who had gotten the call their loved ones were here. They navigated it as best they could, squeezing by people, muttering sorries and excuse mes, until the walkway opened up to a road-width that led to the outbuildings that formed the lesser campus behind it.

He was out of breath. "Admin… building?"

Mischa pointed. She was barely winded, it seemed. "There."

"How do you know?"

"The sign says so."

Zero rolled his eyes as she took off at a sprint, and he did his best to keep up. The administrative building was a squat, one-story structure a few hundred yards behind the main hospital and the ER; its architecture was clearly older, probably belonging to the original few structures that had been built first, before the larger, newer complex. The entire building was beige-colored, with tall, rectangular windows and a sandstone-colored arch at its entrance.

They came to a dead stop at the arch, each of them behind a column, and caught their breath. Mischa pulled out the Glock she had taken from Preston McMahon and handed it to him.

"You'll need this if the fight will be fair," she told him.

"Hopefully I won't." He had to remind himself that the goal was not to kill Krauss. But still, he took it. "Stay here a moment."

He left the cover of the wide column and crept across the vestibule.

Then he stopped in his tracks.

There was a body there, just outside the glass doors to the building. A man in a black suit, his eyes wide, his neck broken.

Krauss was already here.

With the amount of noise down at the hospital, no one would hear shouts or possibly even gunshots up here. They would simply join the cacophony.

And if Krauss was here, that meant Penelope León was almost certainly *not* all right.

He clenched his jaw and gripped the Glock tightly. "I'm going in. I'll try to draw him off. Find another way in."

"Good luck." Mischa darted off around the building. Zero took a breath and pulled open the door.

*

Joanna Barkley drew her trembling knees up from beneath the desk and tried not to breathe.

She had always prided herself on remaining calm and composed in the tensest of situations. But the situations she had found herself in were ones of irate senators, sexist politicians, arrogant pundits, angry detractors.

She'd never had to face down a crazed gunman before.

Nothing about the last thirty minutes seemed real. First was the explosion, right in the middle of the carefully constructed Cairo

Accord. The sound of it—no, the *feeling* of it was unlike anything she'd experienced before, freezing her, rooting her to the spot.

Then her security detail was tugging at her arm, ushering her out, through the maze-like halls of the Cairo International Convention Centre, out an exit, into a waiting SUV. She was not given any answers about what had happened. And then the vehicle had delivered her here, to a small and unused administrative office behind a hospital.

She had, at first, been impressed by the plan; the location was unremarkable. But slowly the noise grew, the sirens outside and the helicopters flying to and from the hospital roofs.

When the first gunshot went off, it sent a shiver down her spine. In this empty building, it was impossibly loud. But out there, she doubted anyone would hear it or heed it. It might as well have been a car backfiring.

Her detail was five people—*had* been five people. One was posted outside. Two more in the halls. Two more in the room with her. She saw the two of them die. Her heart broke at the thought of Agent Mendez, who had grappled with the gunman long enough for Barkley to run, to dash down the hall to an office with its lights off where she now cowered beneath a desk.

That's what she was doing. Cowering, while they died for her.

*Pull yourself together, Joanna. You will get through this.*

There were windows in this office, tall rectangular ones, and if she dared to climb out from beneath the desk she might be able to get one open and scramble out.

*So do it*, she told herself. If Jon Rutledge could survive in the face of being kidnapped and taken to the desert to die, she could climb out a window.

She crawled forward on her hands and knees, out from under the desk. She stood, checked her surroundings, and kicked off her black heels.

As slowly and silently as she could, she opened the blinds over the rectangular window.

Then she took a step back, as her shoulders slumped in a deflated sigh.

There was no latch. This was just a pane of glass. The window didn't open.

Joanna spun at the sound of footfalls in the hall. The door was the only exit of the office. She had nowhere to go. Maybe she could break the glass, throw a chair through it…

The figure appeared in the doorway. He took a step inside, the gun an extension of his silhouette, as if it was a part of him. The open blinds cast light on his face, and Barkley almost gasped. His lips were cracked and broken. There was dried blood on his cheeks. His sandy hair was disheveled, and he had a nasty gash on the side of his neck.

The man looked demonic.

"You," he said. His voice was low, just barely tinged with some kind of accent. "It's your fault we're here."

"Please," said Barkley. She put both hands up. "I don't know what you want, but I haven't done anything wrong."

"Perhaps not intentionally," he said, "but we are all here because of you. The people in that hospital are there because of you. *I* am here because of you. This…" He outlined the scar on his neck with his free hand. "This is here because of you."

"I don't even know who you are," she pleaded.

"Neither do I." He raised the gun, and Joanna Barkley shut her eyes.

*

Zero was kneeling to check the pulse of a downed Secret Service agent in the hall when he heard the footfalls. He quickly scrambled to the corner and peered around it to see Krauss, with Alan's silver Sig Sauer in one hand as he stalked the hall, his back to Zero.

He could do it. He could shoot him, right then, in the thigh or the back, nonlethal. Put him on the ground but not kill him. They were at a hospital, after all.

But when he peered again Krauss had vanished. He'd entered a room. There were voices. Not just Krauss. A female voice.

Barkley.

*She's alive.*

Zero ran then. He sprinted down the length of the hall, and when he reached the open doorway he didn't stop to bring the pistol up or to aim, but instead threw himself at Stefan Krauss.

They collided. A shot went off. Glass broke. Barkley screamed.

The two of them hit the floor and rolled.

Zero still had the gun in his grip. He brought it up, assuming Krauss would get to his feet, but then the assassin threw himself forward with a primal cry and forced him back to the ground. The air rushed out of his lungs as Krauss straddled him, swinging wildly, pummeling him with both hands. It was all Zero could do to keep his hands up to protect himself. The blows were savage, unhinged; most of them glanced off his forearms but some got through. A fist knocked against his chin. Fingernails raked the skin from his cheek.

Krauss was different this time. He was animalistic, ferocious. Gone was the unassuming assassin who used guile, aliases, and subterfuge to get to his targets. This man was part beast. He'd lost whatever had made him, him.

Zero grunted as he flexed a leg, wedging a knee between them as best he could. He pushed hard, putting some space between them. Krauss growled and swung, slamming the butt of his palm into Zero's temple. Stars exploded in his vision.

A shot went off, thunderous and startling. Krauss howled and rolled away. He leapt to his feet, holding an injured shoulder, and dashed for the door.

Joanna Barkley, wide-eyed and panting, held the Sig Sauer in both hands.

"Thanks." Zero scrambled to his feet. There was no time to catch his breath. "Stay here." He wiped blood from his cheek and ran after Stefan Krauss.

*

Mischa had just found the rear entrance of the administrative building—locked, of course—when she heard the gunshot, heard the glass break. But she couldn't tell from which direction it came. She ran around the building, searching for a broken window. She found it, and peered through it to find the Vice President of the United States standing in an otherwise empty and unlit office, her shoulders heaving, holding Alan Reidigger's gun.

"Hello," said Mischa through the shattered window.

The vice president spun, startled.

"Where is Zero?"

"Um…" It appeared as if the vice president was in some state of shock. "Ran off. He chased that man."

"I see. Well, you're supposed to come with me. We have a vehicle nearby. I will make sure you're safe until we can deliver you to the authorities."

The Madam Vice President blinked at her. "But… you're just a girl."

Mischa frowned at that. "Considering your accomplishments in your relatively short career so far, not to mention championing feminism as a cause, I think suggesting I am 'just' a girl is reductive at best, insulting at worst."

"What?"

Yes, the vice president was certainly in some state of shock.

"I am Zero's daughter," Mischa said.

"Oh." The vice president put out a hand. "Okay then, let's go."

# CHAPTER THIRTY EIGHT

Zero burst through the doors of the administrative building and scanned left and right. He spotted him, loping along quickly, holding his shot shoulder as he ran toward the concrete walkway that led down to the entrance of the emergency room at Dar El-Salam.

He gave chase, wishing that saving the world didn't require so much running.

Krauss was heading toward the hospital. Toward dozens of cops and security guards, families and patients. Of course he was; Zero couldn't open fire in a crowded hospital. Krauss was counting on that.

And he wouldn't. He needed Krauss alive. Even if he wasn't the man he'd been before, that information was still in his head. He knew how to find Bright. He knew what Bright had done.

He reached the walkway and battled the flow of foot traffic, not bothering to apologize this time as he shoved and elbowed past people. Krauss disappeared into the hospital, and Zero pursued.

As soon as the automatic doors opened, Zero realized just how difficult this would be. The ER was jam-packed with people, crying out, shouting at each other, shouting at nurses, sitting everywhere, including the floor, as EMTs brought in new injuries on stretchers.

He desperately looked left and right. There was no sign of Krauss.

*Where would he go?*

Zero pushed his way to the far side of the unit just in time to see a pair of elevator doors closing. He jumped toward them, hoping to get a hand in there, to stop them, but not fast enough.

*Up. He's going up.*

He stopped a passing nurse by the shoulder. "Stairs? I need stairs."

"No, uh, no English," she told him apologetically, and then sidled past him.

He spun, looking every direction. There—a door, and the universal zigzag symbol for stairs. He pushed through the door and took them two at a time, as fast as he could.

His own footfalls were echoed in the stairwell. No, not echoed. He stopped, and the other set kept going.

"Krauss!"

The footfalls above him stopped.

He was there, on the stairs, heading up.

"Krauss," he said. "I… I can't imagine what's going on in your head. But I can relate, at least on some level. You don't know who you are. I do. I know who you are."

He listened, but no response came. Only silence.

"You may not remember them," he said, "but there are things in your head right now. Memories, and they can come back. You have information about who did this to you. I want to take that person down. I think you do too."

"You can't help me." His voice didn't sound angry, or confused; it was a statement, nothing more.

"I shouldn't want to help you. I should want to see you dead. But… as it turns out, you might be the only one that can help me now, too."

The stairs were silent for a long moment.

"Everything is jumbled," Krauss said from above him. "That woman? The mastermind. I thought… I thought she would be the woman on the beach."

Zero winced. He leaned against the banister.

Of all the things to remember, he remembered *her.*

"The woman on the beach… she's dead. You killed her."

He shouldn't want to help this man. He should have wanted to see him dead.

"Let me help you…"

"I can't trust you," Krauss said. "Or anyone. Not even myself!"

Feet pounded the stairs again over his head.

"Dammit!" Zero surged upward. He reached the third floor. His legs burned. He got to another landing, and then up another short flight to the fourth floor.

*How tall is this hospital?*

Above him, a door was shoved open. Zero gritted his teeth and forced himself to keep going. He reached the door, and the end of the stairs.

He was at the rooftop access.

He readied the Glock and pushed out onto the roof. The sound of a helicopter assaulted his ears; the wind of the spinning blades ruffled his hair. Krauss was there, yanking the pilot out of the cockpit, throwing him down.

Zero had a clean shot. He aimed…

A flight nurse leapt out of the helicopter and ran, right into Zero's line of fire.

He grunted and dashed forward as Krauss climbed into the pilot's seat.

*Does he remember how to fly a helicopter?* If it had been among Krauss's talents before, was it still?

He got his answer a moment later when the skids lifted off from the rooftop.

Krauss could not get away again. He couldn't let him go a third time, not when so many lives had been lost and more were on the line.

Zero had no choice. He dropped the gun, and he jumped, and he wrapped both arms around a skid as the helicopter leaned sideways.

He body swung with the momentum. His legs kicked out, and suddenly they weren't just a few feet off the ground, but several stories as the edge of the hospital roof fell away.

Zero clung with both arms. He had to hold on.

Above him, the cockpit door shuttered in its frame, unsecure. Krauss leaned over and glared at him, the dried blood on his face and neck making him look maniacal.

He piloted the helicopter over the parking lot, over the lanes of gridlocked traffic, over Cairo. It was all Zero could do to hang on to the skid; falling now would be a death sentence.

*What was your plan here, exactly?* The sardonic voice in his head, oddly, sounded like Sara.

The wind tore at him. The rotors above were deafening. He maneuvered one arm over the skid, around it, and grabbed a fistful of his jacket in the best locking position he could get to under the circumstances.

That gave him a free hand. With it he reached up, and he grabbed onto the edge of the door frame of the cockpit.

The door swung again, and it smashed against his fingers.

He cried out and let go, his arm swinging.

*This isn't how you die,* said a voice in his head.

He'd heard that voice before. It was his own, and in the past it had been reassuring, affirming. But here, now, hanging one-armed from the skid of a helicopter with a homicidal maniac at the helm, things looked pretty goddamn bleak.

Zero gritted his teeth, and he reached up again. He grabbed the frame of the cockpit door. Before it could swing shut again, he pulled himself up, daring to let go of the skid with his secured arm.

The door swung again, smacking against his back. It hurt, but he ignored it. A foot found purchase against the skid, his upper body facing Stefan Krauss.

Zero couldn't let go. Krauss couldn't take his hands from the controls.

"Land it!" he shouted. "Or we'll both die!"

"Then we'll both die!" Krauss shouted back, and he laughed.

Zero brought his other foot up, finding the skid, and with that modicum of stability he dared to let go of the cockpit's frame with one hand. He reached across Krauss and grabbed onto the shoulder harness that Krauss wasn't wearing. He spun his wrist once, wrapping it around his arm. With two feet on the skids and one wrapped in the harness, he could have a hand free.

*But what the hell am I supposed to do with it?*

He did the first thing that came to mind. He reached in, and he grabbed the stick.

The helicopter wavered. Zero swayed with it. One foot slipped from the skid.

"Land it!" he shouted. "I can help you!"

"Help me?" Krauss laughed again, but there was no mirth it. "I remember you. Or… parts of you. We weren't exactly friends, were we?" He grinned, and blood showed between his teeth. "Seems fitting we die together."

Zero glanced through the windshield, and his heart skipped a beat. They were heading straight for the Heliopolis Palace—or, more appropriately, the enormous cloud of thick, black smoke that hung over the palace as it still burned, as fire crews struggled to stifle the blaze.

"Krauss! Don't do this! We'll be flying blind!"

Zero wrenched the stick. Krauss pulled back. With both of his hands on it, it leaned in his direction. The helicopter wobbled and leaned. Zero held on with the shoulder harness as best he could, despite it cutting off circulation to his wrist.

They soared into the black cloud. Their visibility went from clear to gray to nonexistent in the span of a few seconds.

Krauss pushed on the stick. Zero pulled, trying to maintain their altitude, but still he felt the helicopter dip.

"I killed someone, didn't I? Someone close to you?"

Zero ignored him, struggling to maneuver the cyclic.

"Was it the woman on the beach?"

Zero strained, gritting his teeth, trying to fight against Krauss's control of the helicopter. He couldn't see a thing, but he felt their altitude drop again.

"Was she yours?"

He let go.

He didn't want to help this man. Krauss was a killer, and he always would be. He knew nothing else. Zero saw Maria in his mind, saw her in those final moments before her death, walking alongside him on the beach at night. Everything had been perfect then. And a minute later, nothing had been.

He didn't want to help this man. He wanted to see him dead.

He just didn't want to die in the process.

With one hand free, Zero reared back and delivered a cracking blow across Krauss's jaw. He reached for the stick and pulled up.

It was too late. Just ahead, a hazy shape came into view. There was no mistaking it; it was the golden dome of the Central Hall. The highest point of the Heliopolis Palace.

There was no time to pull up. Zero let go of the stick. He let go of the shoulder harness, and in spite of every instinct in his body, he pushed off with both feet against the skid.

He fell backward through thick black smoke. For a moment it felt as if he was floating. Above him, the helicopter struck the golden dome, and despite the low visibility, the orange fireball flashed brilliantly as the helicopter exploded.

Then he hit something, hard, and the air was forced from his lungs. He couldn't move. Nothing hurt. The golden dome burned, and debris rained down on the rooftop around him. He coughed, choking on the acrid air.

*But this isn't how you die.*

# CHAPTER THIRTY NINE

Todd Strickland swiped his keycard through a vertical slot in the wall of a white, cinder-blocked corridor in a sublevel of the CIA's Langley headquarters. There was a loud buzz, the sliding of a heavy electronic bolt, and the steel door unlatched with a heavy *chunk.*

This was just one of four sublevels beneath the George Bush Center for Intelligence—four that he knew of, anyway.

He pushed the door closed behind him and nodded to the single gray-suited security guard who sat behind a beige desk, reading *The Washington Post.* "Morning, Ben."

"Agent Strickland." The retired agent made no attempt to move; there was no need to check Todd's ID or scan his keycard. He was here off the record. "Go ahead back."

"Thanks."

He headed through another set of doors and past three empty cells on each side of the corridor, heading toward the last one on the left. There were no other prisoners on this sublevel; this place had originally been intended as a temporary holding station, usually reserved for domestic terrorists, war criminals, rogue military, and the occasional traitorous agent. It was a way station en route to far worse places, like Hell Six in Morocco—or a simple hole in the dirt. But these days, they hardly used it.

The cell was twelve foot by twelve foot, with a floor and ceiling of concrete and walls made not of bars but two-inch reinforced glass. A grid of half-inch holes in the side facing the corridor made communication possible with the prisoner inside. There were no windows, but far worse was the fact that there was no discernible door. The cell was accessible via a hidden panel in one of the glass facades. It was a psychological maneuver intended to demonstrate to the prisoner that there was absolutely no way out.

Inside was a small cot with blanket and pillow, a tiny bathroom area that consisted of a sink, toilet, and shower head—all open, all exposed—and a single steel chair, bolted to the floor.

The prisoner sat in that chair. He wore simple blue polyester/cotton scrubs, like a nurse in an ER, which lacked pockets or zippers or anything metal. His feet were bare. His trademark trucker's cap was missing; his hair and beard were clean but still unruly.

There was a single metal chair at the end of the corridor. Todd positioned it in front of the glass wall of the cell and sat. "Hello, Alan."

"Todd." Alan Reidigger looked up at him. He looked like he'd aged several years in the three days since they'd been back stateside. "How's the hand?"

Strickland held up his bandaged left hand. "Itchy. But it's healing. You holding up okay?"

Reidigger glanced around at his glass walls and chuckled. "They keep it warm in here. Three squares a day, and I've got my health. So, better than most, I suppose." His smile vanished. "How's Penny?"

Todd looked at the floor. "Better. She's eating solid food, at least. But they're going to keep her on at the hospital for a while. Probably a couple of weeks."

"Give her my best."

"Wish I could. She… doesn't want to see me anymore."

"Oh?" Alan leaned forward. "What happened?"

He shrugged. "Depends on who you ask. If you ask me, she lied and betrayed national security. If you ask her, I didn't heed Zero's advice when I could have. Either way… doesn't matter. She's done here. CIA fired her."

Reidigger stroked his beard and sighed. "Sorry to hear that."

Four days earlier, Strickland had raced back to the Cairo International Convention Centre to find the guard dead and Penny badly beaten. She had refused to tell Krauss where the vice president was—at least she had refused at first, and held out for as long as she could.

Krauss had left her alive. But it would take more than the hospital could offer for her to get over the damage he'd inflicted.

An ambulance had come for her. Strickland wanted to ride with it, to go with her, but as they loaded her onto a gurney, a white Kia SUV had pulled up to the convention center, driven by Vice President Joanna Barkley, who claimed she'd been rescued by a young blonde girl who had shown her to the car and then run off.

Foreign leaders were secure and back in their home nations. Rutledge and Barkley returned to the United States. Egypt condemned the terror attack, of course, but so far the culprits were publicly unknown. The nine would-be member nations of the Cairo Accord agreed, remotely, that they would honor the agreement. They didn't need to sign a piece of paper to hold true to their word.

But the world was still shaken. Forty-seven people had been killed in the bombing of the Heliopolis Palace and more than a hundred injured. The message had been clear.

Before leaving Cairo, Strickland had been contacted by an Interpol director by the name of Baraf, who had Alan Reidigger in custody. They negotiated an exchange, and Reidigger had flown back to the US as a prisoner of EOT.

"And Zero?" Alan asked. "Any sign of him?"

Strickland shook his head. "They're still sifting through the wreckage of the palace. They found the helicopter, but only one body."

He could only guess that the charred remains found in the cockpit of the helicopter were Stefan Krauss. There was no sign of Zero, and only Todd, Penny, and McMahon even knew that he'd been in Cairo.

"The girls?" Alan asked.

"Nothing. Vanished, all three of them." Todd looked Alan in the eye. "You think they're alive?"

Alan nodded. "I do." Todd could tell he meant it.

"I think that's enough small talk." Strickland cleared his throat. "Are you ready to tell me about Bright?"

Alan shook his head. "No."

"Come on, Alan. I can't help you, or him, or stop this, if you don't tell me what you know."

"Telling you anything would only put you on the hit-list," Alan said simply. "Aren't enough people dead?"

"I have resources," Todd argued. "A team. The president's ear—"

"Which is exactly why I won't tell you. Because you'll do the right thing, try to escalate it, tell your bosses. If they're in on it, that makes you dead. If they're not, it might make them dead." Reidigger shook his head. "As it is, I'm already dead."

"No. No one knows you're here but me and Ben, and he doesn't even know who you are. Everyone believes you're in a hole at H-6."

"And if they find out," Alan argued, "it'll be easy picking."

Todd sighed in frustration. Alan had so far refused to tell him anything about the character Mr. Bright, who he might be, *where* he might be. And Todd hadn't said a word to anyone—mostly because he didn't have enough information to go off of. He couldn't enlist Penny's help, not anymore, and his own research had yielded nothing.

"You want to help?" Alan asked. "Then step aside and let him do it. You're doing a job. You're bound by laws. He won't be. Not anymore."

"You're assuming he's alive," Todd remarked.

Alan smiled. "I am, yeah."

Strickland didn't want to say it aloud, but he did too.

"All right, Alan. I've got work to do. I'll come see you tomorrow. And I hope you'll be in a more talkative mood." Strickland rose from the metal chair and started down the hall.

"Todd—wait."

He paused. "Yeah?"

"There is one thing I want to say." Alan hung his head, his beard touching his chest. "Kate… Zero's wife. She knew."

He frowned. "Knew what?"

"She knew what he was. She knew the things that he had done."

Todd didn't understand. "How did she know?"

"Because… she was working for the NSA."

Strickland blinked. "That can't be right."

Alan nodded. "I didn't find out about it until after her death. But it seemed she was on the verge of uncovering something, and I think that something was about Bright. I think she supplied the information she found to the CIA. And I think that's why she was killed. I don't know for sure. But…"

"But all this time," Todd said quietly, "Zero thought her death was his fault."

Alan nodded. "I kept it from him."

"Why?"

"Because," Alan sighed, "he had already created the narrative in his head. And I guess… I guess it was easier to let him think he had done the betraying than to think that she had."

Todd shook his head. "A secret isn't necessarily a betrayal."

Alan smiled sadly at him. "Isn't it?"

He thought of his own life, and Penny, and the secrets he'd kept and the ones that had been kept from him, and he didn't want to admit it, but he couldn't think of a single one that didn't qualify.

"Why are you telling me this?" Todd asked.

"Honestly? Because Zero had a flashback of some sort. I don't think it was real, and he doesn't either. But it could lead to him asking more questions, digging deeper. And… well, I don't think I'm going to make it out of here alive. I doubt I'm going to see Zero again. Someone else needed to know the truth. You know. Just in case."

Todd nodded. "I get it." He stood there for a long moment. "I'll see you tomorrow, Alan."

"Yeah. See you tomorrow."

He left then, past the empty cells and through the door and past Ben the guard. Alan was right about one thing; he wouldn't be seeing Zero again. But if he was still alive somewhere, Todd would find him. That was his goal now.

# EPILOGUE

Joanna Barkley sat on a cushion in front of a picture window overlooking the wide front lawn of Number One Observatory Circle, the official residence of the vice president. She had no spouse and no children; it was a lot of house for one person. Yet she enjoyed her privacy. She liked being alone.

But then again, she was never really alone. She had security. Guards. She'd had security and guards in Cairo, too.

These rare moments of being alone gave her time to think, and she had quite a bit to think about. Namely, the strange young girl who had helped her escape, had led her to a vehicle, put her in it, and told her to return to the convention center where she would find Agent Strickland.

The girl had refused to come with her. She had claimed to be Zero's daughter, and she needed to find him.

But that wasn't all she had said.

The girl had taken her by the hand and led her quickly away from the administrative building, around the main hospital, back toward the road with its clogged traffic, and she'd said some things, some that were lost on Barkley because she had been in a mild state of shock, but some that she remembered vividly.

*"Don't talk; just listen. There is a man who calls himself Mr. Bright..."*

*"...works in cooperation with the CIA, or at the very least, its director..."*

*"...very dangerous. But none are in quite as much danger as you. You represent a direct threat to his endeavors."*

*"...tell no one. Absolutely no one. I am only telling you this because of what it might mean for you. Because you will be a target again, I am certain."*

Barkley shivered, though she wasn't cold.

If the girl was to be believed, Zero had uncovered some sort of conspiracy that involved the funding of terrorism and the unraveling of all of her efforts.

She didn't want to believe it. It sounded insane. She didn't believe in far-reaching conspiracies or shadowy cabals.

But… she'd heard and seen too much to *not* believe it.

For now, she would heed the girl's advice. She would tell no one, not even Jon. But she would look into it herself. She had to do her due diligence. If it was true, it would paint a much bigger target on her back.

If it was true, it meant there were forces working from the inside to undo all they had done and would do.

She couldn't think of anything more frightening than not being able to trust anyone around her.

If it was true, she'd need help.

She could only hope he was still alive, wherever he was.

*

Maya paced the floor of the tiny living room. It was 1:58 p.m. It felt like it had been 1:58 p.m. for an hour now.

The cabin's living room was so small that she could only make two strides before she had to turn around again. Two strides, turn, two strides, turn.

"You're making me anxious," Trent noted from the two-cushion sofa. He was in his boxers and a T-shirt, squinting in concentration as he sewed a patch onto the knee of the only pair of jeans he had.

"Sorry." She couldn't help it; she had energy and she needed to burn it.

The minute hand of the clock on the wall ticked. 1:59 p.m.

Sara burst into the living room from the cabin's single rear bedroom. "Is it time?"

"Almost," Maya told her.

"Ew, Trent, put your damn pants on," Sara scolded.

"I'm mending them."

"Mending? What are we, Amish?"

Maya smirked. She was glad to see her sister's sense of humor had returned somewhat. The last few days had been… trying, to say the least.

Four days ago they'd rescued Sara from the community center. "Rescued" might have been an overstatement; Sara had killed five men to get out of there alive.

From there they drove to Missouri. They changed cars twice and stopped only for gas. They kept to the speed limit and avoided police.

Trent's family owned a stretch of property, thirty-something acres of almost entirely untouched woods in the Missouri wilderness. It had been purchased decades ago by his great-grandfather, who hoped the land would someday become valuable and some developer would offer several times its purchase price to knock down the trees and build a town.

That never happened. So the property stayed in the family. Most of them had forgotten all about it. The only reason Trent knew about it was because his uncle had taken him hunting there when he was a kid. He knew there was a small cabin, with running water and a generator, surrounded by acres of woods and deer and nothing else. The uncle who had taken him hunting was dead now, and the property was neglected and forgotten by everyone but Trent.

The cabin smelled like mildew. There was only one bedroom and a twin-sized bed. The showers were frigid and they had to conserve use of the generator. They had only the clothes on their back and a meager amount of cash that had to last.

But they were together, and they were safe.

Sara had stolen a pay-as-you-go phone from a gas station on their way through Kentucky. They used it as sparingly as possible, turning it on only in the morning and at night so that Maya could check her messages.

Her family had several plans in the event of various emergencies. One of them was the event that they would be separated, cut off from help or resources, and needed to find each other. Maya had found a relatively unknown Chinese messaging app that allowed its users almost complete anonymity. She had created an account, using none of her real information, and shared the user name with her dad, Sara, Mischa, Maria, and Alan.

She had turned the phone on each morning and each night and checked the app. Morning and night, there was nothing. But this morning, she had turned the phone on and opened the app, and there was something.

It was a foreign telephone number, beginning with the country dialing code 2-0. For Egypt. And then a time: *3:00 p.m. EST.*

Finally the clock struck 2 p.m. They were in Missouri; it was three o'clock on the East Coast, and ten at night in Egypt.

Maya powered the phone on. She called the number. She put it on speaker as Sara crowded at her shoulder and Trent leaned forward to hear.

The line rang once. Then twice. A third time.

Then: "Hello."

"Mischa. Oh my god." Maya had never breathed a sigh of relief so heavy before. "You're okay? Where are you?"

"I'm okay. Currently I am at a payphone in Egypt. We are out of Cairo, but I would rather not say where. We were tracked before."

"I understand—"

"And Dad?" Sara blurted out.

"He is with me. He was in a helicopter accident…"

"Sorry?" This time it was Maya who blurted. "A helicopter accident?"

"Yes. Krauss is dead."

Maya and Sara exchanged a glance. She should have felt some pleasure at the statement, some relief that he was gone. But in the moment Maya didn't feel anything but worry for her family.

"Zero is recovering. After the crash he was found by rescue workers and taken to the hospital. He had suffered smoke inhalation and a minor spinal cord contusion. But he could walk, so I broke him out of the hospital—"

"*Broke* him out…?"

"And we fled the city. That's why it took me so long to contact you. He is not well enough to travel yet. But as soon as he is, we will find a way back."

Maya felt her sister's hand on her shoulder. Four days of worrying and not knowing, but they were alive. Maybe not healthy, but alive.

"Listen," Maya said. "We're holed up in a—"

"Don't tell me where you are," Mischa interrupted. "And we shouldn't stay on the phone long. Zero and I will keep moving. You should do the same."

"We will." They weren't staying at the cabin long. Now that they knew Mischa and their dad were safe, they would form a plan and move to another location. "It's good to hear your voice, Mischa."

"It is good to hear yours too. And perhaps you would like to hear this one."

There was a pause on the line.

"Hi, girls."

"Dad." Maya almost shed a tear; his voice sounded so hoarse, weak.

"Can't talk much," he said. "But… will see you soon. Love you both."

"I love you too," Maya told him.

"Love you," Sara murmured behind her.

Then Mischa was back on the line. "We will find a way to come together. Then we will end this. Until then, stay hidden, trust no one, keep moving."

"We will," Maya promised. "Stay safe."

"You too."

The call ended. Maya shut the phone off.

She was right. They would find a way to come together. And then they would end this.

## NOW AVAILABLE!

### ABSOLUTE ZERO
### (An Agent Zero Spy Thriller—Book #12)

"You will not sleep until you are finished with AGENT ZERO. A superb job creating a set of characters who are fully developed and very much enjoyable. The description of the action scenes transport us into a reality that is almost like sitting in a movie theater with surround sound and 3D (it would make an incredible Hollywood movie). I can hardly wait for the sequel."
--Roberto Mattos, Books and Movie Reviews

ABSOLUTE ZERO is book #12—and the series finale—in the #1 bestselling AGENT ZERO series, which begins with AGENT ZERO (Book #1), a free download with over 500 five-star reviews.

**In the shocking series finale, Agent Zero learns of a powerful thermonuclear bomb which, set off in the right place, could kill tens of millions. In a breathtaking twist, he learns of something else that will make it even more deadly.**

**The fate of the world is literally at stake as Agent Zero finds himself in a mad race against time, the only person on the planet with a capacity to find the weapon.**

**Yet, while Zero races to find the location, he is up against other formidable forces: dozens of assassins are dispatched to kill him.**

**And in the midst of all this, the time has come for Zero to have a final reckoning with his own deteriorating health.**

**Full circle from his original discovery of the memory chip, Agent Zero is given one last chance to save the planet—if only he can keep from destroying himself—and everything in his path—in his wake.**

ABSOLUTE ZERO (Book #12) is an un-putdownable espionage thriller that will keep you turning pages late into the night, and the satisfying and stunning climax to a masterful 12-book espionage action series.

**"Thriller writing at its best."**
**--Midwest Book Review (re *Any Means Necessary*)**

**"One of the best thrillers I have read this year."**
**--Books and Movie Reviews (*re Any Means Necessary*)**

**Also available is Jack Mars' #1 bestselling LUKE STONE THRILLER series (7 books), which begins with Any Means Necessary (Book #1), a free download with over 800 five star reviews!**

**ABSOLUTE ZERO**
**(An Agent Zero Spy Thriller—Book #12)**

## Jack Mars

Jack Mars is the USA Today bestselling author of the LUKE STONE thriller series, which includes seven books. He is also the author of the new FORGING OF LUKE STONE prequel series, comprising six books; and of the AGENT ZERO spy thriller series, comprising twelve books.

Jack loves to hear from you, so please feel free to visit www.Jackmarsauthor.com to join the email list, receive a free book, receive free giveaways, connect on Facebook and Twitter, and stay in touch!

**BOOKS BY JACK MARS**

**LUKE STONE THRILLER SERIES**

ANY MEANS NECESSARY (Book #1)
OATH OF OFFICE (Book #2)
SITUATION ROOM (Book #3)
OPPOSE ANY FOE (Book #4)
PRESIDENT ELECT (Book #5)
OUR SACRED HONOR (Book #6)
HOUSE DIVIDED (Book #7)

**FORGING OF LUKE STONE PREQUEL SERIES**

PRIMARY TARGET (Book #1)
PRIMARY COMMAND (Book #2)
PRIMARY THREAT (Book #3)
PRIMARY GLORY (Book #4)
PRIMARY VALOR (Book #5)
PRIMARY DUTY (Book #6)

**AN AGENT ZERO SPY THRILLER SERIES**

AGENT ZERO (Book #1)
TARGET ZERO (Book #2)
HUNTING ZERO (Book #3)
TRAPPING ZERO (Book #4)
FILE ZERO (Book #5)
RECALL ZERO (Book #6)
ASSASSIN ZERO (Book #7)
DECOY ZERO (Book #8)
CHASING ZERO (Book #9)
VENGEANCE ZERO (Book #10)
ZERO ZERO (Book #11)
ABSOLUTE ZERO (Book #12)

Made in the USA
Columbia, SC
23 September 2023